The Jesse Tree

Linda Hurcombe

Orphans
Publishing

First published in Great Britain in 2019 by Orphans Publishing
Enterprise Park, Leominster
Herefordshire HR6 0LD

www.orphanspublishing.co.uk

A Cataloguing in Publication record for this book
is available from the British Library

Hardback: 978-1-90336-037-8

Paperback: 978-1-90336-032-3

Printed and bound by Clays Ltd, Elcograf, S.p.A.

MIX
Paper from
responsible sources
FSC® C018072

For Luba Mai and Venice Caitlin

To Pete Postlethwaite, whose genius inspired the world and whose encouragement sustains me. BFN.

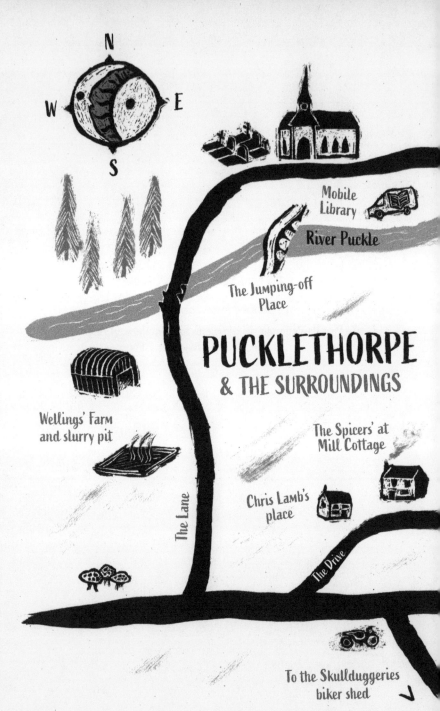

N

W   E

S

Mobile Library

River Puckle

The Jumping-off Place

PUCKLETHORPE
& THE SURROUNDINGS

Wellings' Farm and slurry pit

The Spicers' at Mill Cottage

The Lane

Chris Lamb's place

The Drive

To the Skullduggeries biker shed

Pucklethorpe Castle

High Street

The hatch

Romany Road

Ford

Weir

To school >

Pucklethorpe Manor

The Bakehouse

Limberlost Mill

London Road

To the Airfield
∨

*Your friend is the one who comes in
when the world goes out.*

– anon

Summer Locke nibbled the Scotch egg, first scraping off the crispy crumb coating, then breaking off bits of spicy sausage packed round the boiled egg in the middle.

'Mrs Spicer said you like her Scotch eggs best.'

Summer Locke grinned. 'Yes, this is so. The very best, and always saving the best for last, for good fortune and God bless us.' Summer Locke then ate the white off the egg, finally engulfing the whole of the golden yolk. 'Right, then! Let us be off! But firstly let us tell my folk at the hatch I am still possessed of my skin and the gavs – police, to you – was gracious.' Then, 'Come along, jukel.'

My dog Boddy followed like an old friend, twirling her long snaky tail in that slow-motion lurcher way. Summer Locke took my sticky hand to cross the High Street, which in any other circumstances I would have resented. Summer's hand was cool and confident and somehow familiar.

1

'How are you named?' Summer spoke in a formal manner that reminded me of hand-embroidered waistcoats and Bible stories.

'I'm Robin Swallow. And this is Boddy.' I asked the question I'd been burning to know. 'Why'd you stare through my window the other night and then didn't wait 'til I could say hello?'

'I wanted to set eyes on you but I could not wait about. And you looked frightened.'

'I was so not frightened, not one little bit!' I retorted hotly. 'Maybe just a bit ... freaked out. In London, where we just moved from, most people don't even know their own next-door neighbours. Faces through the window isn't the usual way of things.'

'To be sure. We heard tell you were arriving. You were much preoccupied with settling in.'

'Well, I'm glad I found you. Say, tell me what happened with the police?' Boddy and I had waited all morning for the mysterious Summer Locke to emerge from the police station.

Summer Locke spoke without looking at me as we walked. 'I revealed as how poor blind Mr Brockton and I helped each other and the routines we kept: mowing the manor lawn and tidying the hedges, tending the bees and reading Bible stories and making tea and marmalade and doing the shopping. And how our jukels fetched him shushies and hares and sometimes a pheasant or partridge.' Summer's words were unfamiliar to me but somehow they made perfect sense. 'He would allow our ponies to poove on Pucklethorpe land when the grass was rich. She hated that.'

'She? You mean Mrs Wheatley?'

'The very same. I explained to the gavs how sorely she treated him, stealing his post and setting booby traps meant for him to trip or take a tumble. How he commenced acting strangely toward the end ...' Summer's voice tailed off in a quiver, tears welling. 'Papa Brockton loved me, was father and grandfather and friend all in one. He taught me to be a proper scholar.'

If we have souls and you could paint a picture in one sentence, Summer did just that. I had to choke back my own tears. My brother Zach, who never uses short words when there's a long one, later observed that I had had an epiphany, a special moment when something true writes itself in your soul, never to be forgotten. I felt the real-ness of Mr Brockton Wheatley. I had wanted to play Sherlock Holmes and have a whale of a time. But a living soul had lost his life. Brockton Wheatley was DEAD and he shouldn't be. Just like Rory.

'My father disappeared a long time ago and I don't know whether he's still alive,' I said.

I don't know why but I started shaking and Summer looked kind and ... well, like someone I'd always known, and trusted. 'May I please have a hug?'

'If you like, but only to the counting of three.'

So Summer and I hugged, not too close, up to the count of three.

3

Then, out of the blue: 'Now,' said Summer Locke, 'you stare me in the eye to the count of one hundred, no blinking allowed, and we shall be kin and I will show you magic.'

We stared to the count of one hundred without blinking, Summer Locke counting in a monotone 'one thousand–two thousand–three thousand' and so on. Which is more difficult than it sounds. Summer's hypnotic green eyes were flecked with gold and dark outlines, like shining twin planets. I could see myself reflected back.

Thus began our dear and dangerous friendship.

1
Advent

The journey is the destination.

– Kathy and Dan Eldon

I sat shotgun, which is a fancy cowboy word for the passenger seat, with Indeedy driving the big yellow removals lorry stuffed with all our worldly goods. Boddy posed regally in the middle, clipped in the seatbelt like another human. We made up jokes and sang at the top of our lungs.

When we were about halfway, and just as I was going to ask 'Are we almost there?' to wind her up, Indeedy pulled into a lay-by. There was a big sign of a headless woman in an old-fashioned dress, holding her head tucked under her arm, in front of a shabby looking place called the Silent Woman Café. Why hadn't we stopped at McDonald's or another fast food place? Indeedy didn't like McDonald's. Indeedy didn't like any fast food; she liked slow food. The car park was full of lorries and artics.

'That sign! They've chopped her head off, Mum!'

'Some idiot's idea of a joke,' replied Indeedy. 'Like, women talk more than men? Like, women don't have a sense of humour? I don't think so!' She laughed. 'HAHAHA!'

Zach calls that Indeedy's feminist laugh. One of Zach's favourite jokes to rile our mother goes: 'Question: "How many feminists does it take to change a lightbulb?" Answer: "Only one, and it's NOT funny."'

We both ordered the Full English: sausage and eggs and bacon and fried bread and mushrooms and grilled tomatoes, with tomato ketchup for me and brown sauce for Indeedy. You paid at the counter when you ordered and then the lady brought the food to the table. The lorry drivers mostly had bellies drooping over their belts and some of them wore backwards baseball caps. We got some strange looks, probably because we were the only females in the place, except for the lady behind the counter. She wore her brown hair fuzzed up, with a pencil stuck behind her ear. Her low-necked top and tight short skirt bulged. 'Plumptuous with love handles', I knew Indeedy would call her.

We downed our food without talking. Mum patted her belly. 'Well, my Fruit, that was one fine breakfast. I shall add this place to my list of top notch greasy spoons.'

We ordered two cheese and pickle sandwiches to take away, and a couple of Sprites, and a big sausage for Boddy, wrapped in greaseproof paper. Off we went, over broad hills all golden green in the sun and parcelled like a scrap quilt with stone walls, the landscape altering until gradually everywhere the hills turned blueish and closer to the sky, garnished with hedges and woodland and long curvy lanes. Indeedy hummed as she drove, concentrating on the route and steep gradients. I wish I could read in a car like Zach, who always has his nose in a fat novel or history book, but I get sick, and on long journeys the best thing to do is think what to talk about.

'Mum, do you think Daddy's still alive?'

Indeedy swerved.

'Sorry!' A rabbit skittered into the long grass at the side of the road. 'I guess we'll never know. Officially he's not.' She started to hike up the volume on her favourite Bob Dylan album.

Indeedy never talked much about Daddy, and though Zach was enough older than me to understand more about what happened, he didn't ever explain anything either. Perhaps I never asked. I couldn't remember ever hearing my parents argue, but when I was about six they had sat us down in the kitchen one Sunday to tell us that they had decided to separate for a while to 'clear their heads' and 'give each other space'. It was going to be the best for all of us, they said. Daddy would move away for the time being, and we would stay in the house with Mummy and everything would be fine.

There was no question of who would be looking after us, due to Daddy's job as a foreign correspondent; he was already away on assignments more than he was home. But it felt to me that separating was more Indeedy's decision than his. They never asked Zach and me what we thought. To begin with, Daddy visited whenever he could, bringing us exotic gifts from wherever he was posted. Then one day, another Sunday, there was a phone call and we could hear Indeedy crying. She called us into the kitchen. Daddy had suddenly gone missing on assignment in some dangerous, violent place on the somewhere side of the world. Presumed dead. It was then and there, and I remember the numb feeling as if it was yesterday, that I began to comprehend what 'gone' means – a great dead nowhere hole, worse than a nothing, worse than 'lost'.

Indeedy sighed, as if she was reading my mind, or maybe it was the song Dylan was singing; she didn't speak for what seemed ages. Maybe she was lonely? She hadn't gone out on dates since Daddy's disappearance and I imagine she longed for love, but at the same time I was glad she stayed solo. I wanted her to myself.

'Why'd you split up?'

'WHAT?' She lowered the volume.

'Why'd you split up?'

'Please do *not* say "split up", Robin! You know I hate it. It sounds so violent, like something an axe murderer would do.'

'Sorry. Why did you and Daddy decide to separate?'

'Actually, I'm not sure you're ready to hear the story.'

'That's not fair. I might've never asked before, but you always told me answers should be forthcoming when questions are ready to be asked.'

This is true. Both of my parents always said they wanted to respect us like friends. And we were never smacked; our punishments were never so instant or so quickly over and done with. Once I snuck off with a box of matches and a pilfered cigarette. I was just curious, but I got caught in the act and sent to my room. It was Daddy who came to 'discuss your behaviour like two friends, Robin,' and he went on and on and on. I remember saying something like 'I don't want you to be my friend, I want you to be my Daddy.'

And now, just when I want Indeedy to be both my mum and my friend, she has gone all parental with her *You're not ready.* This is, I think, called irony.

Indeedy took a deep breath. 'OK. Robin, I loved and always will love your father. For a long time I dared to hope that he might still be alive, and there are so many happy memories. Your father is, *was* a remarkable man, devoted to his work and to us.' She paused. 'But I

9

was very young when we married. People change, and I changed more than Rory.'

'Why couldn't you just change together?'

'I truly don't know. It happened gradually. Things just came to a point where there wasn't really a choice.'

'Zach says we always have choices.'

'Maybe he's right. I don't know. You have asked, I can only tell you honestly how I felt. Marriage is serious, Robin, and I went into it for life, "not just for Christmas" like they say in that dog rescue advert. We both *meant* it to be for life–'

I interrupted her. 'Can you give me a "for example"?' I really, really like examples.

'OK. Imagine you're sailing around the world. You check your route, supplies are ample, equipment's in tiptop shape. There are risks and dangers but you weather the storms. Then one day out of the blue comes the mother of all storms and you discover essential equipment is missing – maybe the flares aren't where they're supposed to be, or they got damp. The search and rescue crews keep passing over your heads. Blaming anyone is pointless but anyway you feel it's your fault; it won't save you but it has forever changed your journey. You limp along to shore; when you touch dry land it sinks in that travelling together won't work any more.'

'Mum, you're leaving me and Zach out of the story. To split – I mean seperate when we were little. You were so *selfish*.'

I was thinking with my mouth as per usual. Indeedy slowed down. Her knuckles were white and tight on the steering wheel. 'Perhaps I *was* selfish, but sometimes you have to be selfish.' There were tears in her voice.

I kept my out-loud mouth quiet. Really, I wanted to shout but I didn't want to cause an accident. For a little while we were silent. In my head I was humming the words of a song we sang in school choir: *Be kind to your parents, though they don't deserve it, remember they're grown-ups, a difficult stage of life.*

We lurched round a bend and, pumping the brakes, Indeedy sang out, 'Here we be, Fruit! What a sight for – hell's bells! What's going on here?'

Several police cars were parked up the narrow lane, and those dunce-cap stripy traffic cones lined up everywhere, cordoning off the area. Indeedy turned into the gravel drive over a small bridge leading to some cottages. A police officer approached. In the distance was our family saloon parked outside our new home. Zach had arrived safely.

Indeedy zizzed down the window. 'Afternoon, officer. What's up?'

The officer, handsome like a soldier, tipped the beak of his cap formally and barked, 'I'm rather afraid we have a rather unpleasant incident here, madam, so if you don't mind we'd rather you moved on to your destination.'

That policeman wouldn't last five minutes with Mrs Avey with all those 'rathers', I thought. Mrs Avey was my favourite English teacher.

Indeedy's ears reddened and her ponytail twitched. 'Oh dear. Sorry if you thought we were gawkers but, officer, this is our destination. Note the mode of transport – we're moving here today, first cottage up the drive. What's up?'

Almost as if he hadn't heard, the officer repeated, 'Please move along to your destination, madam. An incident of suspicious intent resulting in an expiry has occurred.'

'You mean a death?'

'Correct, madam, and from questionable causes. Now if you'll just move along ...'

'That's terrible! You're certain there's nothing we can do to help?'

The policeman ignored her. 'You are causing an obstruction, madam. We don't wish to be wasting police time now, do we?' The officer backed away from the window where he'd moved too close to Indeedy's face, shifted a couple traffic cones and motioned her to continue up the lane.

As we pulled away, Indeedy called out, 'Do let us know if you change your mind – coffee, arsenic cocktail, whatever.' Then, under her breath, 'What a pain in the arse! He must be PR man for the "give the cops a bad name" brigade.'

'You just mind out the way, madam,' the officer shouted after us. 'And keep the kiddie and mutt on leads!'

If I were a spitter I would've. Instead I gave him the rude American middle finger sign when he wasn't looking.

Indeedy leaned over conspiratorially and whispered, '"Expiry" for "death". Honestly! Murder, do you think, Fruit? If so it must be the poor old gent at the manor, which is very sad. But hey! I do believe we've driven smack dab into a country crime!'

I gazed across through the driver's side window and got my first sighting of our new home. There it was, even prettier and bigger looking than the estate agent's pamphlet. Rainbow-coloured roses framed the front of the house and the greener than green garden stretched generously round the back where I could see a perfect tree, an oak I think, just waiting to be climbed. What also drew my eyes like a magnet, up a gentle slope and perched majestically like an eagle's nest shining in the afternoon sun, surrounded by a grand hedge with topiary clipped into statue shapes, was Pucklethorpe Manor. I loved it straight away, its windows, doors and chimneys conjuring a generous face despite the sinister news of murder hovering over our new home. My tummy danced.

As we parked, a grey-haired couple emerged from the house next door, waving at us and toting a large wicker basket.

'Welcome!' The man greeted us as we climbed from the lorry. 'Toby Spicer. This is the wife, Margaret. Mill Cottage.'

'Hi! I'm Indeedy Swallow, this is my daughter Robin, the dog's Boddy. Plus there's another family member already here, my son Zach.' Indeedy placed a restraining hand on my shoulder. She knew I just wanted to skip the niceties and skedaddle straight into our new life. 'I knocked on your door when I came to view the house a few weeks back, but nobody was around.'

Just then Zach exploded through the front door. 'What's up with you two, driving backwards?'

'Come off it, Speedy Gonzales!' Indeedy laughed, folding Zach's lanky frame in a bear hug. 'We *were* in a seven-tonne lorry, remember? Zach, say hello to Mr and Mrs Spicer.'

'Pleased to meet you,' chorused the Spicers. Mrs Spicer proffered the basket. 'Thought you might enjoy a little something to keep you going, bit of fresh produce from the farm. The officer told you what's happened?'

Indeedy raised an eyebrow. 'After a fashion. A "suspicious expiry" he said.'

'Well, my dears, it were murder, I fear. Poor, poor Mr Wheatley. Not a happy welcome for you, to be sure. But never mind.'

Mrs Spicer exchanged a sideways glance at Mr Spicer, who was squinting warily at Boddy. 'Dog don't worry sheep, do she?' Like he was changing the subject or something.

'Goodness gracious me, no.' Indeedy grinned. 'Unless they disguise themselves as squirrels or rabbits!'

'Just as well. They're caught worryin', farmers'll shoot 'em without a by your leave.'

Mrs Spicer bent to stroke Boddy. 'I'm sure this one'll be safe.'

Mr Spicer started to turn away, then hesitated. 'T'were no accident,' he said. 'Let's leave it at that. Dinna mix with them up there. You know, toffs. Enough said.' He walked off.

Mrs Spicer blushed. 'My husband, he's a man of few words. Well now, must be getting on now, dears. Chooks to feed and all. Anything you need, just give us a bell or pop round.'

'Why yes indeedy, we certainly will,' Indeedy said. 'And thank you for the lovely welcome.'

In the wicker basket Mrs Spicer had given us there bulged a dressed chicken, a loaf of dark malty-smelling brown bread still warm from the oven, a bendy cucumber and a white cabbage the size of a football. Indeedy said something about kindly neighbours being a good omen.

'I don't know about you, Fruit, but when someone says "Let's leave it at that", well, me, I can't.'

But despite her curiosity, it was furniture shifting time and all hands on deck. A quick cup of tea and then we unpacked the lorry, which had to be emptied for taking to the depot within twenty-four hours to save on hire costs. No time to waste. The bizarre circumstances of our arrival seemed to fade into obscurity.

I couldn't resist sneaking stares up the hill towards the big house whenever I passed the rear window, though. Over the yew hedge bordering the manor garden I could see workmen erecting scaffolding and attaching spotlights along the guttering, presumably making ready for the police to search the whole place top to bottom. There was a police caravan and a huge lorry with a marquee packed on the back. If you didn't know better, you might think they were setting up for a carnival.

Zach caught me staring and tickled me in the ribs. 'C'mon, Fruit, we've got the whole summer to investigate. I mean, you've got the whole summer. Meanwhile, tote dat barge, lift dat bale!'

So I did, because I practically worshipped the ground my brother walked on. Most of the time Zach managed to resist playing substitute dad. Indeedy sometimes teased that we needed counselling for 'excessive sibling harmony'. Not that we didn't have bad patches, especially over Zach's taste in music and his recent condescension towards all my opinions. But in my heart of hearts I dreaded his going off to university, knowing it would mean losing my dearest and closest ally.

By dusk we had all the labelled boxes in their respective rooms. Thank goodness for long summer days! Zach volunteered to drive the lorry back to the depot, saying he didn't mind going alone and was happy to hitch back. Indeedy frowned.

'Shows how much you know about traffic patterns out here, honey. You'd be lucky to catch a passing car every ten minutes this time of day.' No, she would follow him in the car and shouldn't I come too?

I ruffled. Said no thanks, if she didn' t mind I'd stay here and prepare the meal, which I love doing, especially when it's roast chicken.

'Aren't you a bit, er, nervous?' Indeedy asked.

'If I get the whimmies – which I won't – I've got Boddy. Or I could ring the Spicers. What's their number?'

Secretly I relished being on my own, not least to spend time exploring, especially my very own bedroom upstairs. Eventually persuaded, Indeedy hauled me into a big hug and off they drove in a cloud of diesel fumes.

I headed upstairs. My new bedroom, even with all the boxes, was already perfect to me, larger than my London bedroom, painted mint green and smelling of new paint and wood. Indeedy had found time to make the bed up with my favourite candlewick bedspread. I peered out of the big floor to ceiling windows, which doubled as a pair of glazed doors that opened onto an iron stairwell leading down to the garden. The key was in the door. It worked. I could have secret adventures. I'm thinking it's the very best ever room in the world.

I stared out of the windows. Pucklethorpe Manor was lit up like a film set and the big red summer sunset glossed the house with garish orange. The pond gleamed silver in the cloudy twilight. The police marquee was up and the workmen gone. There was just one shadowy someone – a detective? Mr Spicer? – in the manor gardens waving a machine back and forth across the lawn. It looked like a strimmer or something. I longed to explore but stuck to the promised task of setting out dinner, my growly stomach helping me along.

Back in the kitchen I criss-crossed Mrs Spicer's chicken with streaky bacon and bunged it into the Rayburn, one of those country-type cookers that are always hot. I chopped the white cabbage, chomping on the core that makes you fart but I love it, wishing we had some of Aunt Martha's corn on the cob, which you can't get in any supermarket. My corn on the cob job on family holidays in Tennessee was to go out into the field and pick it fresh. The corn grows much higher than me and you could hide in the rows forever if you wanted but you'd be hungry so you'd be quick. I'd pick maybe twenty cobs, take them in, then help Aunt Martha shuck the corn and get all the silky bits off. She'd boil the cobs for five minutes, no more, and lavish them with butter. When you bit them (some people bite in rows and some bite random) the kernels just popped a perfect sweet burst in your mouth. Sometimes Uncle Charlie steamed them in their green husks buried in the barbecue coals.

I was mashing potatoes using too many golden blobs of butter – YUM! – when I felt Boddy slide to my side, hackles sprung, pricking her ears and wagging her tail in a slow, wavy way and gazing at the kitchen window behind us. The hair on the back of my neck hackled too.

Dusk was setting in but not enough to obscure my vision. I turned my head and raised my eyes to the kitchen window – there, behind the glass and about two feet away, not flinching but gazing directly and calmly at me, was a dark brown young face with big greeny eyes and black messy hair going every which way. Instinct prevented me from calling out. The person – girl? boy? – smiled this dazzling smile and mouthed a word that looked sort of like hello. I returned a lippy grin that stuck to my teeth, and half turned away, beckoning this person towards the kitchen door. I was just wondering whether I should open the door or not when I looked again and the face was gone.

I rushed to open the kitchen door, and called out, 'Hello!'

Nothing.

I wasn't frightened. Well maybe a little bit, so I decided not to go out just yet, and checked that the doors and windows were locked. It felt like ages but couldn't have been that long before I heard the crunching of gravel and the hum of our car. Zach and Indeedy returning. What I thought at that precise moment was, PHEW.

We ate our meal in rare comfortable silence broken only by the occasional *Oh my, love that stuffing!* or *Pass the mash, please.* How I managed not to mention the face to Indeedy I'm not sure, but I was thinking she'd just fret.

'Thanks for cooking, Fruit. We'll leave the washing-up for tomorrow,' said Indeedy. 'Time for bed.'

I'd promised myself no matter how tired I was on my first night I would put at least one something up on my bedroom wall, and open my box of books. There was a handy nail and so up went a framed print of a sheer cliff with tiny human figures climbing to the precipice. It was a present from my friend Amelia back in London and the words on it, by Gertrude Stein, read: *Considering how dangerous everything is, nothing is really very frightening.*

I opened my book box, and there on top was my very first diary, a present from Daddy before he disappeared. It was dark green and had a lock and a key that didn't work. The key was tied on with cotton string. My first entry was a note:

I love you Daddy, I don't know where you are but I still love you anyway just like I did when you were here. Do you still love me like you did before? I hope so because I do, goodbye Daddy I love you with all my hart.

I had drawn a picture of a heart. I put the diary under my pillow, slid between my sheets and zonk! I was asleep and dreaming almost the minute I got into my familiar bed in my not-familiar bedroom.

I woke myself calling Zach's name and not sure whether I was still in my London bed or the house in my dream. I think I was sleepwalking. After Daddy disappeared I used to sleepwalk a lot. And stammer. Zach is usually a light sleeper and I found myself in his room.

He groaned but pulled the covers down. I plopped beside him, curling cosy like a koala bear.

'Gettin' too old for this, Fruit.'

'What you mean?'

'Just what I said. Go back to your own bed.'

'Don't be rude, Zach. I didn't know I was coming here. Anyway, now I am here I want to tell you something.' I wanted to share the face at the window with someone.

'Whatever it is, it can wait. Go back to sleep, Fruit.'

'It's now or never,' I said.

'It'll be never then.'

Zach put the pillow over his head. Any other time I'd have just blurted out what I wanted to say. But Zach is stubborn and almost never changes his mind.

'I will never, ever, *ever* tell you anything ever again.' Now I felt wide awake and stomped off and back to my own room.

When I did finally toss and turn myself back to sleep, there came a dream of a house where I got lost looking for Daddy, and then it was the face in the window. The face said, 'Open the door. Go on, open it.'

2
Exodus

Word of the day: empathy.
The ability to understand and share the
feelings of another.

Mum knocked on the bedroom door. She always knocked first. I had been trying to concentrate on my homework, thinking about the father in the book I was reading, which was an assignment from Mrs Avey: 'Was Atticus Finch a good father? Discuss.'

'Robin, what would you say to moving away from London,' said Indeedy, more like an announcement than a question. It didn't really sink in.

'Mum, why'd he say *mockingbird* in the title? Why not an eagle or something?'

'He who?'

'The book writer. Is he from the olden days?'

'*She* is still alive as far as I know. And it's "author" not "book writer", Robin.'

I pretty much thought anybody who wrote a book had to be dead, and I guess they were, mainly – at least the ones we had to read in school. Mrs Avey never told us anything about authors until after we had read the books. She was my most interesting teacher. Even though we all laughed about her dandruff and fat tummy. We called her 'Mrs' but she wasn't married – she'd never had the time, she said. 'I'm very lucky,' she would say. 'I've taught nearly 2,000 children over the years.' She said Mark Twain and Daphne du Maurier and Harper Lee were her joys.

'Now I'm a grown-up,' said Indeedy, 'I think if I were ever lucky enough to meet Miss Harper Lee I'd say, "What a fine book", and ask her to sign a copy. Now. What say you to a move away from London?'

I put my book down and then just thought out loud with my mouth.

'Mum, how can I say 'til I know where and what school I'd go to? And what about all my friends?'

Indeedy put on her worried sympathetic look, produced a leaflet from behind her back and moved closer. She smelled of fudge and vanilla from work. We called her 'the edible mum' as a wind-up – she had a round smell but a thin look.

'Number one first. Here's where. Looks perfect to me. There's even room for a pony, possibly.'

'Pony?'

'Or have you grown out of your pony stage?'

'That makes no sense to me, Mum. A pony is for life not for Christmas, remember?'

'Yes, indeedy. Quite right, Fruit. Well, no bribes and no promises, but we'll see what we can do.' Indeedy spread out the estate agent's leaflet which had lots of colour photos of the place.

On the front page was a red and pink brick house with a peaked slate roof crowned with two chimneys and outside stairs bending round corners, a bit like the fire exits you see on public buildings but pretty, with lacy looking railings. Three red doors were spaced along the front of the house like sentinels, and it had arched windows. The garden was bordered by a dry-stone wall – then, dotted around, climbing trees and a big browny-coloured pond with an island in the middle. And an outbuilding that looked a bit shabby with a chimney stuck at one end described as 'The Old Bakehouse'.

'What do you think, Fruit?'

'It looks ... OK.'

'Look at the name – Limberlost Mill. The countryside is gorgeous and we can renovate the bakehouse for the business. I'll show you on the map.'

I couldn't read maps that well, my idea of north being uphill and south coming back down, but it didn't really matter because I could tell Indeedy had her mind made up.

'We'll not be stuck in the middle of nowhere,' Indeedy said. 'We'll have neighbours, but not too close. In the olden days all the buildings were part of a huge estate. The grand house is nearby and there's someone, an old man on his own, I think, living there in the manor, the big house. It's just chock-a-block with history.'

'What does Zach think?'

'Big bro seems perfectly fine about it. For starters, Pucklethorpe is closer to Bristol.' Zach was off to university in September.

Indeedy was decisive like the rest of her American family. I admit I sometimes wished I was American too, except when we visited the relatives in Tennessee. There I really basked in Englishness because they all loved my accent. *English accents sound intelligent and precise,* says Aunt Martha. The American cousins have good skin and too many big white straight teeth, and they always have a lot of pocket money too. Indeedy's relatives had once been slave owners and still used the 'N' word without the bat of an eyelid. Plus I think they were sort of phony sometimes, like they would say in a drawl, 'Y'all come back soon, ya hear?' to guests, when they didn't mean it. I knew this because as soon as the unfortunate visitors had left, they'd start saying nasty things about them. They had a name for it – 'having the guests over'.

I did think long and hard about why we were moving and whether there is ever a right time to move. I had heard Indeedy complain about some sort of property tax and she said why should I worry about grown-up matters but I did anyway.

I volunteered my opinion to Indeedy. 'I think we *should* move, but,' I said, 'would it make any difference if I didn't?' Indeedy just grinned her big grin again and hugged me, saying that the choice for a fresh start was hers in the end and she would accept the consequences and since I love lists why didn't I make a list of the things I wanted to know and she'd answer them if she could?

So I did:

1. Is there a library? Answer: YES, ON WHEELS
2. Is there a cinema? Answer: YES, IT'S 30 MILES AWAY
3. Are there shops with crunchy peanut butter and popcorn? Answer: TO BE INVESTIGATED
4. Do people have their own horses? Answer: YES AND THEY AREN'T ALL LAH-DI-DAH
5. Do they have homework at the schools? Answer: HIGHLY LIKELY
6. Are there venomous snakes? Answer: YES JUST ONE, CALLED AN ADDER
7. Is my school far from our house? Answer: 4 MILES AWAY AND THERE'S A SCHOOL BUS

8. Is there a school uniform? Answer: YES
9. Will I be able to walk barefoot? Answer: YOU ARE IN ENGLAND! NO!
10. Is there a space observatory? NO

It was all decided. We would move.

Before I left, I wrote Mrs Avey a thank you for teaching me to use indexes and diagram sentences and for giving me a copy of *The Hunchback of Notre Dame* – and most of all for the word book idea.

The word book was simple. It started when Mrs Avey gave us all little red spiral exercise books to copy down a 'word of the day'. She'd ask us to invent our own meaning for the word and then learn what it really meant in the dictionary; a new word greeted us every school day morning written in capital letters on the chalkboard. I keep it up most days, and I can still remember the first word, 'stupefy'.

Kids at school call me a swot but I don't care one little bit. I even thanked Mrs Avey for sending me to the headmaster's office that time the school caretaker died when he slipped and fell off the gymnasium roof. We didn't see it happen but kids said he'd splattered his brains all over the parking lot below, and we were ordered after the announcement of his untimely end to observe three minutes of silence. I got the giggles, couldn't stop. Was in Real Trouble. Mrs Avey quietly approached my desk, took me firmly by the arm and gestured me out of a classroom alive with sniggers. I apologized to Mr Barge, the headmaster, who was not mean at all.

'I'm sorry, Mr Barge, truly I am. I know I shouldn't laugh, but I'm not really sad about Mr Watts because he was mean and smelly and drunk all the time, and anyway all my friends were only pretending to be sad.'

Mr Barge made a tepee with his hands, holding my gaze, and paused for what seemed ages. Then he asked me to sit. 'You are an honest girl, Robin Swallow. Honesty is very important. But so is empathy. I suggest you write one hundred lines: We must show respect for the dead.'

This experience was the first of many lessons in artifice, by which I mean that you're not lying if you keep quiet and just try to listen sometimes, that as Indeedy says you have two ears and one mouth and there's a reason for that. I still don't know whether I could have stopped giggling, but before I wrote my lines I looked up 'empathy' and entered it in my little red 'word of the day' book. Then, painstakingly and in my best writing, but vertically.

we must show respect for the dead
we must show respect for the dead
we must show respect for the dead

Still, I couldn't help wonder what about the living?

I think Mr Watts' death was when I decided not to have kids of my own, not least because I often don't like *being one*. I'd just as soon stick with animals and plants and outer space. How *anybody* becomes a parent is stupefying! I'm happy with Boddy, who whispers like a human, letting her breath out in sort of tuned sighs, altering the shape of her mouth to change the noise. You can't say the word 'walk', and you can't spell it either, because she watches your mouth move *w-a-l-k* and still knows what you're saying. Her favourite word is 'sausage'.

Boddy looks like a big shaggy blue-grey stick insect with four very long legs, a tucked-up tummy and bronze-gold staring eyes. People call her type 'sight dogs' because they see as sharp as humans. Boddy can outstare me – her pupils expand and contract like a cartoon character. And she never gets fat. Even the one time she had pups, her tummy didn't get round like an ordinary dog. Instead the tucked-up bit just gradually went straighter and lower until it was level with her breastbone. She made a good mum. When the pups were naughty she clasped her teeth round their noses with the delicacy of a retriever fetching an egg. Then she'd march them back and forth across the garden until they calmed down. As for moving, well, Boddy loves miles of running space. She looks like a flowing river when she gallops, fast as a racehorse.

By the end of the summer term Indeedy had organized everything and we were packed and ready to go. So it was farewell to our egg-yolk-yellow London kitchen and the park round the corner where it was safe to walk Boddy by myself and the buzz of crowds and cinemas and shops everywhere and the glow of street lamps and Selfridges and Hamleys at Christmas, and especially Mrs Avey.

I said goodbye to my city friends, promised to keep in touch, and tried hard not to look back.

3
Hatchintan

The library is dangerous, full
Of answers. If you go inside,
You may not come out
The same person who went in.

– 'Don't Go Into the Library', Alberto Rios

Tap-tap on my bedroom door. Must be Mum. I opened my eyes to a squinch.

'Where are we?'

'Good morning, Fruitfly! We're right here in our new home.' Indeedy is extremely cheerful in the mornings. Daddy used to call her 'terminally perky'. 'I felt exactly the same when I woke up, *where am I?* Let's have some breakfast, then why don't you and Boddy go exploring, get all the travel kinks out of the system? I've loads of errands and the unpacking can wait.'

Indeedy was right. All those hours in the lorry yesterday had left me, let alone Boddy, itching for a

32

good stretch. I climbed into yesterday's clothes, made a pretence of brushing my teeth, woke my face up with cold water, and bounded downstairs. Indeedy had already finished last night's washing-up.

'Just some toast to go?' I was bursting to tell Mum about the face in the window but a rare pause button between brain and mouth held me back. I didn't want unnecessary explanations to delay me.

'Sure thing, Fruit. Have a good time! Oh, if you go as far as town can you buy a local paper?' Indeedy handed me a couple of pound coins.

Down the drive Boddy and I jogged and up the lane curving towards the village of Pucklethorpe. We crossed a bridge with a perfect jumping-off place and a deep clear stretch of water. I could imagine showing off with back dives and jack knives and belly-flops. Boddy and I are champion swimmers but although it was summer there was still a brr-rrr nip in the air. Later!

In a lay-by after the bridge was a big old-fashioned lorry. It looked a bit like an American yellow school bus but it was white. The door was open. By the fold down steps was a dog bed with an umbrella propped over it to keep it dry, a hook for a lead and a big bowl of fresh water. The sign outside said:

THE BOOK PLACE (BORDERLAND MOBILE LIBRARY) – CASSANDRA KISS, MLS, PHD.

I peeked inside and there she was, the most perfect librarian you could dream of, with a big smile, round old-fashioned spectacles and freckles. A black velvet hairband tamed her long shiny ginger hair. She wore a white shirt, a navy blue pinafore dress and Hush Puppies that Indeedy would call 'sensible', and she was knitting something complicated-looking in bright colours.

'May I come in?'

'But of course, my dear! What can we do for you today?'

Miss Kiss smelled of toast and inside her toasty domain lived all manner and size of books lining the walls and floor of the place. 'I love libraries, they're heaven – which I don't believe in – but I mean that when I die and go to heaven – if there is one – it will be a library and everyone in London thinks I'm a swot but I don't care 'cos I'll find every book possible and I will take them to the meadow outside the library and sit there with my dog who will be there too because if animals aren't allowed in heaven I don't want to be there and we'll read and read and not get in trouble for handing the books back late because we are in forever time.' I stopped when I ran out of breath.

Miss Kiss chuckled. 'Well, young lady! I sometimes think a heavenly library would be one where no one ever checks out any books! People have good intentions but they may forget to return the books in time, and they write in the books, and they fold the pages down like a puppy's ear ... but do please take a seat.'

I had done all those things to books sometimes. Instead of confess, I said, 'We moved here yesterday, Limberlost Mill, the house by Pucklethorpe Manor.'

'Oh, my dear. Such grotesque tragedy and here on our doorstep! The poor man and the downfall of a great house. Mr Wheatley often ordered his Braille books from here. He was, I believe, a historian of some note. He will be much missed.'

I had nothing to add. I wanted to ask if Miss Kiss knew who the face in the window last night might have been, but how would she know? So instead I said, 'Well, Miss Kiss, I want to check books out.'

Miss Kiss gave me a library card to fill in.

'"S" for Swallow. Robin Swallow. Two lovely birds in one name. Do come back soon. We operate the Dewey Decimal System here. Are you familiar?'

'Yes, I am. My year eight teacher, Mrs Avey, taught us.'

'Well done. We're here three days a week, nine a.m. until four p.m. And,' added Miss Kiss, 'we carry only a small selection here in the bus, but whatever the book you want, we will find it for you. Have you something in mind to be getting on with?'

'Is there a history book about big famous houses?'

'Why yes, there is, but not here.' Miss Kiss wrote a note. 'Anything else?'

'Yes please. I'd like a book about space travel.'

'Have you read *A Wrinkle in Time?*'

'Yes. But I'd quite like a factual book.'

'Non-fiction. Well now, as it happens, I've one in stock here, written by a real life astronaut.' Miss Kiss went straight to a low shelf and removed the book. 'Here you are, dear. *The Way of the Explorer*. I believe the author was on one of the Apollo missions. Have you an interest in astronomy?'

'I hope to become a space journalist, Miss Kiss.'

'How exciting! This will be a treat for you then.' Miss Kiss thumped her ink stamp, then stamped a paper glued in the front of the book with a due date, and stamped my brand-new library card too. 'I will ring you when the local history book arrives. I do believe that Mr Wheatley, God rest his soul, was writing a social history of Pucklethorpe Manor.'

'Thank you, Miss Kiss!'

I jumped all the steps at once, holding tight to my first library book, and Boddy bounded up to greet me. We passed a big old church and graveyard and then found the castle. A sign greeted visitors:

PUCKLETHORPE CASTLE, RETURNED TO HER FORMER GLORY
BY ENGLISH HERITAGE.

Someone had struck out the word 'glory' and written 'ruins' and a big smiley face. Boddy and I had a good sniff around the town's main tourist attraction, but having been treated on school trips to places like Buckingham Palace and Windsor and Warwick castles, I failed to see what was so special about this one. I mean, it was a very large pile of stone shaped like part of a castle – still, a pile.

You wouldn't say Pucklethorpe was picture postcard special either. It's one of those places travel brochures call 'sleepy'. It has a police station, a post office-cum-food store, three pubs, a draper's, a sweet shop that's also a newsagent, an ironmonger and a garage where they repair farm machinery. And two churches. We had already passed the first of them, surrounded by yew trees and gravestones, Church of England, very, very old, and there was a Methodist one, not quite as ancient, with its cemetery at the other end of the village.

We stopped by the newsagent's that doubled as a sweet shop to buy Indeedy's newspaper. Front page headlines shouted: LOCAL MAN FOUND DEAD AT PUCKLETHORPE MANOR. I had just started to read the article when a voice behind the counter admonished, 'Young lady, here we encourage customers to purchase what they read. And the dog – only assistance dogs are allowed in the shop.'

The owner of the voice was tall and thin and old and frowny. Boddy's upper lip curled into a silent growly grimace.

'Sorry,' I said. 'We just moved here. Limberlost Mill, by the manor.' I reached in my pocket and paid for the paper, rolling it up and sticking it under my arm.

'A Londoner then, are you?' He looked at the ceiling instead of me.

'Yes, sir.' I said 'sir' but I thought of him as 'Mr Grumps'. 'We just walked here, not from London, I mean, from our house here. What will we find if we wander for a bit?'

Still staring at the ceiling, he replied. 'Out the door, turn left and walk past the pub. When you reach the fork at the top of the road, up left and way up Darky Dale is the school, too far to walk. The right fork will take you out of town on the main road and towards the Gypsy site.'

My ears pricked right up. Gypsies! My imaginary Gypsy fit the face in the window – swarthy, and well, very beautiful. Could the face in the window be an honest proper Gypsy?

Mr Grumps must have seen me look interested. 'I'd steer well clear of them tinkers if I was you,' he warned. 'They'll fetch the shirt off your back before you can say boo to a goose.'

I thought, *Rude!* I could've been anyone; I could've been a Gypsy for all he knew. Boddy and I got out of there fast. I didn't even buy a gobstopper. His warning put wings on our feet. I couldn't wait to get to the Gypsy site. We turned right at the fork in the road.

People talk about Gypsies' wild vagabond ways, which maybe is why I – have you ever? – dreamed about running away with Gypsies when the circus comes to town. But when we got to the place I couldn't see what the fuss was about.

The front garden was tumbly-tidy, with an arch over the main gate laden with white roses and honeysuckle, and though the house looked in need of a lick of fresh paint it was cosy and inviting, and lived-in looking. Piled up behind the house was a stack of firewood as high as two of me. Zach can go to university and study robots or whatever, I thought, but I'll join the Gypsies and learn how to stack logs. The caravans in the field behind the house were bright and shiny like a fairground just set up, arranged in a crescent around a grassy space where about half a dozen hounds and terriers lolled and didn't seem to notice me and Boddy. At the back of the site were piles of metal and bits of wrecked cars, and goats staked on long ropes with spotted ponies grazing free. There seemed to be nobody about, and I didn't knock on the door.

Not this time.

Back home, I was glad to see Mrs Spicer at her front door. 'Your mum says to tell ye she's had to go off on an errand. Fancy a cuppa?'

'Yes, please!' I thought perhaps my new neighbour would be a good source of news about all the things I was dying to ask about – the face at the window, the Gypsy site. And perhaps there would be cake.

'Do come in and take a pew, dearie.'

Mrs Spicer passed me a steaming mug. Boddy leaned hard against my side and then slid in slow motion to a doggy flop across my feet like she wanted to pin me down.

'Here. Give us a hand shelling the peas. I won't look if you pops a few in your cakehole.' She smiled. Then, out of nowhere: 'It's true what they say about murder, my dear.'

I was bursting to ask her about the Gypsies but instead I asked, 'What do they say?'

Plink plink went the peas from their pods into the big brown bowl.

'High society and lowdown deeds. Folks get more het up over property and money than a human life. Me? Borderland born and bred I am, only moved away in the first place to marry my Toby, and now here we are, back home.'

'I don't understand killing someone.'

'Ah now, nor do I. When her Ladyship left Mr Wheatley she tried to sell the house outright, but he refused to budge. Sitting tenant, they call it, I do believe. She got proper outraged and vowed to sue him, have him evicted.' She gave me a knowing look. 'But then, who am I to say?'

I chewed on a pea pod from the rising mound beside the bowl and slipped one to Boddy, who likes peas: *crunch crunch.* Mrs Spicer sipped from a purple drink she called her *dy-jes-teef.*

'He loved that house, Mr Wheatley did, the grandness and all, so fair enough. Loved it more than she did, I dare say. Put his life's work into it, but he was stubborn to boot while she was one of them nobs – folk who see 'emselves as above the law and better than everyone else. And like I said, money, my dear, all of it from her side of the family. She was the brass and him the brains, more wishbone than backbone, if you ask me – but he was harmless, like.'

'They must've been rich to own a place like that,' I said. 'So many rooms!'

'My giddy aunt, yes! Back in the day these houses down the lane, yours and mine and the one up the way, was all part and parcel of the one estate. And then there's a tale me mum told me, sticks like treacle.'

Mrs Spicer leaned close. 'Me mum, she said the last Lord Pucklethorpe buried treasure somewhere in the manor grounds during the last war, so's if we was invaded, like, his money would never help Hitler. Gold bars it was,' said Mrs Spicer, lowering her voice to a whisper. 'Me mum, she was housekeeper at the manor. Lord Pucklethorpe's wife's maid was having an affair with his Lordship's valet. The valet told the maid and the maid told me mum that the reason for the gold bars was he didn't trust paper money, so he brought them bars over here from Europe and hid 'em away' – she lowered her voice – '*somewhere in the manor grounds.*'

Mrs Spicer sighed, wiping her hands on her apron and taking another glug of her drink. Her cheeks were going pink. 'I expect it's a load of balderdash, but it makes a ripping yarn, don't it?'

I nodded yes. I was fascinated. Gold bars!

'I'd love to hear lots more stories! The librarian Miss Kiss said Mr Wheatley was a historian.'

'Well, yes, my dear. That's why he liked living there, I s'pose. The history, and the stories. Now, what can I tell you?' She sipped again from her glass. 'Ah, yes. Very sad this story is to tell. The last Lord Pucklethorpe, he had only one child, a lad called Jesse – named in honour of the Jesse Tree in the cellar of the great house, I believe. The poor chook died after a fall from his pony. After that, Lord Pucklethorpe renovated the ancient chapel in the cellar, and he planted that beautiful topiary hedge round the estate you can see now. He and his wife, Lady Eleanor, poured their energies into doing good. They endowed colleges and hospitals and orphanages, and treated their well-paid staff to glittering parties. But they never had more children, so eventually, when they died, the manor was up for sale. And that's when Lady Charlotte's family bought it.'

Topiary – another one for the word book, I thought, remembering the elaborate hedges I'd seen from my window.

'Any road, back to now, and poor old Mr Wheatley. When her Ladyship left him, it seemed his eyes got worse, *masculine* degeneration or some such. He never felt sorry for himself, used to say it was a lovely part of the world to be poor and that he could remember what seeing was like.'

'Did Mr Wheatley know about the gold bar story?'

'I'm not sure about that, dearie, but most likely yes. He did keep digging around the grounds. Had a Gypsy child at his side most days helpin' him.'

At last!

'Gypsy?'

Mrs Spicer put some potatoes in a colander and handed me a peeler. Her eyes softened with affection. Another glug on the purple drink.

'Name of Summer Locke. Lives about a mile up the Romany Road by an old house the far side of Pucklethorpe. Proper Gypsies they are; keep their caravans painted bright as cathedral windows and clean as a whistle. Summer's bright as a button but never been to school, an orphan they say, taken in by the Romanies. Most likely that child was the best friend poor old Mr Wheatley had, right up to his passing. Summer Locke was his eyes and his messenger. You'd see 'em together, trimmin' the hedges and tending the hens and bees. Did some of his shopping too, and frightened off burglars more than once, so I'm told.'

'I think I've seen Summer Locke,' I said excitedly. 'Last night. The man in the newsagent's said to stay away from the Gypsies but I want to meet them.'

'Well, my dear, you will discover soon enough. Most folk, includin' our own police, don't abide easy with those who keep on the move like Gypsies and their now you see us now you don't.'

'I went there to find them, wasn't anyone there.'

'I'm not surprised. It's the time of year when they'll be goin' off to some Gypsy horse fair or other. They'll be back soon enough.'

'I truly want to meet Summer Locke,' I said.

'In that case, my dear, I shall make you my famous Scotch eggs tonight, in case you go soon. Summer Locke swears by 'em. Tell Summer I sent them. That child is always welcome here.'

Hearing the sound of a car outside, I sped up with the potato peeling and wiped my hands dry on my trousers. 'Better go. Mum'll think I've run away.'

Mrs Spicer chuckled. Her drink was empty and her button nose shone as pink as her cheeks. 'Well now, you've done more than enough, chook, thankin' you. You're always welcome too.'

Boddy and I went next door to greet Indeedy. I still didn't mention the face at the window.

Later, tucked all cosy in my bed in my new room, I opened my very first library book about space exploration. I must have dozed off after only a couple of sentences. Country air helps you dream better, I suppose.

I am lost in a dark forest. I come to a window without a house around it. I try to look inside but it's like the window is wood and I have to open it like a door. There's Daddy, he is reaching for me from a bridge and I run towards him but he keeps going backwards and I can't catch him. I trip over a book on the ground and fall into waking up.

4
Open the Door

This is the house where Ridey Didey died. Stand on the fallen door and look inside.

– 'Ridey Didey's House',
The Barrow Poets

Next morning we did more unpacking. I kept staring out at Pucklethorpe Manor, which was off-limits during the investigation, bursting to sneak a close look. Just in case people didn't understand the KEEP OFF message, the police had brought in a dog patrol, which appealed to Boddy's flirtatious nature. She was up in my room, whimpering at the French windows and getting in the way, ears up and askew. That dog almost always gets her way and I wanted an excuse anyway, so I turned the key and exited down my bedroom escape steps, letting Boddy take the lead. She cavorted and twirled her whippy lurcher tail at the German Shepherd dogs with

46

their bandit faces and shiny *Granma, how big your teeth are!* grins. The police dogs didn't move a muscle, bandit face markings inscrutable, panting, hackles raised in an involuntary message: STAY OUT. Me, I was thinking that Boddy might be able to keep them at bay when the police go home, and I'd work out a way to get close to the big house. But not yet.

Back inside, Indeedy had her nose stuck in yesterday's paper.

'Interesting. Look at the headline, Fruit: "Murder at the Manor: Correspondent Chris Lamb Investigates." Chris Lamb lives in the cottage just up the way here. She left a message for us introducing herself and I'm meeting her later. But I digress. It says here they've arrested some Gypsies as well as Mr Wheatley's ex-wife for questioning. In my opinion, that woman deserves locking up just for the names she gave her kids.' Indeedy pointed at the article. 'Look. Bathsheba, Zadok, and Delilah!'

'Oh, really?' I was only half-listening. My mind was on the face in the window and the face now had a name: Summer Locke. I needed a plan.

'Mum, guess what? Yesterday I found the library. It's a mobile library in a big bus and there's this brilliant librarian called Miss Kiss who will help me find any book I want, so is it OK if I go there now and check some books out?'

'Sure, honey. Any unpacking we haven't done will still be here waiting for us whenever.'

I wasn't exactly deceiving Indeedy because I truly did want to check more books out and soon. I just had to find Summer Locke first.

Mrs Spicer caught me outside on our driveway. 'Got somethin' for ye, dear. I've made you some Scotch eggs in case you find young Summer.'

I looked over my shoulder to check that Indeedy wasn't in earshot. 'Er …well, I was going to the library but I could fetch them specially to the Gypsy site for you now you've made them.'

Have you ever noticed that once you sort of cover up the truth you have to keep on covering up and it can get complicated? Indeedy always says that if you tell the truth you don't have to have a good memory. And the fact is that there was no good reason why I didn't want to tell Indeedy about the Gypsies, not really. Some people think you just start lying automatically when you become a teenager; maybe it happens a lot, even though I wish it didn't.

The Scotch eggs smelled delicious, like bacon and chips, and Boddy's wet black nose twitched with pleasure. Mrs Spicer had wrapped five of them individually in greaseproof paper.

'Two each for you and Summer Locke, and one for your lucky dog.'

Boddy and I tore down the drive, up the lane, past the jumping-off place, behind the mobile library – so that Miss Kiss wouldn't see us; I felt bad for not stopping – along the High Street through town and straight along the Romany Road to the Gypsy site.

Today the Gypsy encampment was as full of life as it had been empty yesterday. My heart raced as I opened the gate, and a man's voice boomed out. 'What you want, chavvie?'

I jumped. Boddy slid herself between me and the owner of the voice, her lips curling up quietly over her teeth.

He was a big muscly man standing beneath the rose arbour, arms crossed over an open-fronted check shirt. There was a gorilla tattoo on his forearm. 'Excuse me, sir, my name is Robin, and I'm looking for Summer Locke.'

'Say so, chavvie? What you want with Summer?'

'Well, sir, Summer came to see me the day we moved in and said "Hello" through my window but we didn't chat properly.'

'Whereabouts you moved to, then?'

'Down the lane, sir. Limberlost Mill. Our house is below Pucklethorpe Manor.'

The man stiffened. 'Them's tried to see us evicted more'n once.'

'Sorry, sir. I'm glad they didn't. From what the papers say you're not the only ones they wanted rid of.'

He nodded a measured yes, as children from the caravans formed a circle around me and Boddy. One of them tried to stroke her and Boddy ducked her head away.

'Sorry,' I said again. I was apologising a lot. 'Lurchers do that, don't feel bad.'

Immediately I felt stupid because of course they'd know that, Gypsies being lurcher breeders for millions of years. I felt small, like my Fruitfly nickname, even though nobody was threatening me. One little girl, about five or six, with big green eyes and long blue-black hair all tousled and wild, touched my single brown plait. I had pulled it over to the front of my shoulder, twisting it round my fingers.

'I like your hair, missy.'

'Thanks. I hate it myself, my hair, that is, but Indeedy – she's my mum, we call her Indeedy because she's always saying "Yes, indeedy" because she's American – she won't let me cut it yet. Wants to see if it'll go down to my bum. It gets in my way most of the time. I'll plait yours, if you like, would you like that? It doesn't take long if you hold still.'

There I was prattling on again, talking whatever came into my mouth from my head. The little girl eyed me steadily, twisting a lock of hair.

'Summer ain't here since morning. Been tooken away by the *gavs*.'

'Sorry – taken by who?'

After a brief glance at the man, the girl continued. 'The *gavmush* – coppers.'

'Oh, I'm so sorry,' I said, remembering that Mrs Spicer had warned about keeping Summer Locke away from police. 'Is there any way I can help?'

The man scowled, rubbing his tattoo. 'Day after they found the *puro moosh's* dead body they swooped in here, arrested the lot of us. They always do, any excuse. Summer was off somewhere and got missed. Not so lucky this time.'

The little girl added, 'We always tried to stop Summer going to the big house but Summer and Mr Wheatley was fast friends.'

'Yes,' I said. 'My neighbour Mrs Spicer says Summer looked after him.'

'Well,' said the little girl, 'long time back, Mr Wheatley caught Summer tending his beehives and after he shouted at Summer they made friends, because Summer mostly never runs away from nothin'. Summer won't tell the *gavs* nothing neither, King says,' she added proudly, nodding to the man.

'Would you come with me to the police station to find Summer?' I asked the girl.

King intervened. 'No. Our Ditty won't be no way going near there.'

'Sorry, sir. Well, please just point me in the direction,' I said, even though I already knew really.

Boddy, who had been introducing herself to the other dogs, trotted unbidden to my side. Ditty took my hand and walked me to the edge of the road, pointing directions to the High Street and assuring me I couldn't miss the police station. 'Cheers!' I said, glancing over my shoulder. 'Thank you, Mr King!' But Mr King had gone.

It wasn't far at all back into town. How long would we need to wait for Summer Locke? I found the grumpy newsagent and tied Boddy up outside, then spent my pocket money on a magazine, a bottle of fizzy Vimto and a lemon sherbet fountain. Ditty was right, you couldn't miss the police station, diagonally down and across the street from the post office, even though it didn't look very official to me. There was a big sign saying 'Police', and in Welsh underneath, 'Heddlu'. It was an ugly grey place, totally unlike the nearby timbered buildings leaning comfortably against each other along the length of the street.

Around the side of the police station was a grass verge and a bench where we made ourselves comfortable. I couldn't wait any longer to taste Mrs Spicer's Scotch eggs, and divided one to share with Boddy, then opened the Vimto for a few tugs and prepared to wait as long as necessary. The sun warmed us like basking seal pups. I read my magazine and Boddy dozed off.

I must have dozed, too. When I opened my eyes there Summer was, standing above me. Alluring.

'Some dream you been dreamin', missy. Are you sound?'

'I've been waiting for you,' I said. 'You are Summer Locke, yes?'

'The one and the only,' Summer replied.

The *gavs*, Summer recalled as we walked on out of town, had been reasonable and hadn't asked any no-go questions. Summer, they said, would henceforth be eliminated from police enquiries.

'What do you mean "no-go" questions? You mean because you are a Gypsy?' A bit blunt, me. Summer Locke didn't seem bothered.

'I do not know whether 'twas ...' Summer left the sentence dangling.

'Go on!' I begged. 'Please tell me a "for instance" no-go question.'

'I shall, when I see that you are worthy.'

'How'm I supposed to prove that?' I said. 'Ask my brother Zach, he'll tell you I'm the world's best-ever secret-keeper!'

'But you are a *gorgio*. A housedweller.'

'So?'

'All right, then. I shall offer one example: I could not tell the *gavs* that Mr Brockton Wheatley was planning to adopt me and see to it that I would be the first ever Romany to attend Oxford University.'

So Summer is an orphan? I'm kind of like, half an orphan, I thought.

'Want a Scotch egg?'

'Yes, please!'

We had not walked far out of town when I was seized with curiosity.

'Listen, Summer, shall we go now and see if we can get into the manor?'

'I must first speak to the elders at the *hatchintan*. They will wish to know that I am safe and sound.'

We backtracked to the site and Summer reported the police interview to King, out of my earshot. Frankly I felt a bit of a plonker just standing there waiting. King's dark face remained impassive, broken only by an occasional truculent nod. When Summer finished, King offered a cool, 'Joller along with the chavvie, then. See you when we see you.' Summer's little lookalike Ditty scampered after us, begging to come along. Just one 'No' from Summer and she turned back in a skulk to the site.

'Why'd you turn her back?' I asked.

'We do not let our girl children loose to roam round, and that is that.'

So was Summer Locke a boy? Not that it mattered one little bit. I let the subject drop.

The afternoon sun beat down and I was all sticky and hot. When we reached the jumping-off place I was ready for a swim.

'Hey, Summer! What say we go for a dip?' Without waiting for a reply I stripped off to my vest and knickers. 'I'm a junior life saver, so don't fret.'

Summer shrugged comfortably. 'I shall not fret.'

'Let's go then! First one in's the champ!'

I clambered onto the coping stones of the bridge and leaned over at a daring angle. Still no movement from Summer so I upped the odds: Boddy sprang up on the wall beside me, putting me off balance. Saving myself from a precipitate plunge, I glanced at Summer. 'I'll count to three. On three it's jump!'

'Understood.'

'Boddy too – in the water, Bod!' I planned a foot-first entry, remembering Aunt Martha's cautionary wisdom about shifting rocks in running water and the way swimming holes and jumping-off places can turn into deadly traps if the rocks shift during floods. From the bridge's wall the water looked a very long way down.

'One, two, therr-ee JUMP!' I shouted. I pointed my toes for entry and felt the cold wrap my body. Opening my eyes in the green icy water, I finally hit the bottom with my feet and pushed off hard from the smooth round rocks. The time between slicing into the water with my toes and reaching the river bed seemed to take more seconds than a single breath could hold. Heading for the light, I burst through the surface of the water, looking around me for Summer Locke. Boddy had jumped with me and already scrambled up on the bank, where she was now shaking herself like a levitating kitchen mop. There stood Summer, statue-still, on the jumping-off place wall, unapologetic, smiling and, of course, dry.

'Could not jump, no dry clothes.'

'No problem,' I lied. 'Boddy and I are the champs. Let's go!'

As we reached the lane, the hornet sound of a motorbike cut through the quiet, speeding round the corner towards us. The rider screeched to a halt too close for comfort. Summer froze like a fawn caught in headlights, looking right and left for an escape. The bulky biker raised his hand, made a slicing move in slow motion across his neck and growled, 'You! Mind your back, you gyppo gobshite.'

'Don't you be rude to my friend!' I yelled, moving protectively in front of Summer. Boddy, hackles raised, tail up, stuck by my side, silent and menacing.

The biker was wearing those goggles that you can't see their eyes through. He revved his engine and looked me up and down. 'As for you, you mimsy blow-in, if I was you I'd lock my doors as well. As for your mangey hound, it's cats what has nine lives!' He spit on the ground. 'Remember, you dirty pikey, open your mouth and you're dead meat!' And off he screeched, as suddenly as he had arrived.

'Who was that?' My heart was pounding.

'A *dinlo chal* named Meat Loaf. He is well known to our people. A nasty piece of work is Meat Loaf.'

'What's a blow-in?'

'It is a local term for any newcomer to the area. Also for my people.'

'Why does he hate you?'

'Because he is an evildoer and knows that we know.'

'Know what?' I didn't know much of anything.

'That my people know. More of this I cannot say.'

'But I thought we made a pact! You said we were kin.' I thought of how we had stared into each other's eyes; of the twin planets. I felt betrayed, although our friendship was not yet hours old.

Summer Locke just looked at the ground.

I was exasperated but had something more on my mind. 'Summer, please, please when you meet my mum don't let's tell her about Meat Loaf and being blow-ins. Not that I'm scared,' which I was, 'but she wouldn't like this, not one little bit.'

Summer squeezed my hand. 'We shall not speak of this to your family or to anyone. Now then. Shall I show you a pleasing new route to the manor?'

'You bet!'

'We needs must retrace our steps into town. Across from the Red Lion is a stile leading to a ford in the river. Come along.'

Summer Locke's shortcut led us through a field, then a wooded area. Boddy loved it, chasing squirrels and rabbits and ... was it a deer? It was a much quicker route than the lanes, heading in the direction of the back view of Pucklethorpe Manor. Past a dovecot, past the beehives and approaching the hedge bordering the mansion, we were in for a surprise. The grounds appeared to be empty. No police, not even the police dogs. Too good to be true!

'Summer, when were you last inside the manor?'

'Why,' Summer hesitated, 'the day Mr Wheatley ...'

'Oh. Could we have a look?' I asked. 'I don't mean, I mean, well, there's no one here to stop us and, well, I would so love to see it.'

A look of desperation flitted across Summer's face. 'I am not sure.'

'Please.'

Summer considered for a moment, then fumbled about and produced a key on a long string. 'This is a skeleton key: it fits front and back. We shall enter from the front.' We skirted round the house to the front. 'Here.' Summer handed me the key. 'You may unlock the door.'

The key turned easily in the massive door. I pushed it open expecting a loud creak but it slid smooth and soundless.

My *wow!* echoed and bounced off the walls.

'Shhhhh.'

'Why? There's no one here!'

'Shhhhh!'

I had never seen an entrance hall like this one. Boddy's toenails echoed click click on the parquet floor. This hall was at least as long as an Olympic swimming pool, the walls all panelled in wood and full of dark important looking portraits, with a white ceiling carved with animal and plant shapes. The hall went on and on, right to the back of the house, and ended with a massive window where the light flowed in motes through the leadlight window panes.

'Let us step quickly. Here on the left is the small study.' Then there was a huge dining hall and a room which Summer called the Rocking Horse Room, scattered with a couple of forlorn looking toys and now echoing with emptiness.

'What about these?' I pointed to my right, and began walking with Boddy in that direction. Did I imagine a cold feeling in the air? Boddy froze, hackles up and refusing to go further.

'No. We go up these stairs, to my room of the sky.'

Up the massive curved flight of stairs we went, two treads at a time, Boddy taking at least three. I stopped on the first floor but Summer urged me to keep going, dismissing this floor as 'a parcel of bedrooms'.

Summer took my hand when we reached the top landing.

'Here. My sanctuary, my room of the sky. It is here Papa Wheatley bade me rest, as it is nearest the roof and not so like a housedweller's room. Look here, there is a poem on the wall.'

In childlike block letters, with a frame around it like a painting, were the words:

> *A-hunting we will go,*
> *A-hunting we will go,*
> *We'll catch a fox, and put him in a box,*
> *And then we'll let him go.*
> *— Jesse P. 1940 A.D.*

'Papa said here was the very room where a young child rested his sweet head. Was many a long year past when young Jesse died, in a fall from his pony. Tragic it was.'

'Yes, so sad. Mrs Spicer told me about Jesse.'

'But come. Feast your eyes.'

The view took in the grounds and horizon, a perfect spot. Winding its way up the drive was a big white police van.

'Uh-oh, Summer! I think we'd better leave,' I said. 'Like, now.'

'This way!'

Summer grabbed my hand and we ran like the wind down the stairs.

'I didn't lock the front door when we came inside!' I remembered, panicked.

'Shhhhh! Follow me!'

The sound of voices and heavy footsteps echoed as we flew silently down a darkened corridor and out of a door at the back. I stopped to catch my breath but 'Keep going!' Summer said.

'D'you think they were looking for us?' I asked Summer. 'I mean, d'you think someone saw us and reported us?'

'It is of no consequence. We will hasten now to your house; here, through the kissing gate.'

'My mum thinks I've been to the library!'

Summer Locke was solemn. 'Yes.'

5
Sleuth

Home is the place where, when you
have to go there
They have to take you in.

– 'The Death of the Hired Man',
Robert Frost

We breezed in, trying to look relaxed.

'Hullo, kids.' Indeedy greeted us as if she were expecting Summer Locke already. She was slumped on the sofa, looking exhausted and beautiful and old as a mum. The dining table was set for a buffet, with cold ham, potato salad, coleslaw, a pile of peanut butter cookies and a big jug of apple juice.

'Robin, you look like a damp puppy! How'd you do it on a hot dry day?' Without waiting for an answer, 'Go loose your plait and dry your hair. You know how easily you catch cold.'

'Mum, please, it'll dry itself.'

'Don't argue, just get it dry. And change those filthy clothes.'

I blushed. In front of Summer and everything!

Then, like an afterthought, Indeedy said, 'Who's the friend here?'

Summer grinned back at Indeedy's question. 'I am named Summer Locke.'

I left them to it while I darted off to change. I freed my plait and fluffed my hair up with my fingers, changed my shirt and flew back downstairs. It took about thirty seconds.

'I was just asking about Summer's name,' Indeedy said.

'Papa Wheatley said that whoever and wherever they were, my parents must have desired their child to be a season of the year, and my Romany folk say the name derives from this very truth, as I was born in the time of the swallow and swift, who, like the Gypsy, move freely but in the sky.'

Indeedy smiled. 'How lovely! No one's ever going to mispronounce your name. Hey, let's eat. It's a buffet today. Zach will be here soon, with Chris from up the lane.'

'Chris?'

'You know, the journalist, up the lane at West Mill Cottage. She's offered to help with the bakehouse. Help yourselves to some grub!'

Summer hesitated.

I've been told some American ways are quite strange to the English, like being spur-of-the-moment. That's Indeedy. She likes the unexpected.

'Go on, Summer,' she urged. 'You are an honoured guest!'

Summer selected a modest slice of ham and a spoonful of coleslaw.

I was fidgeting and not hungry, but spooned some potato salad on my plate. Boddy's gourmet doggy meal waited at the foot of the dining table; she always waited until invited to begin sharing her teatime meal with us humans. Some people disapproved, especially when Indeedy would allow Boddy to pre-wash the plates before everything went in the dishwasher.

Zach and Chris Lamb arrived from working on the bakehouse and dived straight into the grub, neither of them even glancing our way. Chris was tall, lean and blonde, and quite pretty in a no-nonsense sort of way.

'You must be Robin.' Chris smiled warmly and extended her hand.

'Hello, Chris. This is my friend Summer Locke.'

Summer grinned. 'We have met.'

'Mum, can Summer spend the night?' I didn't need to give Indeedy advance warning because I knew Summer would be welcome. I was thinking it might not be safe to go back to the hatch. I didn't think about asking Summer first.

'Sure, but the spare room's not ready.'

'Summer can stay in my room.'

'OK.'

'Begging your pardon, and many thanks for your kind invitation,' said Summer gently, 'but it is best tonight I return to the hatch.'

As usual I hadn't engaged brain and mouth. If I think it's a good idea I just presume it will be. My face felt hot so I took a big bite of potato salad. 'Sorry, Summer! I'll walk you back. Thanks, Mum. That was scrummy,' I said.

'Robin, please don't talk with your mouth full. I want you back before dark. And stay away from Pucklethorpe Manor.'

'Will do!'

I liked it that Indeedy didn't ask what library books I'd checked out, where we'd just been or where we were going.

The white police van was still parked out in front of the manor, blue light flashing and motor purring. Someone inside switched the downstairs lights off and two shadowy figures emerged from the front door, closed and locked it. Then in a whoosh, they were off.

'Summer, this is our chance!' I wanted to go back inside so badly. 'Please, please will you show me more? Pretty please?'

Summer paled but agreed. 'Aye, when it is safe to do so. There is indeed something I did not think to fetch earlier.'

'No time like the present! What do you want to fetch? Where is it?'

'It will likely be in Papa Brockton's study. I pray the *gavs* have not removed the history book Papa was writing.'

'Miss Kiss the librarian mentioned he was a historian. He checked out Braille books.'

'Yes, it is so. Papa had already left his journal with me, for safe-keeping he said. He did not feel safe in his own home ...'

'Let's go!' I urged.

'Thanking you but no. It will not be safe now.'

'But the van is gone!'

'Truly, but 'tis too dark.'

'I'll fetch a torch!'

'No.' Summer was adamant. 'But soon.'

I was not happy. Summer squeezed my hand.

'OK,' I said, reluctantly. 'I'll walk you as far as the kissing gate?'

'Excellent.'

Summer was right. Even in high summertime the night comes. The dusk was gathering.

'When will I see you?'

'Tomorrow mid-morning. There are many things I wish to tell.'

'Me too!' I wanted to know everything about Summer Locke.

Back home, I went straight to my room to plan my way to sleep.

'Brush your teeth, Fruit!' shouted Indeedy.

'Yes, Mum.'

I made a pretence of brushing my teeth. In my bedroom I opened the curtains wide, and plopped onto my bed, turning on the bedside lamp. Here is my plan. I will be a sleuth, Sherlock Holmes to Summer Locke's Doctor Watson, or perhaps the other way around. We will solve the murder and maybe even find the treasure. Nothing can bring Mr Wheatley back but the criminal will be brought to justice. I remember seeing a metal detector propped by Mrs Spicer's door; perhaps it was Mr Spicer I had spied in the grounds on the first night? He may know something. Summer and I will do wonderful things sharing the reward money, if there is any, and we will travel the world and find my father. He won't be dead he won't be dead he can't be dead.

Feeling the lump under my pillow I fetched out my old diary. All those little girl words and thoughts scribbled down. My throat tightened.

After Daddy vanished I had problems with stammering, especially when someone asked me a question and I tried to answer. It would go something like this:

Teacher: 'Robin, have you decided what you would like to draw for today? To go with your lovely poem?'

'Y-y-y-yes.'

'Good! What will it be?'

'I d-d-don't know.' And then I'd start crying.

At night Daddy would be right there in my dreams, so real, but I'd wake up and go to school the next day and he wouldn't be there. I thought that sleep time was my real time and daytime was a dream. I'm glad I didn't tell anyone because they'd have put me on drugs, or so I've heard. Instead, Mum had asked would I like to go and stay with Uncle Charlie and Aunt Martha in Tennessee over the summer holiday. If I liked it there, I could have a term in a Tennessee school. 'Would you like that, Robin?'

'I d-d-don't know.'

Mum took this as a yes, and at the end of the summer term, which is about the middle of American school's summer vacation, off I flew on my own in a jet plane, with kind stewards making certain I was safe. Mum and Zach stayed behind in London. I will always remember the sky, being *in* it, flying. I loved that picture from space where Earth looks like a shining Christmas ornament. Even in the normal sky and in a jet plane, that picture from the moon was hard to beat.

Sometimes you have friends who say nothing ever happens to them and that they are bored and have boring lives. And sometimes I wished that nothing ever happened to me and then I would know what it meant to be bored. Tennessee should have been one of those places where nothing ever happens. It was damp and drowsy with lightning bugs, and hot at all hours – so soggy hot at night you couldn't even keep a sheet over you without feeling like you would melt to a puddle. In the daytime it was chiggers and mosquitoes, but not too bad.

What happened to make me certain I didn't want to stay in Tennessee was about snakes. Cottonmouth water moccasins, to be specific. They are called 'cottonmouth' because when they hinge their mouths open to show their fangs, the inside is pure white, like cotton bolls. Cottonmouth water moccasins are venomous (poison being what you eat and venom being injected in your bloodstream, as Mrs Avey would tell us) and venom is worse than poison. It is true that if they strike you, you may die, even if you're a big grown-up. And there are lots and lots of them all around Uncle Charlie and Aunt Martha's place.

Aunt Martha and Uncle Charlie had a worker called Moses who lived in an outbuilding on their one-time family plantation.

Once, Aunt Martha asked Moses in my presence why he wanted to stay with them 'when y'all've been free for more than a hundred years', and he said something like, he didn't understand why his own kin left, because he was 'happy as a chigger in a henhouse'. Aunt Martha said, 'Well, boy, ah am honnuhed! And thinkin about it, all freedom has limits.'

Moses never once set foot in the big house. When I asked him why, he said, 'Honey chile, I ain't no house nigger and don' want it. No way.' I was shocked at the way he used that word but, coming from Moses, I guess it seemed fair enough.

At Sunday school in Tennessee we sang, 'Jesus loves the little children, all the children of the world, red and yellow, black and white, we are precious in his sight, Jesus loves the little children of the world.' But all the faces at the local church were white faces; I asked why, and was told that the likes of Moses would be attending another church up the road and that 'everyone' liked it that way. Aunt Martha didn't explain who 'everyone' was, and I didn't ask. It just felt to me like it was white folks doing all the choosing.

Moses had skin as dark as a blackbird, and he smelled sort of nutty, like Cheerios. He took my hand one day and showed me how to fetch Julie the mule from her field with a bucket of bran mash and a long piece of baling twine. There Julie was, a good distance away, long ears pricked forward, not moving. We squatted on the grass. Moses called out, 'Now, Miss Julie! Miss Robin's come to see you, all the way from Englun'! Fetch up here now!' Then he made a noise like part horse and part donkey. Julie 'neigh-hawed' back, echoing Moses and trotting straight to us, her muzzle disappearing into the fragrant bucket of bran. Moses tied the baling twine round her neck and off we went to her shelter in Aunt Martha's yard.

Moses had taught Julie to smoke Camel cigarettes and drink Coca-Cola from a bottle. He called it her 'pahhty trick'. He would light the cigarette and then give it to the mule, who would puff away then pull the cigarette into her mouth far enough to bite off the lit end, before eating the cigarette. 'Isn't smoking bad for her?' I asked.

'Well, now, honey chile, she older than you 'n me combined, so I 'speck she all right.'

Have you ever had a dog or pony who walks *you*? Julie walked me. I'd lead her to the fence and slide onto her warm bare back and she just went where she wanted to go and then turned for home when she was ready. I didn't have a saddle or a bridle, only a piece of baling twine tied in a rough semblance of a halter, and we wandered along sweet as a pea.

One day Julie and I were heading for Nolan's Creek and a few metres away was Moses, demolishing a tree by the water. It was cool and shady where he was working, and Julie made a gentle beeline in his direction. As we approached, I could see something in the water moving in a swirly swim and getting close to Moses.

'Moccasin!' I shouted. 'Cottonmouth!'

Moses jumped but the snake sprang, hitting Moses' thigh. He dropped his axe, looking to the sky and cried 'Help! Dear Lawd! Get help!'

The cottonmouth freed itself from Moses' leg and landed on dry ground. Julie went straight at the snake, and trampled it until it stopped moving. I was holding on for dear life, legs clamped and frozen to her back, terrified to move or not to move.

Moses looked at me then and spoke calmly, very calmly. 'Robin,' he said, 'please give me your shirt, and I will make a tourniquet. Then run to Miss Martha.'

I tore my cotton shirt off.

Go, Julie!

Julie saved Moses' life.

People say that mules are aloof and cold and stubborn and that they scarcely ever gallop, but people are wrong. Julie galloped like the wind. For a while the doctor thought Moses might lose his leg – they called it a 'threatened necrosis'. His leg might turn black and then they'd have to amputate. But it didn't happen. Moses got better, and my stammer stopped that day. Now it seems hundreds of years ago. But I knew then that I wanted to fly back home to England, where there are no cottonmouth water moccasins and where children of every colour go to school together.

Moses would like Summer Locke. And Daddy would be proud of me.

6
The Jesse Tree

My mother said I never should
Play with the Gypsies in the wood.

– anon

'Wake up, Fruit!'

Indeedy was in perky top gear. She and Chris Lamb, she said, would be turning the old bakehouse into a new cookhouse for the business. 'And Zach too.'

As I ate breakfast, my brother sloped downstairs looking like an unmade bed.

'Hey, sunshine, grab some grub and we'll be off.'

Zach grunted an incoherent something.

'Chris Lamb is the spitting image of Sigourney Weaver, don't you think, Fruit?' enthused Indeedy.

'Who?'

'Remember *Ghostbusters*? She was in that one. Plus some films you are too young and tender to remember.'

Young? Fair enough. But tender? Huh.

'Hey-ho, I'm off,' Indeedy said. 'In the bakehouse if you need me. Zach! Shift.'

I decided I'd mooch around 'til Summer got here, unpack some more stuff. Back in my room, I opened the French window and slipped onto my little balcony. The manor grounds were absent of the police crews and dogs who'd greeted us on our arrival. Perhaps they'd finished the searches already?

Downstairs the phone rang. I raced to pick it up.

'Borderland 116, Robin speaking. Oh hello, Miss Kiss. My book has arrived? Thank you so much, I'll be round to collect it, hopefully this afternoon. Thanks again. Bye for now.'

Miss Kiss is so efficient. In London usually it takes a week or more for a specially ordered book to arrive. I hope *An Architectural History of Borderland* has lots of pictures.

By mid-morning Summer hadn't appeared. I decided to follow the shortcut from the house. Maybe we'd meet halfway, or I'd walk at least as far as the kissing gate. Boddy and I slipped through and past the ornate hedge bordering the grounds. The police had left a big mess for someone else to clear up; the garden was torn up by tyre marks and littered with plastic cups and bits of paper. Roof slates and guttering were dislodged by the scaffolding. Boddy took a good sniff of everything I'd allow, reading her canine newspaper for the day.

Boddy suddenly took off ahead of me and around a corner, then back in a noiseless flash, tail and hackles up.

'Check it out, Boddy, good girl!'

There by the bracken in a pool of bright sunlight, zigzagged in copper and black and sunning itself lazily in the middle of the path, was a snake. We froze on the spot. My mind flashed to last night when I'd trembled myself to sleep thinking about snakes and now, here in England on a footpath, was a big fat snake with a triangular head, meaning venomous. It was like I'd dreamed it into being.

Also there was Summer Locke, smiling a greeting.

'Ah, hello, my beauty,' Summer whispered, wide-eyed and fearless, approaching the creature, then squatting close by. 'She is an adder,' Summer told me.

The snake, still coiled, raised her perfect head and began hissing and puffing up.

'Summer, are you crazy?'

'If I do not harm this fine *sap* she will not harm me. See?' Summer gazed steadily into the adder's eyes. 'She hears without ears and through her whole body. *Joller* along then, my beauty.'

Black tongue flicking, the snake eased away into the bracken as if she understood everything Summer said.

'Summer, that snake could kill you,' I protested.

'Yes, she is venomous. But she will not strike unless she is harmed. Now then, Robin. Follow me. Let us enter by the back door.'

I made a mental note to tell Summer about cottonmouth water moccasins.

We approached a doorway round the corner at the back of the house. Summer tugged on the keys. For some reason, I assumed that today we would be climbing like spies through a window or sneaking through a trap door, which is always exciting.

'This is the servants' entrance to the kitchen – where Papa Brockton ...'

'Where he died?'

Summer nodded. Yes.

'Well, you are very brave, Summer, but how d'you know? Where he was killed, I mean? Did the police tell you they've arrested Lady Charlotte?'

'No. The *gavs* do not tell nothing to Gypsies; but they ask us much. My people would rather crawl into a viper's den than help the *gav*.'

'Indeedy said it was in the newspaper about Lady Charlotte. But what do you have against the police?'

'We have our ways, and our ways do not fail.' Summer gently took hold of my shoulders, turned me so we were face to face, and passed me the keys. 'Now, my friend, you will unlock the door, please. At this door you undo with the big one first, then the small one.'

I commanded Boddy to *wait here*. She crouched in the daylight like a sulky statue, ears loppety-doodle, eyes glowing amber and green.

The doorway's sprawling pink roses contrasted with the scene I imagined might lay inside. How could someone walk through a door like this – surrounded by nature – with murder in mind? Had I ever been angry enough to kill something, anything? Slugs and flies maybe, but a grown-up human with blind eyes and a kindness for children? I turned the key. My hands shook. I had not dared to ask whether entering the house was permitted by the authorities; all we had was Indeedy's prohibition and the KEEP OUT signs on the grounds. On the other hand, Summer was virtually Brockton Wheatley's only family at the end. After all, isn't family supposed to be forever?

The door creaked open and I gestured to return the keys to Summer, who took them but then placed them round my neck. Here was a small porchway with a brass coat-stand at the far end. Summer pressed the light switch. Nothing happened.

'Plenty of daylight, anyway.'

Summer shrugged. 'Perhaps they disconnected the electrics last night.' Summer drew a deep breath, tentatively turning the doorknob on the left, then hesitated. 'I have not been here since ...'

'You said.'

The door swung inward into a spacious kitchen with a refectory table in the middle. On the flagstone floor was the white outline of a human form. I almost stepped on it before I saw it, the chalked-in border of Brockton Wheatley's body, where he fell dead. Summer's voice choked, 'Please please, let us keep moving.'

My turn to be the grown-up. Since I didn't have a clue as to just where we were going, I squeezed Summer's hand and said, 'Just point me to where we need to go.'

My legs shook, and I felt almost sick at my stomach. Summer directed me towards a door at the far end of the kitchen into the main dark oak-panelled hall, and knocked at the fourth panel which, on pressing, swung open to reveal a miniature doorway. Summer backed away and pointed to a brass ring on the bare, shiny floor. 'Please pull it.' The door opened up on hinges to a set of stone steps down to the cellar. You could see where the stone had worn away from hundreds of years of feet going up and down. A waft of musty air hit my nostrils.

'Look,' I said, 'it's too dark down there. We should've brought a torch. Why not the upstairs first? I want to go back there.'

Summer made no reply but darted around the corner and returned in seconds with two candles and a box of matches. 'There. You shall soon know.'

'OK,' I said, summoning courage from somewhere or other. 'I'll go first.'

Summer struck a match and lit the candles. Initially the cellar looked and felt dank and airless. 'It seems both big and small at the same time,' I whispered, sweeping the candle back and forth and casting our shadows into long dark ghosts.

'And so it is,' said Summer. 'For every room on the ground floor there is a cellar room beneath, each with its concealed entrance.'

I wondered aloud how many people in the world live in houses with multiple cellars and more than a dozen bedrooms. Plus a grand ballroom and too many bathrooms?

'I asked Papa Brockton about houses, and why people live in them at all.'

'Surely you know the obvious answer to that?'

'No,' Summer replied. 'Romany homes are everywhere and anywhere and nowhere. It is complicated.'

'Well, most people live in houses for shelter and protection, of course. Your people are living in a house just now!'

'No,' Summer repeated. 'The hatch on the Romany Road is an ancient stopping place; we are always on our way.'

'Will you be allowed to stay if you wish?'

'We will move on as and when we must. We are not here to speak of the future.'

'You mean you are going away?' Already I felt I had known Summer all my life. This was a thunderbolt.

'People in houses and countries have taken over the world and forever wish to disappear our people. Why do you think Papa Brockton was killed?'

'I don't know why, Summer.'

'For property and I hate it!'

Tears began to well up again. 'Well your name is Locke so you have keys to something!' I was at a loss. What should I say, or do?

'Summer, please. Where is this incredible thing anyway? Why are we here?'

'Hearken with your eyes,' Summer said. 'Papa Brockton's treasure.'

'Where'm I s'posed to?'

Summer slipped to the centre of the cellar and lay down flat on the cold flagstones, face up. 'Come, lie you down by my side. Close your eyes until I tell you to open them.'

So I did. Then a whispered command, 'Open your eyes.' I did. 'Lift your candle high and you will see the Jesse Tree.'

I didn't know what a Jesse Tree was, but I imagined an old evergreen-shaped tree like a fir or spruce, the kind you bring into your house at Christmas. This wasn't a tree at all. Instead I saw a brightly coloured painted ceiling full of crowned human figures with lions and unicorns by their sides, some with wings. The image above us was surrounded by flowers and connected by a great vine-like stem that grew from the belly button of a sleeping male figure. Around the outside were petals ticked in gold; even in the gloomy candlelight I could see the colours were as bright and clean as a fairground carousel.

'Why do they call it a tree?'

'You see here the very first family tree in the world, in pictures and not in words. It is Our Saviour's family tree, joined with his forebears back to the root and stock of Jesse. Jesse is the one lying asleep. Jesse is the father of the King of the Jews.'

'Spooky!' I shivered.

'"Twas Lord Pucklethorpe's chapel. Papa Wheatley said this Jesse Tree is hundreds of years old. Look, Baby Lord Jesus is there at the top, see, in the arms of Blessed Mary the Mother of God.'

'I'm an agnostic,' I said.

'Well, then, I expect I am wasting my time telling you much of anything Papa Brockton ever taught me.'

'Sorry,' I could tell I had offended Summer. I tried to make it right. 'All I mean is religion gives me the heeby-jeebies, like you feel about houses. Indeedy prays all the time but me and Zach, we don't believe.'

'*Mooshabove* is accustomed to not being believed.'

'That's what you call God? Look, Summer, I don't want to argue.'

'And nor do I. But if you want to know about the Jesse Tree you will be obliged to listen to some religion.'

'Course.' Time to change the subject. 'Do you know what that writing means?' I said, pointing to words scripted in a gold crescent around the top of the Jesse Tree.

'I have heard the words, yes. It is Latin, and Papa has written them down in his journal but I do not recall. He thought the Jesse Tree and the poem were some sort of key to finding an ancient site called Camelot here at the manor. But let us be going. It is cold as the grave in here.'

'My brother knows Latin,' I said. 'We could ask Zach.'

We headed back up into the oak-panelled hall. Summer started in the direction of the kitchen. Then I remembered.

'What about Mr Wheatley's history book notes?'

'Thanking you. We will fetch them now. His study room, there, near the main door.'

Mr Wheatley's manuscript lay apparently undisturbed on his desk, in a fat folder labelled 'Camelot'.

'Should we take his journal too?' I asked, thinking of the poem.

'That I already have,' Summer replied. We went into the hall, where the front door beckoned out into the daylight.

'Oh! I almost forgot,' I said. 'I need to collect a book from the mobile library. For our murder investigation. Will you come with me?'

Summer paused. 'I have no need to investigate.'

'What do you mean?'

'It sorrows me, but I can say no more.'

'You won't help?' I was baffled. Didn't Summer want to find out who killed Papa Brockton?

'I did not say I will not help. I said I cannot now speak.' And then Summer would say no more.

Cross and confused, I headed off in the direction of the lane and Miss Kiss and her library on wheels, not caring whether my complicated friend came or not. I glanced over my shoulder to see Summer Locke following, Boddy in tow. I had forgotten to fetch her from the back door where she would have been waiting patiently, but Summer hadn't forgotten. A brief wash of guilt passed over me.

'Hello, Miss Kiss. This is my friend Summer Locke.'

'Hello, dear. Here's your book.' She stamped the book's due date and handed it to me. She had marked the page discussing Pucklethorpe Manor. 'I fear you may be disappointed with the information you seek. Only one paragraph about Pucklethorpe Manor, and not very complimentary.'

'Thank you, Miss Kiss.'

'And how are you getting on with your space exploration book?'

'It's great,' I fibbed. My effort so far got me only to page two.

'Well, dear, be certain to return the books on time. We have stiff penalties for late returns,' said Miss Kiss, eyes twinkling.

'What?'

'Fifty lashes with a wet noodle!'

7
Genealogy

Sometimes I feel like a motherless child,
sometimes I feel like a motherless child,
sometimes I feel like a motherless child,
a long way from home, a long way from
home.

– traditional African–American spiritual

When Summer and I returned to the cottage, Indeedy
and Chris Lamb were curled on the settee near the
inglenook, sipping tea and watching the news.

'Hi, guys. All right? We're a bit zombified,' Indeedy
said. 'The bakehouse conversion is a bit of a mega-
project. What have you been up to?'

'Miss Kiss rang earlier today. The book I ordered
has arrived. Look.' While Indeedy leafed through the
book on architecture, I dashed upstairs to stash Mr
Wheatley's manuscript in my room.

'Hey, Fruitfly! Pucklethorpe Manor is in here. Not much but it's here.'

'Yeah, Miss Kiss marked the page. Mum, where's your Bible?' I knew we had one but we never read it. 'Summer's going to read something called the *Begats*.'

'Have I unpacked it?' Indeedy said. 'Check the pile by the book case in the study.'

I returned with the big black family Bible.

'Are you referring to the "begats" as in Abraham begat Isaac and Isaac begat Jacob?' Chris asked.

Summer Locke smiled. 'The very same, Miss ...'

'Lamb. We have met, it was a while back when I wrote a feature on your people. I live up the drive at West Mill Cottage. Please call me Chris.'

Summer and I sat cross-legged on the floor with the Bible in front of us. Summer opened to a page headed *The Gospel according to Matthew* and, pointing to the desired passage with ease, said, 'Here is the story of the Jesse Tree: "Abraham begat Isaac, Isaac begat Jacob, Jacob begat Judah and his brothers, Judah begat Perez and Zerah, whose mother was Tamar–"'

'Why only one woman?' I interrupted.

'The Jesse Tree is about fathers.'

'Well. They all had mothers.'

'Shh-hh. They are called the Patriarchs. Hearken now ...'

Summer droned on. And on ...

'"... Jacob the father of Joseph, the husband of Mary, of whom was born Jesus, who is called Christ."' So. A genealogy, a Jesse Tree in words, nearly a thousand years.'

'So what? So does the English royal family.'

Summer sighed. 'My people have no written history. Your people have twenty-six letters and millions of words written down from your alphabet. Papa Brockton taught me his love of history. Robin, may we speak alone?'

'No one's listening.'

Indeedy and Chris were riveted to a television documentary. A blurry film of mounted police swinging at people with truncheons flashed on screen. Zach was hunched over a book as usual.

'Anyone for Ovaltine?' I asked the room, to a mumbling of vague no tas. 'I'll just make some for me and Summer then.'

We moved into the kitchen. Summer began tracing the square outlines of the gingham tablecloth with a forefinger. I put the milk on the Rayburn to heat.

'What's the story, then?'

'I have been thinking where to commence.'

I stirred the milk faster. Eventually Summer spoke.

'As I told you, Papa Brockton believed that Pucklethorpe Manor is the true seat of Camelot. He left me with something to be going on with. He believed that the Jesse Tree in the cellar provided a key to Camelot and to the Holy Grail.'

'Oh.' I remembered Mrs Spicer or someone saying half the grand houses in England claim to be home to the Holy Grail.

'But hearken. When they first settled here, Papa Brockton was in possession of his sight. In the early days, he sketched the Jesse Tree in his journal, and with the Holy Grail in mind. Then the doctors diagnosed 'macular degeneration'. Papa would go completely blind and there would be no cure. He was trying to teach me how far he needed to go towards working it out when ...' Summer stopped.

'In that case I think we should find out what the poem means.' I love a mystery, and the poem sounded like a clue.

'Fair enough. We will check first in Papa Brockton's journal.'

'My brother knows Latin. He could help. Summer, did anyone ever tell you the gold bar story?'

Summer shrugged, *do I care?* But I was chuffed to think I might have knowledge that Summer maybe didn't.

'Well, Mrs Spicer said Lord Pucklethorpe bought gold bars during World War Two and hid them here somewhere. Then their little boy died and then Lord Pucklethorpe died at war and then his wife went potty and then everything went to hell in a handbag. Do you believe that?'

'Aye, Papa Brockton spoke somewhat of it. But he leaned to the Camelot legend. I believe that to

Papa Brockton the gold bars were little more than an interesting distraction.'

'But what if the opposite is true? What if there's really gold there? Didn't you help him dig holes in the garden?'

'Yes, we did dig holes,' Summer said, but we were searching for the Holy Grail, with its miraculous powers to cure blindness and all sorts.'

'Here in Borderland!' I scoffed. 'Have you ever seen *Indiana Jones*? Everybody thinks they know where the Holy Grail is hidden.'

'I have not seen this, no.'

'OK, sorry,' I could see Summer was irritated. 'What's the *something* Mr Wheatley left?' I asked. I poured the steaming Ovaltine into mugs and sprinkled cinnamon over the top. 'Marshmallow?'

Summer ignored the marshmallow offer. 'I have said. It is Papa Brockton's journal. Will you help me?'

'How?'

'When you see his journal you will know. It is in a safe place at the hatch. I shall fetch it.'

'Look, Summer. I'm really and truly confused. I thought we both want to find out who murdered your Papa Brockton and all you're talking about is Jesse Trees and Holy Grails! The journal can wait,' I scolded, looking over my shoulder to the very same window where I first saw Summer. 'You can't go back to the hatch now.'

'Best time, darkness,' smiled Summer, swilling the Ovaltine. 'King is hiding it for me, no worries. I will just slip out.'

'I'll go with you then.'

'Never. Forgive the rudeness, but Gypsies do not trust any *gorgio* lacking an invitation on the hatch past daylight. However, I will stay the night here if I am welcome, and it will be most helpful if you prepare our sleeping things. We will need midnight nourishment and a torch. Pencils will be useful. And a sleeping bag for me, if you please.'

'All right,' I relented, grateful and offended at the same time. 'You're right, Summer. There just might be important clues in the journal, like who killed your poor Papa.'

Summer's direct gaze wavered.

'No. Yes ... well, I will be off and return presently.' Summer slipped like a cat out of the kitchen door and into the darkening dusk.

I brought the Bible back to the lounge, Chris Lamb was standing by the front door, her head almost scraping the ceiling beam. 'How tall are you, Chris?' I asked idly, plopping myself down by Indeedy.

'Six foot something,' smiled Chris.

'I always wanted to be tall like Zach and Daddy.'

'Truth told, it was hell when I was your age,' Chris said. 'Head always in the clouds, they'd say, and look at the size of my feet. But hey. See you tomorrow, Indeedy? We'll tackle the tiles.'

'*Ciao*, Chris!' Indeedy's voice warmed affectionately. 'Remember, we're interviewing at nine a.m.'

'Absolutely. I'll be here. Toodle pip, Zach.'

Zach unglued his eyes from his book long enough to glance Chris's way as she left. 'See you.' Then he noticed me. 'Where's the young friend gone?'

'Er, Summer? Just slipped back to the hatch, I mean the site, for something. Be back in a tick. Mum, what's this about interviewing?'

'Let's see,' said Indeedy. 'I've some catching up to do with you, my Fruit. We've advertised for couriers to deliver the food. When that's done, we are ready to rock and roll. As for Chris, what a godsend.' She smiled. 'We're going into business together, me supplying the art and cooking skills, Chris taking care of the business side of things.'

'I thought Chris was a journalist.'

'Well, yes. But she's self-employed and could do with another day job. We get on like a house on fire. Fruit, sometimes you just know when something is right, and Chris is right.' Indeedy unfolded herself, tugged her ponytail tight and switched off the television.

Zach peered over the top of his owl-like specs and rolled his eyes. I thought to myself that usually people said that about someone they fancied, which meant that Indeedy was meaning something else.

'Who's coming to be interviewed?'

'We've only had one response from some bikers, call themselves the Skullduggeries. They phoned to say they'd put in a quote for the job if they like what they see. A bit over-familiar, but ...'

I heard the kitchen door squeak open. 'C'mon in!' Summer was carrying a fat leather-bound book. 'That was quick! Guess what? My mum's opening shop soon and tomorrow they're interviewing for couriers.'

Indeedy beamed. 'Thanks to Chris's networking, we already have a wedding and birthday on the books. Would you like a tour of the bakehouse tomorrow?' Not waiting for an answer, 'Never in a thousand years did I think we'd be so quickly off the ground.'

'May good fortune bless your days,' said Summer, in that formal way.

'Golly gosh,' said Indeedy. 'D'you realize it's past bed o'clock? I presume you will be staying the night, Summer?'

'Yes, Mrs Swallow, if you please.'

'To bed with you both then, me as well. Robin's room for now, if you don't mind. We'll clear the guest room for you as soon as.'

Mum fetched the sleeping bag from the loft. We sat beside each other on my bed, Summer cocooned like a chrysalis in the zipless sleeping bag.

'I think we should tell Zach about the Jesse Tree, Summer,' I whispered. 'He might be able to help.'

'All right then.'

Mum rustled up a late-night snack of popcorn and more Ovaltine, brought it up and bid us good night.

'Mum, would you mind asking Zach if he can spare us a moment?'

'Sure.'

Zach peered through the bedroom door. 'We were talking about you. Want some munchies? Listen.'

My brother folded his lanky body on the floor near the bed and took a handful of popcorn. 'OK, Summer?'

Summer nodded yes. I went on quickly.

'There's this carved ceiling in the cellar of the manor and ... look, here's a sketch right here in Mr Wheatley's journal ...'

I took Zach through the essentials – how old the Jesse Tree was, Mr Wheatley's obsession with Camelot, that his refusal to move out wasn't about being blind and alone with nowhere to go, but more about the history backed up with his theory about King Arthur.

'Bear with me,' said Summer Locke, leafing through the journal to a page near the back. 'Here it is, the poem. 'Tis Latin. Papa Brockton has not translated it here:

> *Unitas in Trinitate*
> *Tres in Uno ambiant*
> *Circum Jessis arborem.*
> *Tres personae unum sunt*

GENEALOGY

Una sit substantia
Lauda aurarius Trinitatem
Alma Redemptoris Mater

Closing the book, Summer sighed.

Zach yawned and stretched himself upright. 'I'll take it to my room and have a go.'

Summer Locke reluctantly handed the journal to Zach.

'Robin, I must say my prayers,' Summer told me as my brother left.

'Whatever.' I wiggled down under my blankets.

'I must speak them aloud.'

'Whatever.'

Summer, head bowed.

'Ten little angels round my head, two to the foot, two to the head, two to watch, two to pray, and two to keep all bad away. Amen.'

'Is that it?'

''Tis usually five angels but I doubled up the angels for you, Robin. Good night, and God bless.'

I dream a ladder. I climb up to the top of a tree like a totem pole of cherubs lying on their sides, each holding a branch in one hand and a book in the other and piled up on top of each other. A vine growing so fast that as I climb I can actually see and feel it growing, like Jack and the Beanstalk. The vine is trying to grow around my body like a snake, trapping me.

I scramble to reach the top of the tree fast enough to clasp a golden skull perched on the fingertip of the topmost angel. From the forehead of the skull glows a serpent.

I woke, frightened. Summer was sound asleep on the floor by my bedside. I wouldn't be sharing this dream with Summer Locke.

8
The Polymath

Q: Robin Swallow: Who would I be if
I wasn't me?
A: Rory Swallow: You could be anybody.

Indeedy hustled one of her 'mega breakfasts' for
Summer and me – buttermilk pancakes with maple
syrup, home-cured bacon from the local butcher and
fried eggs sunny-side up, plus fresh percolated coffee.
We were cleaning up when the roar of motorbikes
blasted up the drive.

Summer peered out of the window at the arrivals,
ran back into the kitchen and blurted, 'Please forgive,
I must take my leave now.' Then, to me, quieter, 'Keep
Papa Brockton's book in a safe place, Robin. I will
explain everything later.'

'There's gratitude for you,' muttered Indeedy, as off
Summer ran, around the corner and out of sight.

'There *is* a reason Mum,' I countered.

'Oh, yes? And that would be?'

I was saved from inventing an answer by the doorbell's ding-dong.

'Where the heck is Chris?' muttered Indeedy as she tidied her ponytail and tucked her shirt into her jeans. I stopped in the kitchen doorway in order to duck out of sight if necessary. Sure enough, at the door was the very man in black leather bike gear, the one who had terrified me and Summer. No way did I want him to see me here. Today he wore reflective sunglasses too small for his round, flat face.

'You're the lady wanting food deliveries,' he stated as fact, shouldering his way into the house, before Indeedy could invite him in. He was followed by two identically clad but leaner cronies. Indeedy stood still momentarily, ponytail still as a bone. Then Chris Lamb swept breathlessly through the door.

'Sorry I'm late.'

I hid behind the door so I could see and hear but remain unseen.

'No probs.' Indeedy breathed a sigh of relief.

Meat Loaf spoke first. 'Saw your ad about food runs. We can spare us three.'

'Hang on a minute,' said Indeedy, mustering formality. 'Let me introduce myself first. I'm Indeedy Swallow and this is my business partner, Chris Lamb. And you are?'

'Meat Loaf at your service, missus. And my colleagues, Rock On and Twitch.'

Rock On managed a one-sided smile; Twitch, a peremptory nod accompanied by a shift of the shoulders.

'Please do take a seat,' invited Indeedy, eyeing Chris in an exclamation point look that said, 'Is this a joke?' The three squished onto the sofa, Meat Loaf in the middle. Twitch lived up to his nickname, a study in perpetual motion – hands, biceps, thighs, neck. In contrast, Rock On crouched smooth and still, a lop-sided smile frozen on his face.

'Coffee?' Chris offered.

'White, three sugars, me,' said Meat Loaf. 'These two take tea, same but only one sugar. Right, lads?'

'Right,' chorused Rock On and Twitch.

'Right then,' echoed Chris.

'Right then,' repeated Indeedy. 'Robin, where are you? Did you hear the orders?'

'Sure, how many?' I called, still out of sight and annoyed at being mentioned.

Three teas, three coffees counting Zach. I made coffee and put teabags in mugs, watching through the window for Summer Locke.

Woken no doubt by the roar of motorbikes, Zach sprang down the stairs three at a time.

'I've made you a coffee.'

'Thanks.' He peered into the kitchen. 'Harley Davidson fans, eat your hearts out.'

'Will you hand out the drinks?' I said.

Zach gathered the coffees and teas on a tray, which he plonked on the table, then sat on the floor beside Indeedy. She was going through what she called the necessaries about the business: who her first clients were, how a suitable employee would need to be up and about early and take work on a month's trial on commission, deliveries as and when until the business got on its feet.

'Suits us, eh, lads?' said Meat Loaf, looking to right and left for the required affirmatives.

My mum was in the process of employing the very man who'd threatened me and Summer at the jumping-off place for reasons I could not begin to comprehend. But then, I'm thinking, she doesn't know what happened. Because I haven't told her.

'Well, Chris and I will consult and when we have completed interviewing the other candidates we will contact you,' said Indeedy. 'If you are successful, we will supply customized panniers for your motorcycles. But you must use and maintain your own bikes.'

'And,' Chris added, obviously noting the trio's economy with personal hygiene, 'Clean turnout is essential.'

'Suits us, yes, lads?'

'Suits us.'

'Any further questions?' Indeedy edged towards the front door, ready to usher them out.

Zach intervened. 'Do you mind if I ask something?'

'Be my guest, son.'

'How well do you chaps know the area?'

Rock On spoke solo for the first time, from the sneery side of his mouth. 'Like the backs of our hands, matey. Borderland born and bred, me.'

'Yep,' said Meat Loaf, finally removing his sunglasses and revealing small reptilian eyes. 'Like the backs of our hands,' he repeated, winking at Indeedy.

The threesome rose in unison.

'Right then,' Meat Loaf said. 'When do we start?'

'As I have just explained, I will contact you as soon as we've interviewed the other candidates – either way.'

I peeped out, noting the logo on the backs of their jackets as they headed to the door: a human skull, top-hatted, with a huge roll-up cigarette sticking out of the gaping mouth. Beside the skull was a green leaf with seven serrated sharp points, and underneath it all, in ornate letters: SKULLDUGGERIES.

They roared down the drive on bikes as immaculate as their owners were scruffy. Indeedy and Chris sighed at the same time, as if they'd been holding their noses through the interview.

'Well, what do you think?'

Chris breathed in, then, in a cascade of giggles, 'Not the most attractive prospects around … on balance, "Hire in haste, fire at leisure." I know a bit about this lot from the days I was working up hours for my pilot wings.'

Ears burning, I emerged at last. 'You're a pilot?'

'Yes, qualified a few years ago at the local airfield,' Chris said. 'I was writing a feature for the local paper on pilot training when I stumbled on gossip about these chaps trafficking shady deals here and on the continent. Meat Loaf was boss back then too. Lady Charlotte had flying lessons too, around the same time. And her son. Just thought of that. Anyway, not sure.'

Indeedy frowned. 'This sounds crazy. Do *you* believe the rumours?'

'Well, rumours are just that – rumours.'

'Shall we see who else applies for the job?' Indeedy said. 'They won't be a first choice, but frankly, beggars can't be choosers.'

Zach was slack-jawed. 'You should most definitely find somebody else. Those blokes are pond life.'

Chris laughed. 'Go easy on our freshwater friends!'

I had managed so far to engage the pause button between my brain and my mouth. But I did want to speak.

'Why's Summer afraid of them, Chris?' I asked, pretending to know nothing.

'Don't know any specific reason, Robin, but as a general rule bikers don't have a reputation for kindness to Gypsies. Gypsies have been wary of housedwellers from forever, and the feeling is mutual. Clearly your friend is quite exceptional, mixing with us *gorgios*, as they call us.'

I was trying to work out a way to prise Zach outside when he seemed to read my mind. 'Say, Fruit, I'm up to the eyebrows with highbrows. How's about you show me a Borderland beauty spot or two this morning?' Zach glanced at his watch. 'I mean with what's left of the morning.' In an aside, 'I've translated it. The poem.' *Wink wink.*

'Let's go! Fancy a dip at the jumping-off place?'

'Sounds intriguing. Long's we're back for lunch.'

Zach ran upstairs to fetch his togs. I shouted after him to bring 'that book' from his room, and fussed around my neck, checking that Summer's keys were still there as Mum and Chris continued to debate the pros and cons of the Skulduggeries' suitability as delivery drivers.

We dog-trotted up the lane to the jumping-off place, settling under an oak tree with a girth so big it would take two grown humans holding hands to embrace it. Zach drew Brockton Wheatley's journal from his duffle bag.

'Weighty tome, this, from what I've seen so far.' Zach scrunched to the grass, bracing his back to the tree, and opened to a page with a marker.

Summer materialized as if from nowhere, flushed and panting. 'Yes, it is, God bless Papa's soul.'

'Am I ever glad to see you!' I said in surprise. 'How d'you know we were here?'

Summer smiled and ignored my question. 'They have gone away.'

'They who?' I asked.

'The elders.'

'Well, you're travellers, aren't you? You said so. I expect they'll be back in no time.'

Zach intervened, patting the ground. 'Take a pew, you two.' We nestled on either side of him. 'Here. *Unitas in Trinitate*, that's "one in three".' He showed us what he'd written down.

Unitas in Trinitate
ONE IN THREE
Tres in Uno ambient
THREE IN ONE
Adempleat Jessis arborem
FULFILLS THE JESSE TREE.
Tres personae unum sunt
THREE PERSONS IN ONE
Una sit substantia
ONE IN SUBSTANCE
Lauda aurarius Trinitatem
BLESS THE GOLDEN TRINITY
Alma Redemptoris Mater
DEAR MOTHER OF THE REDEEMER

'I thank you, Zach.'

'No problem-o, Summer. Not sure about the Latin grammar but this is the gist of it. Just one thing,' Zach said. 'Did you say Mr Wheatley connected the Jesse Tree and this poem with some sort of Camelot notion?'

Summer frowned in concentration. 'I believe he did.'

'Well, just to say, I'm sure your Jesse Tree is probably very, very old, but the poem is not. Witness the date, and the initials.'

'Yes,' said Summer. 'I believe the marks stand for Rupert Jesse Taliesin Pucklethorpe.'

Zach nodded. 'You mean "initials". So we can conclude that, for whatever reason, Lord Pucklethorpe added the verse.'

I began to feel the heat of the sun and the monotony of my polymath brother. 'Let's take a cool dip.'

'You're on!' Zach couldn't resist. 'Last one in's a loser!'

I donned my togs and cannon-balled the river from the bridge in Zach's wake. Summer sat beneath the beech tree, leafing through Mr Wheatley's journal and staring at the water. Boddy waited by Summer's side as long as she could bear, then leapt in the river to greet us as we clambered to the edge. Returning to the oak tree she baptized Summer with a great shaking shower from her coat. Summer laughed and ducked to protect the journal. I cocooned myself in a towel and plopped between Zach and Summer.

'Zach, do you have time to see something positively amazing with me and Summer?' I glanced sideways at Summer for affirmation. Summer nodded yes.

'I can give you half an hour,' said Zach.

'Let's go then! Still got the key.' I grasped the thong round my neck.

'I know,' said Summer Locke, stroking Boddy's blue-grey head.

Summer managed somehow to ignore the stark chalked outline on the kitchen floor this time and we were soon in the cellar of Pucklethorpe Manor, lying on our backs like three sausages and gazing up at the Jesse Tree.

'Yes. Yes. Yes. It is quite something else,' murmured Zach, sounding a bit like Prince Charles on television. 'Yes, quite something else, not just the Bible connection, you know. It's dynastic. Saw my first Jesse Tree in Granchester Cathedral, A level history. There aren't many left in all the British Isles, a few stained glass windows dating from the Middle Ages, perhaps earlier. Unless I'm mistaken this one's not made it into any of the history books.'

'Summer has explained the Bible bit,' I said, 'but what's so special about Jesse Trees?'

'Quite simply, they are priceless visual narratives,' Zach said. 'This one looks like plaster ... yes, a coffered or decorated plaster ceiling.'

Zach, stood, reached the ceiling and touched it. 'Never heard of a plaster Jesse Tree ... and whyever in a cellar, where no one can see it?'

'Papa Brockton said it was Lord Pucklethorpe's family chapel. This cellar is in the oldest part of the house.'

'Ah. Makes sense, especially if they were a Catholic family. In any case, Robin, to answer your question, they were designed to show the Messianic promise of Christ's birth in pictures. Messiah meaning saviour. How does that Bible prophecy go?'

Summer, instant response. 'The Book of Isaiah, Chapter 11, Verse 1: "And there shall come forth a rod out of the stem of Jesse, and a branch shall grow out of his roots."'

'Yes, something like that,' Zach agreed easily. 'They're picture stories for the peasants who couldn't read, and street cred for the nobles of the time. What's the saying? "What I read I forget, what I see I remember."'

'My people are not peasants but we are not readers of words.'

'But you can read, Summer.' I couldn't imagine the world without books.

'My people are not always welcome in the schools of housedwellers, and we move on from stopping place to stopping place,' Summer said. 'But Papa Brockton taught me to read because I wish to learn everything.'

'Well, the fancy word is *genealogy*,' Zach told us both. 'You always read a Jesse Tree from bottom to top, from Jesse lying on the ground and sprouting a tree to the Queen of Heaven with her baby God at the top.'

'Can't make much difference on a ceiling,' I said.

'Possibly not.' Zach's eyes settled on Mary. For moments, he said nothing. Then, 'Staggering. Absolutely staggering.'

'What?'

'If you look carefully you'll see she's no ordinary BVM. That's Blessed Virgin Mary to you, Fruit. She's holding the Christ child in her arms, quite traditional, but look at her belly.'

In an oval, carved where Mary's lap should be, was the head of a bearded man. 'That would be God the Father. So she is truly the Mother of God here,' marvelled Zach. 'The quintessence of the Holy Trinity. And it explains the last line of the Latin poem.'

For an agnostic, Zach knows a lot of religion.

'I think there's a statue of her on the little island. On our pond,' I said.

We left the cellar with a new confidence. I threw the keys to Summer, and broke off the conversation by challenging a dash back to Limberlost Mill. Zach won, Summer came second, Muggins third. Boddy beat us all, of course. I blamed my slowness on a backache, which was only partly true. Indeedy indulged in a little whinge about 'you kids' being half an hour late for lunch, but then with Chris's help laid out a pile of chubby tuna sandwiches, crisps, cold milk, brownies and fresh fruit.

'Chris and I have come to a rapid and thorny decision,' Indeedy said. 'We've decided to hire the bikers – on trial – for one month.' Zach opened his mouth to protest but Indeedy pressed on. 'We've discussed the risks, but the fact is that no one else has answered the ad so far, and time isn't on our side. Anyway, the whole darned venture will be risky – and before anyone says anything, I *am* concerned, Summer, that we don't know why you ran off when you saw them.' Indeedy directed her laser gaze at Summer, who was toying with the lettuce spilling out of a very fat tuna sandwich.

'Gypsies do not really take to bikers,' said Summer, looking down, avoiding my mum's eyes.

'Do you know Meat Loaf, Summer?' Chris asked.

'They have brought trouble to the hatch in the past. Many is the time King has warned them off. King says Meat Loaf is a drug dealer, and his *mullamooshes* give the Romany a bad name.'

'What'd they want with people at your hatch?' Indeedy wondered.

'That I cannot tell, but my people never forget a wrong doer; it is also true that evil doings may be cursed,' said Summer. 'King says they are bad *baxt*.'

'What's "baxt"?'

'Romany for fate or luck.'

'I'd never even cross the road if I paid any attention to that sort of superstitious twaddle.' Indeedy wasn't very sensitive sometimes.

'Ease up, Mum. But I think you're making a mistake,' said Zach. 'Not about superstition, just your judgement.'

'Well, you're entitled to your opinion,' smiled Chris. 'I'll be keeping my beady eye on that lot, so no frets, no worries, young Summer.'

But Summer looked worried nonetheless.

9
Revelation

Q: And did those feet in ancient time
Walk upon England's mountains green?
And was the holy lamb of god
On England's pleasant pastures seen?
A: No

> – 'Jerusalem', according to Zachary
> Swallow, with apologies to William Blake

'I do not know where to commence.'

'How about the beginning, Summer? Like, why did Meat Loaf threaten us?'

'There is knowledge too dangerous for you to know.'

'We made a pact, Summer Locke, remember?'

We were sat on my bedroom balcony, looking out over to Pucklethorpe Manor.

'My heart is filled with heavy stones.'

'Please,' I begged.

'Bear with me.' Summer sounded old and tired. 'If you are to know, it is our forever secret.'

'Please.' I looked Summer straight in the eye. 'Shall we count to one hundred again?'

Summer squeezed my hand, then, taking a deep breath, began.

'It was dusk, and the commencing of the week Papa Brockton died, I was settling the hives and feeding the chooks. Papa, I believe, was in the kitchen at the rear of the house. I heard the sound of a motor, and spied Lady Charlotte's car driving up to the front of the house.'

I glanced from my balcony perch and across the grounds. Last week already felt like a hundred years ago. Last week we were packing to leave London for a new life in Borderland and I had not yet met Summer Locke.

'There she was, and with her was a big man carrying a torch. Your very Meat Loaf, it was.'

'What were they up to?'

'Mark it, there were no lights come nightfall at the manor. People don't think but why would Papa, being blind, need to switch on lights? Anyway, I tiptoed closer and hid in the yew hedge and what did I see? Meat Loaf climbing in through a darkened side window, and her, why she was pushing a big heavy object into the middle of the drive.'

'What was it? And what was it for?'

'She was blocking the drive to prevent comings and goings. I took courage, and made myself visible, and asked would she like assistance with the big object, which I believe was a water butt.' Summer paused. 'This was a mistake, for she cursed at me. I will not repeat her words. Then Mr Meat Loaf emerged from the main door carrying a large fire grate. "Is Mr Wheatley aware of this?" I asked, at which point Lady Charlotte threatened to have me arrested for trespass, and Mr Meat Loaf, well, he ran at me shaking a poker, I believe it was.

'When next morning I told Papa Brockton, he said did I not know there was nothing new about her nasty pranks? Did I not know she was setting booby traps, stealing his post and sneaking things from the house and did he pay any notice? He did not really mind about the things she pinched from the house as long as he had a place to lay his head and I to lay mine, and nor did he wish to frighten me, he said, and he would always see to my safety, but he felt it his duty to inform me that his life was in danger. I was to keep well clear of that lot, especially Mr Meat Loaf, "A man of very dangerous leanings, even deadly deeds", he said. I asked Papa what he meant and Papa said Meat Loaf was a coward, but he was a man of "nefarious leanings".'

'You mean, like a killer?'

'I believe so.'

'Did you tell the police? About him sneaking through the window and coming out with stolen goods?'

Summer Locke managed a pale smile. 'This would be a no-go question. As I have said, Romany are honour-bound not to seek help from the *gavs*.'

'They only want to protect us!'

'*Gorgio* law deprives us of our freedom,' said Summer Locke.

'I really haven't got a clue what you mean.' I was frustrated again with the riddles in Summer's world.

Just then Indeedy called us down for tea.

Later, after a stroll with Boddy chasing shadows in the woods, we were back in my room and Summer Locke was solemn. 'Robin, I am thinking I shall not be biding here.'

'Don't be daft. You said there's no one at the hatch! You're safer here.'

'I did not say "no one", I said no elders.'

'Whatever! Please, please stay,' I implored. 'I've got an idea. Let's leave the journal for now and look at Mr Wheatley's history stuff. We very nearly have a library of our own now!' I'm trying to keep Summer's mind off the subject of murder. Mine too.

'I will stay for now,' Summer said.

I removed the manuscript from its folder. *Pucklethorpe Manor: True Camelot*, partly typed and divided into chapters.

'Papa had a secretary, once a week for three hours,' said Summer. 'She typed his handwritten notes. She would say, "Mr Wheatley, you should have been a doctor, for your writing is inscrutable!" and Papa would laugh his grand HA HA! and say, "I believe you mean 'illegible', Mrs Corfield!" Mrs Corfield, she was a lovely lady; she called me Papa's eyes. She promised to teach me touch-typing "so as to help when Mr Wheatley sends you to Oxford University". And of Papa's efforts she would say to Papa, "you've got it all down pat, Mr Wheatley", meaning Papa truly knew what he was talking about.'

'And did he?'

Summer began to read aloud. "'Introduction. This book is not a guide book, and nor is it a historical news report …'"

'My teacher Mrs Avey would say we should never write about what we aren't going to write about.'

'May I continue?'

'Sorry.'

"'… rather it is the record of a great and noble family home from its earliest days. Most importantly, it is a quest for an answer to this question: with apologies to the great mystic William Blake: *And was bright Camelot builded here, In Pucklethorpe's dark peculiar hills?*'"

'Summer. Zach knows almost everything there is to know about King Arthur and the Round Table and such.' I dashed across to Zach's room and found him sloped across his bed reading *A Hitchhiker's Guide to the Galaxy*.

'Zach, Summer says the manor is ancient.'

No response.

'We've got something else we want you to check out. It's Mr Wheatley's notes about Camelot and the Holy Grail.'

Zach peered at me with his young fogey look. 'Let me guess. The poor codger thinks ... sorry, *thought* that King Arthur's Round Table was here?'

'Yes, and he believed the Jesse Tree was a key to finding the Grail.'

Zach slammed his book shut. 'What do you want me to do about it?'

'Just come and have a look at Mr Wheatley's notes? Just this one more time? Pretty please?'

'You owe me.' A reluctant Zach followed me.

'Look Summer, I need to say that stories of the location of Camelot are as rampant as sightings of the Loch Ness monster or the Abominable Snowman,' Zach said.

'Yes,' said Summer Locke, 'but you are speaking of mythical and fantastic creatures. Papa Brockton was speaking of a locality on a real map.'

'Have you any idea how many places make a claim on Camelot? I'll tell you, there are dozens – Tintagel in

Cornwall, Glastonbury in Somerset, Caerleon in Wales, Castle Cadbury in Somerset, Winchester, to mention a few. There is almost certainly no Camelot in Borderland!'

'It is true not many people agreed with Papa. He carried on, saying to me, "Absence of proof is not proof of absence".'

'Fair enough. I'll have a look. But don't get your hopes up.'

'About what?'

'I don't know. Anything! Now I'll be returning to Mr Adams if you don't mind.'

This set me thinking. To Summer, the manor and Papa Brockton Wheatley were interconnected, and now Papa was gone, what was Summer to make of the manor and how to carry on Mr Wheatley's wishes? What was I to make of Summer Locke? Was the pretty carving in the cellar a red herring to take our minds off the goal? I wanted to solve a crime, not play riddles over a bunch of cartoon characters growing from a Bible man's belly button. Not that I'd say this to Summer Locke.

'Summer, do you believe in ghosts?'

'There is a spirit in everything.'

'Even stones?'

'Yes. And mountains and flowers and bees.'

'Do you believe the Jesse Tree has anything to do with why your Papa Brockton was murdered?'

'I do not know.'

'But you do know that Lady Charlotte wanted rid of him, yes?'

'Yes.'

'And do you know why she wanted rid of him?'

'Not really, but I do believe she wanted money-money-money.'

'You never finished telling me what happened after you saw Meat Loaf stealing stuff.'

'We must wait.'

'Why?'

'Because I do not feel very well.' Summer looked flushed, snuggled already in the caterpillar sleeping bag.

'Let me see if you have a temperature.' I placed my wrist on Summer's forehead. 'You do. Mum!' I shouted downstairs. 'Summer's got a temperature.'

In no time, Indeedy was in the room with some Lemsip and a cool cloth for Summer's forehead.

'I thank you, Mrs Swallow.'

Indeedy smiled. 'Let's hope this does the trick.' She left, closing the door softly.

We lay still. Then, 'Summer, is it OK if I just have another chat with Zach?'

'Good night and God bless,' said Summer, murmuring a mantra: *Ten little angels round my bed ...*

'I've seen enough already,' said Zach, before I had a chance to open my mouth. My brother pulled out a few papers from the stack. 'These are rejection slips from five learned societies and journals, saying very politely but firmly that, whereas Mr Wheatley's social history of Pucklethorpe Manor was well-documented and fascinating, his Camelot "hypothesis" was frankly little more than pie in the sky.'

I settled beside my brother. 'I don't mind, really, but Summer will. Zach, have I told you about the gold bars?'

Zach ignored me. 'Let me finish. Your Gypsy friend has much to learn. At Summer Locke's age I already accepted the *Hitchhiker's Guide* theory of being human, that we may have big brains, but are ultimately little more than weeds in the timeless bog of the universe, cowpats in the meadows of infinity, rescued from chaos by illusion.'

Sometimes my brother sounds like a comic book minus the humour.

'Zach, you sound like ... like an old man!'

'I take that as a compliment, Fruit. Just listen to this,' he ordered, dropping *The Hitchhiker's Guide*, then retrieving and leafing through Mr Wheatley's manuscript. I spied my newly checked out *Architectural History of Borderland* on the floor.

'I was looking for that!'

Zach is good at ignoring me these days. 'Here are some good bits from Wheatley's manuscript: "The connections of Pucklethorpe Manor go back to Civil

War times, when Borderland soil was steeped scarlet with the blood of enemies who literally tore one another apart."' Zach paused. 'You know Red Lake, up the hill?'

I shook my head.

'Named Red Lake for why? Because the soldiers' blood turned the lake water crimson, is why.' Zach read on: '"In the Civil War winter of 1643 tragic events came to a head in a bloodbath at Pucklethorpe Castle, reported by some to have been joined by a tunnel to Pucklethorpe Manor ..." Pucklethorpe Castle's only half a mile down the road, so I suppose it's possible,' he mused.

My eyes began to glaze over.

'But listen to this, Fruit: "One siege ended in horror, when twenty-four Parliamentarian soldiers were tied back to back and then some of them had their hands cut off, and ..."' Zach stopped. 'It's too awful.'

'I'm glad people aren't like that any more.'

'Excuse me! What makes you think we're any better these days?' Zach frowned. 'But wait, this is interesting. Says here that before razing the castle to the ground they removed the grand staircase and moved it to Pucklethorpe Manor – "where it remains to this very day". I didn't notice a staircase today.'

'Because we went in the back door and straight to the cellar, duhhh. I need to tell you about the gold bars, Zach.'

'Sure. If we have a Holy Grail why not treasure? Why not Fort Knox? Or Atlantis?'

I ignored his sarcasm. 'Well. I know for certain that Lord Pucklethorpe buried gold bars somewhere, because Mrs Spicer's mum worked there and heard first hand. It was during the last war, I think. Lord Pucklethorpe didn't want his English money helping Hitler if England was invaded.'

'Yes. That would be World War Two.' Zach tried to pat me on the head but I dodged. 'Frankly this sounds like more unsubstantiated Camelot twaddle. Gold bars!'

'But,' I spluttered, 'Mrs Spicer heard it first hand from her mum who was Lord Pucklethorpe's housekeeper here at the manor! He didn't trust paper money.'

'So you said. How many gold bars?'

'I don't know but she called it treasure, which sounds like a lot. And also you said the poem isn't old? The one above the Jesse Tree, which is old?'

'Yes?'

'And it's Lord Pucklethorpe's initials by the poem?'

'Yes?'

'Well! Lord Pucklethorpe had a little boy named Jesse and he died after a fall from his pony, which is why Lord Pucklethorpe went off to war and died and then his wife went crazy and got sent to a loony bin and that's how it all ended.'

Zach yawned and stretched and picked up *Hitchhiker's Guide*. He was like a long thin cat. 'OK, Fruitfly. Let's take up the story anon then? You don't want to turn into a pumpkin.'

'Just one more thing.'

'It'll wait.'

10

Toffs and Tinkers

The dead don't go 'till you do, loved ones.
The dead are still here holding our hands

— 'Darling', Jackie Kay

Through the night I heard Summer coughing and tossing and turning. In the morning, I checked Summer's forehead again.

'You still have a temperature, Summer, and you're shivering. Hope you don't have the flu.'

'Please may I have a glass of water?'

'Indeedy will have you better in no time.'

Indeedy loved to minister to the sick. *Are you warm enough, Summer? Are you thirsty, Summer? Hungry yet, Summer?* Indeedy made chicken noodle soup and reserved the broth, insisting that Summer sipped it as often as possible. She readied the spare bedroom next to Zach's and Summer moved to the bed there.

'Your mam says it is my room for as long as I wish.'

'Great.'

The guest room was all cosy, with just a normal window and bed and dressing table and wardrobe. I was lucky to have my bedroom with its big windows and adventure steps. Mainly Summer slept and slept through the day and the night, and the next.

Time stretched and melted.

I opened the French doors of my room to let the morning air breathe. Another beautiful day. I checked on Summer.

'Summer,' I called. 'Are you awake? Summer?'

'I am.'

'Come into my room if you feel up to it.'

'I am now well,' said Summer.

But Indeedy insisted on one more quiet day and Summer didn't argue. We shared toast and tea, and then I went off for a stretch with Boddy to return the architecture book.

'Hello, Miss Kiss.'

'Robin. How lovely to see you. Would your dog like a treat?'

'Yes, please.' Miss Kiss extracted a very smelly tripe stick from her bag. Boddy loves them.

'Was the book helpful?' Miss Kiss asked.

'Not really, not meaning to be rude. There's only a tiny bit on Pucklethorpe Manor. It says the manor house is Grade II Listed, but it is "not very impressive as an example of its period".'

'I'm surprised to hear that. I believe it is Jacobean, and some say it is built on Norman or even Saxon foundations.'

'Well, can't win 'em all,' I said offhand. 'Miss Kiss, do you remember mentioning Mr Wheatley writing a book?'

'Yes, indeed.'

'We've found the manuscript. There are loads of notes on the Pucklethorpe family lineage.'

'Marvellous. You will have all you require then, Robin.' Miss Kiss busily organized shelves as we spoke.

'Did he ever speak to you about King Arthur?'

Miss Kiss tutted. 'Oh the dear man, he was quite obsessed with –'

'Camelot?'

'Indeed. It was difficult to sway him from the notion.'

'Well, what do you think?'

'With all respect to a man of great intellect, I believe Mr Wheatley was on a hiding to nothing. I never saw the chapel he spoke of, apparently in the manor's cellar. Have you seen it?'

'Yes. Are there any books on Jesse Trees?' I asked. 'There's one in the chapel on the ceiling.'

'Allow me to check.' Miss Kiss tapped away on her big computer. 'I've just checked by the name "Jesse Tree". No luck. I'll cross-reference and let you know. How are you getting on with your astronaut book?'

'Thanks! I love it. Must rush home!'

Did I have to rush? Not really. But I didn't want to talk about the space book just now.

'Summer. Isn't it time to tell me what really happened?' I demanded, rushing into the bedroom. 'After the day when you saw Lady Charlotte and Meat Loaf?' I suddenly felt I could not wait any longer to hear the story.

Summer nodded a hesitant yes and motioned me to sit on the bed, 'So as to look you in the eyes.' I love Summer's steady gaze.

'All is as clear to me as is this very moment. I lay awake on the morning of the day, staring through the manor window at the dawn summer light creeping through the dark copper beeches, watching shadows on the fruit trees all abuzz with bees, catching the animal shapes of the yew hedge, light sneaking into the house …'

Mrs Avey would have given Summer an A+ for description.

'Emptiness is king in all but two of the thirty rooms. Papa Brockton was sad that these rooms were now bare but for a few pieces of furniture and all save one of the bathrooms empty of soap or towel or toothbrush.'

I wanted to say 'cut to the chase' but instead unlocked myself from Summer's steady gaze and fidgeted with the appliquéd nobbles on Summer's fluffy bedspread.

'Must've been spooky. In such a grand house.'

'Ghosts in every nook and cranny. All along the grand staircase to the public rooms – see there is the great hall, and the study, and the drawing room, and the library –' Summer gestured the shape of this invisible tour – 'and the vast master bedroom where nobody has slept for longer than you or I have been on this earth. There was this emptiness and I thought, if *gorgios* must have houses, the houses must have folk living in them.'

'Shall we go to my room? Then you can see everything while you tell it.'

'Yes.' Summer stretched and rose. In my room we went straight to my open French windows, looking out across the grounds.

'So, when the light slanted through the window of my attic room I would rise.'

'Then what?'

'I recalled that this day was special. I dressed in a flash and ran down the echoing hall. "Six o'clock and all's well!" I sang through the doorway of Papa Brockton's bedroom, then I dashed to the landing, slid down the banister of the grand staircase, ran through the main hall into the kitchen, filled the kettle with water and placed it on the Aga to boil. Papa Brockton claimed tea tasted better brewed with water from the Aga than from the electric kettle. I sliced three thick slabs of high-baked sandwich loaf. These I would place in the Aga toaster, which is like a tennis racquet' – Summer made a tennis racquet-sized circle – 'two hinged wire mesh circles with long handles which open and close over the pieces of toast.'

The thought of toasting bread made my mouth water. 'Fancy a piece of toast?'

Summer gave me a no-thank-you look. 'You will turn into a piece of toast if you do not take care. Now then, speaking of toast, Papa Brockton is pernickety about his toast; it must come out hot and nearly burnt, and criss-crossed with black square marks from the mesh. The butter must be spread while the toast is hot. Out to the very edge. Two pieces for Papa and one for Summer. Marmalade for Papa, honey for Summer.'

'Have you tried honey and peanut butter on toast?'

'No.'

'Would you like to try it some time?' I was still thinking about toast.

'I thank you, no. Papa loves our breakfast. He says that when he is alone breakfast takes much longer, though to my mind he moves with grace for a man robbed of vision. He says that with the aid of his contact lenses and thick spectacles he is just able to shape a thick blur and a pinprick in front of him.'

Summer stretched an arm straight out and raised a forefinger. Mrs Avey's shadow tapped my shoulder and whispered a silent correction in my brain – why is Summer speaking of Papa Brockton in the present tense?

'Papa feels his way round the shutters of the kitchen, closes them every evening. Then each morning he releases the catches and allows the light in. "To the blind," Papa says ...' Then, Summer read my mind and self-corrected. 'I mean "said", "the warmth of sunlight is very important."'

'You must have been like his very own child!'

Summer brightened, affecting a Queen's English accent. 'Yes. "Top of the form, young bean!" he'd say in his big booming voice and then he would gather me into a grand hug.' Summer smiled. 'The top of Papa Brockton's head was shiny like a mountain's top. He taught me so much; he said he'd see to it I would attend Oxford University, and he said also that I could help him save the house, "and my tough old pelt too, young bean!", by being there with him when Lady Charlotte made her unwelcome visits.' Summer paused. 'And I *shall* attend Oxford University some day.'

'When did she start her bad turns?'

'When first she began her trips to the manor she would fetch up with her children Zadok and Bathsheba, sometimes Delilah, all courteous like, and Papa Brockton he was welcoming. He would invite them into the kitchen for tea and scones. But it never felt quite right, he said, and he soon caught her main purpose.'

'Which was?'

'Everything wretched – to mock him, set booby traps, steal his post, take away furniture while naming me a thief. I have told you of the water butt to block visitors from gaining access. Later this same week she shouted at him she was going to arrange an accident, so as to repossess her property.'

'You heard her say that?' I was incredulous. '"Arrange" an accident?'

'She did. This time she did not see me there, for I hid myself after her threats. Papa Brockton lost his temper then, he felt in the compost for a rotten apple and threw it in the direction of her voice. The lump met with her nose: SQUISH. "Wretch!" she screamed out. "Wretch! Just you wait! I'll see you laid in your grave!"'

'This is terrible, Summer.'

'On my life so I did hear the very words.'

I'm thinking, Hell's bells! I draw a mental image of Lady Charlotte. She would be all tall and pale with flashing eyes. She'd drown puppies for a lark and make dog-fur coats like Cruella de Vil in *One Hundrend and One Dalmations*. She would be very sure of herself, and she would not stop until she got her way.

'What was she up to on … on the last day?' I hated the way the word 'last' felt coming out of my mouth.

Summer coughed and heaved a deep sigh.

'Well, she arrived with Bathsheba and Zadok to paint the windows. They brought ladders and such.

Lady Charlotte was very restless, like, and dashed back and forth shouting orders. I asked Papa if I should make myself scarce, but he said please not to leave, my presence might help.'

'And did it? Help?'

'I do not truly know. But I reminded Papa Brockton that we were planning the mowing of the great front grounds and that I did not really wish to leave him in any case.'

'How does a blind person mow a lawn?'

'Aha, this was clever. She was mocking away and we ignored her. Papa used his push mower that was made "when Jesus was a boy, young bean!" We'd make straight rows with a big white yoghurt pot which I would move so as to keep in his view. We commenced mid-morning, it took us some few hours. Lady Charlotte became harsher in her mocking as the day passed – "Thank you very kindly, *sir*, for preparing the property for your imminent departure." And, "I cannot imagine, *sir*, why you are troubling to entertain your so-called friend tonight. You shall be out of this house within the month." Then she left. Papa, he laughed his grand HA HA! "That woman honks like a goose, don't you think, young bean?"'

'Did the children stand up for him?'

'No. I think it pained him that his own children did not defend him – never once did I hear a kind word uttered on his behalf – eventually Papa did not attempt to speak to them. They seemed frightened.'

'That is so sad,' I said.

'This is why we became so close,' said Summer. 'We retreated to the kitchen for lunch and then Papa went to his study, while I set off to the village for his shopping.'

'Was she still at the house when you left for the shopping?'

'Yes. And on my return, she said to me, "Tinker baggage" as I took Papa's goods through to the kitchen. And I answered her back directly – we Gypsies are not tinkers, Robin.'

'What did you say?'

'Says I, polite like and pointing to my parcel, I says to her, "Yes, madam, here is the baggage, and here is your Gypsy toting it." As I went in I noticed her large crowbar propped up against the stone steps leading to the outside door but thought no more of it at the time. I should have twigged ...'

'Twigged what?'

'That she left it there for a reason. She always hooked it over her arm like a walking stick, she said she might be needing it for self-defence, you know, as if Papa Brockton might attack her.'

'And would he ever?'

'Never. Just that rotten apple the once, and he would have missed her if he could have seen proper.'

'What a meanie.'

Summer yawned and leaned back. 'I am tired, Robin.'

'Do you want to wait 'til tomorrow to tell me the rest?'

A knock on the door. 'Come in, Mum.'

Tucked under Indeedy's arm was a fluffy new pillow for Summer. She carried a tray. The scent of chicken noodle soup and toast wafted our way. She left the chicken bits and the noodles in the soup.

'Lunchtime.'

Mum at her top-notch.

'Here's another pillow for you, Summer. Take it back to your room when you go back to bed.' Indeedy tossed the pillow Summer's way, and turned to go, ponytail swinging. 'I'm off to the bakehouse. Do try to take it easy.'

'Thanks, Mum.'

'I thank you, Mrs Swallow.'

Summer waited for the door to close, making finger patterns on the surface of the soup. 'Papa Brockton was most excited about this Dr Whelan's visit. They were friends at college and had once planned a coffee house in Oxford they would call The Whale and Wheat. The project never materialized but the friendship lasted. "A man of intellect and considerable influence, young bean," Papa said. He felt as if Dr Whelan could aid him in realizing his Camelot dream.'

Lunch seemed to give Summer a second wind.

'Don't you need a rest, Summer?' I felt ready for a snooze myself.

'I am revived, thanking you. Dr Whelan arrived at half past four. But suddenly, as he parked in front of the water butt obstacle, herself appeared.'

Summer again affected the upper class accent. "If you are the *visitor*, you should be aware that you are trespassing on my property, sir, and I would be obliged if you would turn your motor around and depart *now*." Dr Whelan, he seemed nervous. He did not look her in the eye, but proceeded to set the car's burglar alarm and central-lock. Then he said, "Madam, I am not in the habit of breaking appointments, so perhaps you will forgive me." And then she said to him, "Suit yourself, sir, but there is no point whatsoever in seeing him. Very soon he shan't be here." Then off she went.'

Summer returned to the big windows and breathed deep. 'Ah, the sweet rain has come.'

We could hear the delicious pitty-pat of raindrops hitting the roof.

'Go on, Summer,' I urged. 'What happened next?'

'Well, now. Papa greeted Dr Whelan at the main door and introduced me as his "young bean" and "third eye". He poured us each a glass of sherry, which was terrible tasting. "Dr Whelan and I shall slum it for high tea in the kitchen, my young bean. Toad in the hole with fine claret, HA HA!" says Papa.

'There was nothing left of the meal or the wine when Papa guided Dr Whelan round the house. He saved the cellar for last, telling Dr Whelan how the estate was restored by Lord Pucklethorpe during the Second World War and all. "This inscription," says Papa Brockton, pointing to the Latin script beside the Jesse Tree, "is fascinating." Well then, Dr Whelan, he took off his specs, he stroked his chin and scratched his head.'

Summer Locke mimed the same.

'Papa Brockton, his eyes flashed. "Why, sir, I am persuaded the place will easily rival Camelot! With sufficient funds we might be able to re-open the tunnel connecting the manor to the castle." "Tunnel? Don't be daft," says Dr Whelan. "You do know, my good man, that many grand estates are rumoured to connect to that castle, and that not one has yet been discovered?"'

'So Dr Whelan was another doubter?'

'Sad but true, a nay-sayer.' Summer paused, spooning soup and dipping toast. My eyelids felt like heavy weights.

'Then and of a sudden and before Papa could reply, Lady Charlotte's face appeared in the ground-level screen covering the cellar window.' Summer's voice went high and nasal again. "He's ruining the house, you know, you're bound to carry off vermin on your trail." Well, Dr Whelan, with the grill between them, he eyed Charlotte straight. "Not to fret, my dear lady. I'm extremely fond of small creatures. Now, with all due respect, if you'll forgive ..." then he just carried on with Papa.

'When we left the cellar, Papa asked me to fetch another bottle of sherry, which I did. But then I made a grievous mistake. Feeling the fidgets, I asked to be excused from their company to visit the hatch. Papa reminded me I had promised to sketch the shape of the Jesse Tree in his journal, so I swore to return presently, and draw it tomorrow. As I left, Lady Charlotte was heading down the drive. So off I ran to the hatch. Little did I know that I —'

I interrupted. 'So Papa Brockton never mentioned the story of the gold?'

Summer seemed annoyed. 'The gold? Have I not said before that the gold was not important to Papa Brockton? I was no more than an hour at the hatch, but I was never to see Papa alive again.'

'Oh, Summer.'

'Which remembers me, I must needs go to the hatch now and discover if my elders have returned.'

'May I come with you?'

Summer sighed deeply. 'I prefer to attend on my own.'

'Are you strong enough?'

'I am sound.'

Did my friend no longer trust me? Feeling the tension tighten like a noose, I dug deep to hide my disappointment.

11
Perspective

Suddenly, from behind the rim of the moon ... there emerges a sparkling blue and white jewel, a light delicate sky blue sphere laced with slowly swirling veils of white ... this is earth, home. My view of our planet was a glimpse of divinity.

– Dr Edgar Mitchell, Apollo IV

Chris Lamb eased the Grumman Tiger off the runway at Green Man Airfield, climbed steadily, then banked north through the summer sky. The day was mist-free, dazzling. 'My very favourite machines,' Chris said. The Grumman Tigers were trim single-proppers with a special place in local history; the first to land at Green Man when the airfield opened.

The River Puckle shimmered, a silver thread below. I scanned the toytown landscape of twisting lanes, castle ruins, clustered roofs and woodland. Summer was immersed in Brockton Wheatley's journal and scarcely looked out of the window.

'Summer! You're missing everything!'

Summer glanced at me. 'How high would we be flying now, Miss Chris?'

'Several football pitches stacked end on end,' said Chris. 'Amazing, isn't it? I never get over the buzz.'

Summer returned to the journal, I to my eagle's eye view. The flight was my surprise birthday present from Indeedy and Chris. Indeedy teased that she'd never known a child turn fourteen and forget the fact, but I had. Where would we like to fly? Dublin? Glasgow? Paris? There was no competition.

'Over Pucklethorpe Manor, please!'

'Easy peasy lemon squeezy.'

'Can I bring Summer?'

'Sure, Fruit.'

Below us lay the green stretch of Pucklethorpe Manor, surrounded by outlying buildings. 'Look! Our house. Summer Locke! If you miss this you'll miss why you wanted to fly in the first place. May we fly lower, Chris?'

Chris banked sharply into a circular descent. 'I'm afraid we aren't allowed to fly lower than 500 feet.' A miniature Indeedy emerged from the bakehouse. You could see her ponytail, her gingham shirt had merged into a solid blue. She was waving frantically and jumping up and down with Boddy's wiggly blue-grey speck dancing circles round her. We waved back, just in case Indeedy could actually see us too.

Summer Locke took in the view this time. 'Would it be possible please, Miss Chris, to circle round the manor a few times?'

'Certainly,' grinned Chris. 'Should be fun. I'll just pretend I'm on a roundabout and not taking the exit 'til you give us a nod. We used to play roundabouts when I first earned my wings … round and round until someone plucked a word from somewhere, like, "Aberdovey!" If it was a lucky day we'd set off to the spontaneous destination, charting as we flew. Naughty but nice. By the way, I heard an amusing story about the old girl who's inside for murdering your friend. I've interviewed her, you know.'

Summer continued to peer out of the window, sketching on a blank page in Mr Wheatley's journal. 'Oh?'

'I almost took pity. Apparently Lady Charlotte had no friends and nor did her mother, who had only one friend, and nobody liked her mother's friend either! But then I don't suppose aristocrats worry their pretty little heads about being liked or not, their sense of privilege and entitlement is genetic.'

Summer cast an odd look at Chris. Then at me. Was this supposed to be funny, or was it news?

'That's quite sad,' I said, pointing out of the window. 'Look, Summer.' Beneath was the roof of Pucklethorpe

Manor and its outbuildings, genuflecting in the midst of the elaborate garden design.

'Summer? I'm talking to you.'

Summer, scribbling frantically. 'Follow the line of the hedge round the great house, Robin, starting at the front gate. There.'

At first it looked like a lot of greener than green to me, other than the buildings. Then, lightbulb moment. Yes! The longer I looked, the clearer the shapes, ornate, tidy and symmetrical.

'Tell me what you see, Robin,' said Summer, sketching away.

'I see the house. Look how big it looks even from up here! It's in the middle of the border. It's squarer than you'd think ... I mean, more rectangular.'

'The border, the border,' urged Summer.

'Got it! Kind of like a four-leaf clover and a big square at once. With four small box squares in each of the corners.'

'What are you two up to?' Chris said. 'Sounds like a game of aerial Cluedo.'

Summer ignored her. 'Yes, Robin. Now will you please count the trees round the house, inside the hedge?'

'You count. I'll take your word.'

'Including the four box hedges in each corner. Thirty-nine, forty ... forty-two.' Summer nodded and produced the sketch. 'What shape do you see now?'

'Scribbles. What do *you* see?'

'The very same shape as the Jesse Tree in the cellar. The top of the tree bit with the Mother of God is *your* garden, Robin. See? The pond? That's at the top bit.'

'Ah!'

Summer smiled. 'Many thanks, Miss Chris, we can exit your roundabout in the sky now.'

'Wait a minute, Summer!' I protested. 'Whose birthday is it anyway?'

'I am sorry,' said Summer, smiling radiantly and not looking sorry, not one little bit.

Chris guided the craft and caught a tailwind back to the airfield. As she readied to land, a freak thunderstorm, the first fall of rain in days, pelted down. 'Now there's a baptizing for your day,' said Summer Locke, as the craft juddered to safety on the steaming runway.

'Time for birthday lunch in the tea room with Indeedy's very first customers,' Chris grinned, ushering us towards the airfield cafe.

The Green Man Airfield and Hospitality Centre consisted of a converted hangar housing a tearoom-cum-cafe and airfield office. Pictures of all manner of aircraft and a bulletin board advertising 'Flying Machines For Sale' decorated the end wall, painted in magnolia and grown grubby with age.

Chatter morphed into silence amongst the small group of aged and ageing men, goggles perched on foreheads and dressed like versions of Biggles. Cups of tea finished quickly, moves made to vacate the room.

Chris Lamb assumed a look of horror. 'We aren't much accustomed to seeing females here!' Winking at us, she leaned on an invisible zimmer frame. 'Far as I know there's only one other lady pilot here now, called Beryl. She goes wild every time we meet.' Chris gestured over her shoulder. 'And then there's our Doris here, who doesn't count as she suffers from aviophobia – fear of flying to you.' Chris directed my gaze to the food counter. 'Robin. Doris makes perfect fish and chips.'

Yes, please, to fish and chips.

Chris perused the contents of the glass cooler and beckoned us to have a look at the sweets. Behind the bar loomed Doris, wearing a badge declaring "I am NOT your mother". Doris wore her hair tightly pulled back and combed into a severe ballerina bun. Her faded apron stretched tightly across an impressive mono-bosom.

'Fish, chips and peas times five, please,' beamed Chris. Indeedy and Zach had not arrived yet.

Doris nodded tersely.

'No peas for me.' I hate peas unless they're raw.

'Please keep your peas, Robin. I will eat them,' said Summer.

I tried to cheer Doris. 'For my fifth birthday we had fish and chips. Also peas. I said to my mum, "Mum, I

HATE peas!" and she said, "Let's compromise, Fruitfly. Just five peas?" And I said, "When I'm twenty-five will I have to eat twenty-five peas?"'

Doris almost smiled and I smiled back. She looks pretty when she almost smiles.

Chris shrugged. 'To pea or not to pea ... that is the question!'

Groans all round.

'Now *there's* an interesting somebody,' said Chris, pointing to a photograph on a panelled door. 'One Commander Gordy Garden. Gordy logged over twenty thousand flying hours in thirty years – and almost as many lady friends. Handsome devil, eh?'

Chris tried the door. It was unlocked. 'Come on in here, I'll fetch us our drinks and show you around the *inner sanctum* while Mrs Happy Hour rustles up our grub.'

She went behind the bar to pour our drinks: Vimto on ice for me, cream soda no ice for Summer. Chris allowed herself a large whisky.

'Commander Garden was my instructor,' said Chris. 'He also enjoyed an intriguing connection with Lady Charlotte Wheatley.'

Summer nursed the cream soda, sucking foam from the top. 'What connection, Miss Chris?'

'Well, Gordy taught Charlotte's son to fly. He – Zadok, was it? – won his wings about the same time as I earned mine. He seemed a lovely young chap, if a bit more wishbone than backbone. I'm not entirely certain Lady C ever received her certificate, but she did have lessons too, and 'extracurricular' flying jaunts. Gordy was driving Lady Charlotte's car on the last night of his life.'

'He died?' I asked.

'Yes. I covered the inquest. One of the flying instructors found him lying face down and dead as a post on a disused edge of the runway. There was one witness, a local who said he'd been standing in his garden late at night, watching the flood rise on the back road to the airfield. He saw a saloon struggling to cross the ford, in spate it was, conditions requiring a four-wheel-drive vehicle. He saw the car stall. It was too dark to identify the driver, who tried to re-start the car, failed, then abandoned the car. It was still there next morning in the middle of the ford.'

Chris took a sip of her drink, then went on: 'The coroner concluded death by misadventure, accepting the version that Gordy was drunk and had died from exposure after abandoning the car in floodwater to reach his caravan on the airfield.'

'Do you believe it was an accident, Chris?' Summer asked.

'Not for one instant, and I'll tell you why. His body was a mess, his face bloodied and his nose broken. And –' dramatic pause, deep breath – 'the moss on the runway where they found him was scraped for several yards, as if he'd been dragged along. There was moss on the backside of his trousers. How could he beat himself up and drag himself along on his back?'

It was all so grim. The countryside was beginning to feel more dangerous than I had ever dreamed.

'Well,' I said. 'It's my birthday and I want to be happy so I don't want to think about it.'

'Sorry,' said Chris.

'I'd like to have flying lessons some day,' I said quickly, changing the subject.

'We need more women with wings,' Chris agreed.

'Like Amelia Earhart?'

'Yes, Robin, much like Amelia Earhart.'

'Mrs Avey, my English teacher in London, she told us about Amelia Earhart. She said that Amelia showed girls we have the power to achieve our dreams with hard work and dedication.'

'What happened to Amelia?' Summer hadn't heard of her.

'Miss Earhart disappeared in 1937, no one knows exactly where. She was attempting to fly around the world. She disappeared somewhere in the Pacific.'

I felt a sick sensation about how Daddy disappeared. About how to stop thinking that Rory, like Amelia Earhart, might still be alive somewhere. How old would Daddy be now? He'd be forty-eight, I think.

Chris crunched on an ice cube. 'Mrs Avey sounds like a good teacher. Come to think, Lady Charlotte had an Aunt Diana, the duchess who flew. After Charlotte moved to these parts her aunt the duchess would fly to Pucklethorpe from Sussex. She'd sweep low over the manor in her Hornet Moth, flapping her foils. Then she would touch ground here.'

A knock on the door. Mum!

'Grub's up! You first, birthday girl.'

Chris ushered us all back into the cafe, Summer bringing up the rear. At the far end of the room, balloons now festooned a dining table topped with a giant white cake. Indeedy was radiant, grinning ear to ear at their surprise for me, Zach too. In raucous chorus, they sung, 'HAPPY BIRTHDAY TO YOU, YOU WERE BORN IN A ZOO! YOU LOOK LIKE A MONKEY AND YOU ACT LIKE ONE TOOOO!'

I hate the feeling you get of not wanting people to sing to you. I felt too old. Still, it was candles out in one breath, the cake set aside for afters, the fish and chips and peas for all. Doris managed something like a smile, and the ragamuffin hangar cafe became a party. My party.

'G'won, Fruit, make a wish,' teased Zach, when it was time to cut the cake.

'One moment,' said Summer Locke. 'I have an idea. On Romany naming days everyone must make a wish out loud except,' nodding my way, 'the birthday person. She must keep her wish to herself.'

'And do the out-loud wishes come true too?' asked Zach.

'Yes, I do believe it is so.'

'And are the out-loud wishers allowed a secret wish?' I asked.

'Yes, I do believe it is so.'

'I like that idea. As it's my birthday may I go first?'

Collective nods. I squidged my eyes shut, wishing more than one thing – that Rory would walk through that very door at this very moment, that September and school would never happen, that Zach wouldn't go away to university, that...

Zach glanced at his watch and cleared his throat. 'Ahem! Fruit, how many wishes are you wishing?'

I opened one eye. 'Your turn, Summer. Out loud.'

'If you like,' said Summer, all seriousness. 'I do wish most sincerely that King and the other elders from the hatch would allow me to know they are safe and well and returning shortly.'

'We go from youngest up,' I said. 'Your turn, Zach.'

Unhesitatingly, Zach said, 'That I can fit in all the courses I want to study at uni.'

'Geek.'

'I do love compliments, Fruit, but OK, I wish that I'll meet the girl of my dreams? Satisfied?'

Indeedy eyed Chris. 'Your turn.'

'Mum, hang on. Who's older, you or Chris?'

'Me,' said Indeedy. 'Don't look it, do I?'

'Age before beauty. Please proceed.'

'Right,' said Indeedy. 'I wish that I didn't have a wish. Your turn, Chris.'

Chris fetched a bottle of sparkling apple juice, popped it open and poured equal portions as she spoke.

'I'm a hack. I wish to see the murderer of Brockton Wheatley brought to justice. And, that Yes Indeedy Cakes & Bakes breaks even in our first year of operation – at which point I just might be able to consider giving up the day job.'

'That's two wishes. Never mind. Before we raise our toast,' said Indeedy, drawing a parcel from the satchel at her side, 'here's something for you, Robin.'

The parcel was in a bubble bag with American stamps:

<u>Book Rate. Handle With Care.</u>

Par Avion.

Sender's address: Monroeville,

Alabama USA

'Sorry I didn't get round to wrapping it,' smiled Indeedy.

I picked slowly along the heavily taped lip of the envelope. A book.

'Open to the title page, Fruit.'

To Robin Swallow. Thank you for sending your fine essay titled
"Was Atticus Finch a Good Father?"
— Nelle Harper Lee
PS yes he was.

To Kill A Mockingbird, by Harper Lee. My favourite book in the world – and with a note from the author!

'Mum, thank you! Mrs Avey would love this so much!'

'Write and tell her then.'

I raised my glass. 'Here's to the coming true of all our wishes!'

'To the coming true!' came the chorus.

A roar of motorcycles drowned the gentler buzz of small aircraft outside. Moments later the new employees of Yes Indeedy Cakes & Bakes strolled in carrying labelled boxes, and headed straight for Doris. Meat Loaf plopped his burden unceremoniously on the bar and pulled an invoice from the pocket of his black leather jacket. 'Three rounds shortbread, two toffee crumbles, two dozen fat rascals, one summer fruit cake, one Death by Chocolate brownies. Right?'

Doris pulled a pen from her apron pocket, scrutinized the contents of the boxes and laboriously ticked off the items on the invoice, moving her lips over each word. Finally, with flourished formality, she signed for the delivery. Meat Loaf glared loathingly at Doris before snatching the paper, tearing a piece off the bottom, leaning over the bar and dropping it deliberately to the floor.

We were heads down and paying a great deal of attention to the contents of our plates. Especially Summer, who, having looked desperately for an exit at the arrival of the trio, sat quietly. Nowhere to run this time. Oblivious to any potential audience, Rock On pleaded in a mocking tone: 'Ain't you got a treat for us, Doris? Just a little drinky?'

'I do not. You can pay like everyone else.'

'Well, ain't that a shame?' chided Meat Loaf, heaving his bulk round to address anyone present. 'Now don't you think we deserve a cup of tea from Doris on this fine ...' His eyes roved the balloons, his boss, his boss's partner, me, Zach, and then settled on Summer. Motioning to Rock On and Twitch to stay put, he swaggered over to the birthday table, stopping a hair's breadth away from Summer.

'Well, well, well now, if it isn't the prying little tinker gobshite partying with the hoity-toities. Now then, where have we been hiding ourselves?'

Indeedy stood. Chris followed suit. Indeedy raised her hands as if pushing an invisible barrier. 'Whoa now! Mr Meat Loaf, it's me, Indeedy Swallow, your employer, remember?'

'Keep your Yank nose out of it. This is between me and the gyppo.'

Zach raised a hand and positioned himself between Meat Loaf and Indeedy. 'Mr Sykes,' he said, resorting to the biker's proper surname, 'there is no need for rudeness or nastiness here. We are celebrating my sister's birth—'

Meat Loaf shoved Zach sideways back into his chair. 'How's about a nice bit of cake, then?' he sneered. The table creaked with his weight as he leaned and slowly shoved his fist into the middle of my cake. Then, licking the crumbs and icing off, 'Cake, lads?'

Chris placed a restraining hand on Indeedy's shoulder and beckoned me and Summer to stay seated. Summer's hands trembled.

'Mr Sykes,' croaked Indeedy, in a voice caught between outrage and fear, 'I do not suppose it is necessary to point out to you that your trial contract with my firm ceases forthwith.'

Rock On and Twitch *tsk-tsked* their way menacingly towards the table. Meat Loaf stopped licking his hand and feigned a tragic face. He glanced over his shoulder and conducted his mates to repeat after him, 'Dearie me, has one lost one's job?' Then far too close to Indeedy's face, 'You can piss off with your gobshite job and your gobshite gyppo friends! We were quittin' anyway.'

He then swung round with his friends in tow and made his exit. As he reached the door he sniped, 'We won't be forgetting, Gyppo. Catch you later.'

Then came a roar and the whoosh of fumes through the open door.

'He won't half get sticky handlebars now, eh?' Despite his humour, Zach was quite shaken.

Doris upped periscope from behind the bar. 'They gone? Never could understand why you hired such as them,' she frowned. 'Done no good to nobody. Why, Commander Garden, God rest his soul, he banned 'em for holding races on the runways with their awful bikes. And see what good it did him.'

Chris, still sheltering Summer, fetched another chair. 'Come join us for an apple juice, Dot, tell us all about it. And please be a pet and bring us a plate of brownies? I fear the birthday cake is beyond rescue.'

Doris removed her apron, smoothed her pink nylon dress and joined us, placing the plate of brownies in the middle. Indeedy removed one candle from the ruined cake, stuck it in a brownie, lit it and gestured my way.

'Blow it out, Fruit, make another wish.'

I did. Silently, I wished Summer Locke would stay safe from harm.

'Well, I don't mind sayin' my ears was burning,' Doris said eagerly. 'Poor Mr Garden. I had a bit of a soft spot for him myself for a time.' Doris blushed. 'He was one devil of a good-looker.'

'Yes,' said Chris, gesturing to me and Summer. 'I was telling the children.'

Doris was in her element. 'They'd been courtin' for some time, Mr Garden and Lady Charlotte, from up at the manor. Credit where credit's due, she was quite a beauty in her time. But no way were it an accident, his death.' Doris sipped her apple juice, dropping her voice to a conspiring whisper. 'And she had something to do with it.'

Indeedy leaned forward. 'What do you think really happened, Doris?'

'He must have known something about her, I don't know – something she needed to hide. So he had to go.'

'And where does Meat Loaf come into it?'

'You need look no further,' Doris said, enigmatically.

'Why do you say that?' asked Zach, engulfing a brownie.

'That Sykes man stops at nothing, do anything for money, he would. And before you ask, I can't prove it but where there's smoke there's fire. He's a tea-leaf from down south, never fear. People thinks we're all peace and quiet here, but no, you couldn't make it up.'

'Tea-leaf?'

'Tea-leaf, thief – rhyming slang,' said Zach.

Indeedy frowned. 'I've made some silly mistakes in my time, but I think hiring the Skullduggeries takes the cake, if you'll pardon the expression.'

'Not to worry,' said Chris. 'They worked long enough to kickstart the business. Anyway, needs must, as they say. But I think now we should purchase our very own YES INDEEDY van.'

'With what? My stunning looks?'

Chris laughed. 'I'll take care of it.'

12
Peripatetic

I'm a Romani Rai, I'm a young didikai
I travel the roads with me dogs and
*   me grais.*
I don't pay no rent 'cos I live in a tent
And that's why they call me the
*   Romani Rai.*

— traditional Gypsy song

Chris kept her word about a van. Within days a smart cream-coloured Bedford van arrived, decorated in forest green lettering ticked out in gold:

YES INDEEDY!
CAKES & BAKES
SOURCE LOCALLY, DINE GLOBALLY, ALL YEAR ROUND.
DELIVERY FRESH TO YOUR DOOR.

Indeedy asked Toby Spicer to knock some shelves together for the back of the van and Mrs Spicer offered ten hours a week cooking time.

'Between ourselves,' she said, 'I'll make no secret of it, I was glad to see the back of them biker boys. They was no good through and through.' She would help out until Indeedy found a suitable full-time cook, and weren't her own fat rascal scones already the best in all Borderland?

Summer was never explicitly invited in so many words to live with us. One day Indeedy just told both of us to hop in the car to fetch Summer's belongings from the hatch. The spare room was already a 'Summer' space. Summer Locke did not like undressing in front of anyone. I thought Gypsies must be super modest, which was fine by me, although in our family the facts of life and turning into grown-ups were common conversation as far back as I can remember. Whenever we asked questions, 'Peter Pan's a great story,' counselled Indeedy, 'but growing up is compulsory.' Sprouting hairs and getting girly curves, periods and erections were all just the source of much laughter.

Indeedy pulled up at the lay-by bordering the hatch. The caravans were still in place, ponies in the field, lurchers and terriers and children lolling. Little Ditty trilled her delight to see her beloved Summer again. I noticed someone had tamed Ditty's explosion of black hair into a single plait down her back since the last time I'd seen her.

'Oh, Summer, we've missed you. There's scarce nobody here now, except Mrs Boswell and Mr John Pockett. Oh, and Bibi Esmeralda – she's come back!'

Summer lifted Ditty off the ground and twirled her round. 'Esmeralda's back? Which explains why your hair's gone all tidy,' teased Summer, tugging Ditty's plait. 'Any word from King and the elders?'

Ditty frowned. 'No. They left no *patrin* nor nothing, but Bibi, she says bring your friend and visit her before you go off again.'

My ears perked. 'How'd she know we were coming?'

'Once you meet our Bibi you'll know the answer,' replied Ditty, pirouetting to emphasize the mystery. 'She'll be *dukkerin'* for you, I expect.'

'*Dukkering*?'

Summer mimed an invisible crystal ball. 'Fortune-telling to you, Miss Robin.'

Indeedy, who had remained silent during our greetings, smiled indulgently.

'Mum, would it be all right if we stay here for a bit?'

'Is it safe to leave you here?' she wondered. 'You know. Meat Loaf.'

'We will be safe here, thanking you kindly.'

'Well, OK. I really must get back to the bakehouse – we're totally snowed under, or should I say "doughed" under? Plus Zach's packing for college. But let me take your things back, save you lugging stuff across the field.

How's about if you're not back at the Mill by six I'll come back and collect you?'

'Yes, please!'

Indeedy eyed Summer's belongings as she opened the bag brought for the purpose. 'No one can say Gypsies don't know how to travel light,' she smiled. Into the bag went one pair of jeans, two pairs of underpants, one plaid flannel shirt, three t-shirts, some socks, a pen knife, a slingshot, a rosary, a box of pebbles and feathers, a Latin primer from Miss Kiss, and Brockton's journal. 'This all?'

'That is all, thanking you.'

Children and dogs rushed to the lay-by, waving Indeedy off like a film star. Summer Locke called them back. 'Tell you what, chavvie,' said Summer, 'I will storify a bit about Esmeralda Locke.'

Summer motioned us to sit round the open fire in a circle.

'Bibi Esmeralda is "real deep Romani". Some good Roma found her when she was only a wee *rawnie*. Orphaned she was, as was I, and wandering round the ruins of some war – in Germany, I do believe. They fetched her over the channel and the Lockes adopted her as their own, giving her the Locke name, as they gave their name to me and to many a rescued babby over the years. Esmeralda, she was a natural born nimble-footed chavvie, so Fiddler Locke began to take her on his musical adventures.'

'I'm cousin to the Lockes!' beamed a small boy.

'Yes. Lockeses and Pocketts are family. Your very cousins once travelled the hills of Borderland with twenty or thirty donkeys in scarlet harness, some of the finest fiddlers in the wide world. Fiddler John Pockett, he would call round the pubs with Esmeralda; he was famous, you know. He would find his cider laced with spirits and his bow primed with bacon fat to keep the music sweet. His finest piece was the "Dance of the Three Jolly Black Sheepskins". Esmeralda, she'd place three fleeces on the pub floor and dance around them. A bit like this.'

Summer Locke smiled, rose and, arms still and relaxed, performed an agile step-dance round invisible sheepskins. One of the children began tapping *fiddledy-diddledy-diddledy-diddle-diddledy-fiddledy-rat-a-tat-tat* repeatedly on a tin with a stick. Twirling and twirling, feet tapping, criss-crossing and circling, like a spinning top and leaping higher than you'd think possible, *sprong-sprong*, with arms almost still and lowered.

Summer stopped for breath. 'The guests, they would try to imitate Esmeralda's dance. But one foot wrong and the next round of drinks would be on the guest, so Fiddler John, he was never short of a drink, you see.'

I startled to the sound of applause behind me.

'There's dancing for your dinner, my fine *didekoi*,' said a lean old woman, nursing a pipe.

'Bibi Esmeralda!' Summer Locke sprang over the invisible sheepskins and ran to the woman, embracing her so fiercely she nearly tipped over. The sweet smell of pipe tobacco, like ginger biscuits baking, tingled my nose. I stood.

'Bibi Esmeralda, this is my friend Robin. Robin Swallow.'

'Hello, Bibi Esmeralda,' I said, extending my hand.

Esmeralda smiled warily. 'Ah then! One little bird with the name of two. No need for the "Bibi". No unkindness meant, my chavvie, but I'm not your auntie.'

I saw Summer blush. Esmeralda tidied her jet-black plait and adjusted the scarf knotted turban-style behind her head. A jagged scar marred the aquiline symmetry of her nose.

Admonished, I felt small and slipped into pidgin American. 'Sorry, ma'am, I don't know Romany. Yet.'

'Not to fret, child. Just so's you know your proper place.' Esmeralda looked into my eyes, took hold of my hand and turned it palm up. I returned her gaze. *What burning amber eyes you have, Grandma!* Then I looked down, taking in Esmerelda's lavish shawl, pinned by a brooch of gold crown pieces inset with coloured stones; the shawl rested over a fine white apron with two deep side pockets bulging with I wished I knew what.

'You've no common hand, my *rakli*, you know? Come to my waggon for a brew, the both of ye.'

Esmeralda released my hand, lifted the corner of her long black satin frock and swept away towards her caravan. The children scattered across the field. Summer took my hand and followed Esmeralda. Tethered nearby were Esmeralda's horses. Unlike the usual sturdy painted Romany cobs, Esmeralda's animals were white and of finer breeding.

'Those ponies there?' said Summer, reading my mind. 'They must be near twenty years old, called Andalusians. A Gypsy from Spain brought them over as a gift for Esmeralda. Told her they stepped high and danced like her.'

I ran over to stroke the white horses. They nuzzled fondly like old friends, poking for titbits. I breathed in their sweet smell. 'They're beautiful.' For the first time since moving to Borderland I recalled Indeedy's vague promise of a pony. It seemed a million years ago, a childhood time when life was ordinary. 'Do you think Esmeralda might allow us a ride?'

'That would be tidy,' said Summer. 'Let us see how we go here first.'

Summer led me to the fold-down steps of the old-fashioned waggon.

'Wait a minute! Look at these decorations, Summer. They're awesome!'

Esmeralda's waggon cut a more elaborate outline than the surrounding caravans. Green canvas tightly covered the rounded roof and a metal chimney poked from a top corner. A weathervane composed of sun, crescent moon and stars perched on the chimney. The caravan was a rich, deep plum. It was so shiny and clean it looked like it had been through an enormous dishwasher. 'Look at all the gold curlicues and flowers and birds. And those horses!' I had never seen anything like this. The carvings of doves, horses and sunflowers were flashed with gold leaf, low-lighted in dark green, scarlet and cream.

'Yes. Mr John Pockett painted them for Esmeralda,' Summer told me. 'Have a peep inside. Most waggons are long gone or tucked away in museums and theme parks. This one here is a bow-top, shaped like the fat end of a fiddle. When the horse was king of the road the Gypsies round these parts favoured this sort.'

I felt a precise chill of excitement, and maybe dread too, run through me, just like the time Summer's face beckoned me through the kitchen window. As we mounted the waggon's wooden steps, the vessel gave slightly, like a dinghy in a sea breeze. And another precise sensation: I am growing up, I am more than Fruitfly weight.

'Enter, my chavvies.'

The waggon's immaculate interior took up an area of approximately ten feet by six. Esmeralda read my face. 'Us Gypsies are very particular about cleanliness. Living like we does, you got to keep clean. Go on now, you have a good look for yourself.' I caught the scent of cloves and vanilla as Esmeralda spoke.

I didn't feel relaxed, not one little bit, but I moved towards a wardrobe with a small boot cupboard below. Next to it, a boxed-in fireplace with miniature cast-iron cooking range, and above the range a mirrored overmantel. A brass bracket lamp lit the overmantel. On the nearside, a glazed bow-fronted china cupboard, a seat with a lock opposite the fire, and a chest of drawers, the top of which appeared to double as a table. Across the back of the waggon were the two-berthed bed-places and above, an open sash window. Esmeralda sat at her table surrounded by her possessions: gilded carvings, brilliant-cut mirrors, French-polished mahogany and ornamental brasswork, delicate china, lace trimmings, family photographs in ornate silver frames.

'This is … this is … it's … regal.'

Summer squirmed and gave me a sweet knowing look. 'Shall I fire the kettle, Bibi?'

'Fine idea, my *raklo*.' Esmeralda smiled at me. Maybe she was pleased to see that here was one housedweller who appreciated Romany life. 'Yes, mine is the best of the best, and there'll not be boasting as I say it.' Esmeralda paused, settling her direct gaze on me. 'Now. I'd be pleased to *dukker* for you, Robin Swallow.'

That blunt. That sudden.

'Thank you very much for offering, but, you see, I … I'm …'

'Robin says she is an atheist, Bibi.'

I felt my face heat up. 'I wasn't going to say that. "Agnostic" is what I meant.'

Esmeralda smiled. 'Why, that's no reason not to *dukker*, and the dear *Mooshabove* loves atheists the best. What I can tell you is, is you'll call to rememberment all your life what Esmeralda tells you this day, as I've been blessed with the second sight.'

'How do you know?'

'If I told you the stories you'd be thinking I made them up now, wouldn't you? We Gypsies believe everybody's got an evil spirit and a good spirit. If a person commits evil – commits murder, say – we believe that the evil spirit provokes them to do that. And if someone does a kindness, the good spirit provokes him to do that good.'

'Can a person control their spirit?'

'Mostly. But some let the bad or the good take over and then you're in trouble. Gypsies included.'

Summer Locke poured tea into three delicate china cups. 'That's more or less the same as Christianity. Papa Brockton said it is a matter of willpower and prayer and Bible study.'

'My brother Zach says it's all a load of old cobblers. Religion's a crutch for cripples, he says.'

'Well, there you are then.' Esmeralda sipped her tea. 'But if you ponder it you'll notice we all need propping up from time to time due to the occasional limp. *Dukkerin's* different than the business of religion, though. It's my gift I was taught, and then I'm to pass it on. It's old as the hills. Why, when they opened the pyramids all those yonder years ago they found the impress of the hand in the marble slabs.'

All the way back to Egypt? I extended my right hand. 'All right, then.'

'You right-handed?'

I nodded.

'Then it's your left hand I'll be reading.'

I closed my eyes and felt Esmeralda's cool hand supporting my palm. I thought, I'm glad it's not sweaty for once. Esmeralda hummed to herself as she explored my hand. Almost sing-song, she noted, 'This little Robin bird is impetuous and cheerful ... artistic, tactful and tolerant ... at times easily influenced and inclined to laziness ...' Esmeralda twisted my thumb about. 'Robin is loving, wilful and sympathetic. She bites her nails, which reveals a critical side to her. The bumps on her palm disclose some kind of nervous tension. Her lifeline manifests a desire for solitude and a deeply religious nature.'

'Deeply religious!' I broke the calm of the session. 'How can you say that?'

Esmeralda patted my palm gently. 'Sometimes a fightin' against can be a way of finding something important, my chavvie.' She returned to tracing the lines of my palms. 'Oh, my dearie. You have lost someone very dear, you've called forth a deep sadness for a long while in your young life.'

'My daddy,' I whispered, feeling unwanted tears well up, my throat tightening.

'Well, now I am sorrowed and it's the God's truth I'm telling ye, you shall be comforted and you shall be surprised by joy.'

'Is my father still alive?'

Esmeralda concentrated. 'My dear little *cheriklo*, I think not, I believe he's passed over, it sorrows me to say.'

Esmeralda moved over on her bench and motioned for me to sit beside her, giving me her lace handkerchief. I wiped my eyes and glanced towards Summer. I felt no shame for my tears, but I did feel I had heard enough to be going on with. I turned to Summer, 'Your turn now.'

'Another time,' said Esmeralda. 'There's something else for you, my chavvie. Trust your own rememberings. You're likely to be saving a life sooner than you think, not an easy task for a young *rawnie*. Now you listen to me.' Esmeralda placed her hands on my head. 'I am the *Phui Dai* of our tribe and I'm blessing you now. That way you'll be ready for some hard doings to come. But never fear, there will be luck in your lovely life, you understand what I mean, my *rawnie*?'

Esmeralda closed her eyes and stayed her hands on my head. I felt the tingly sensation again, then a warmth and calm all through my body. For just a brief moment I felt as if the whole world were inside me, and *for* me.

Esmeralda removed her hands gently and fetched two amulets from her apron pocket, placing them around our necks. 'For your good health and fortune,' she explained. I fished a fifty pence piece from my pocket and passed it to Esmeralda.

She put the coin in her apron pocket. 'It'll be best luck your havin' now, for sure, for crossing the old Gypsy's palm with silver. Now, be off with ye.'

We took our shortcut through the back fields, silent the both of us. I didn't feel like talking at all. Suddenly I missed having Boddy with us, her quick body running ahead, and wished we had not left her behind when Indeedy drove us. Summer broke the silence as we climbed the home post-and-rail fence by the pond. 'You would like to know what happened to Bibi's nose, yes?'

'What?' I was thinking no such thing. 'Can't say that I do, and anyhow it would be too rude to ask.'

'I wish that you shall know. It was a jealous lover slashed her nose with a knife, though Esmeralda swore her innocence.'

'How cruel!'

'Aye, there is cruel and kind in our people, and in everyone. The men to the womenfolk stands out. Until your grandparents' time men had total power, even to the death, over women. Now the women have risen up. Esmeralda, she is *Phui Dai* now, but when she was young she had no power; something to do with womens' bleeding being a curse.'

'You're meaning periods. Indeedy says they can't be avoided, but it's the one girly thing I sort of hope never happens. I hate even thinking about it. Let's go to the kitchen for some lemonade.'

Summer persisted. 'Surely your mam is right, it is the way of nature. Women who bleed for life while the men must tear the flesh by fighting or sport, or bringing cruelty and harm.'

'Don't preach at me, Summer Locke.' I started to say count yourself lucky you're a boy, then. But for a change I buttoned my lip, remembering my father saying to me, 'You have two eyes, two ears, two nostrils but just one mouth, and there's a reason for that.' Instead, wanting to change the subject, I just said, 'I'm thirsty.'

In the kitchen Indeedy and Chris and Zach sat at the breakfast table. Indeedy's face was buried in her hands.

I looked hard at Zach. 'What's the matter?'

'Boddy's gone missing.'

'But – but she never ever strays.' I could not understand it.

Summer looked at me. 'Let us seek her out now.'

'Wait. When did she go missing, Mum? Have you called her? I'm sure she won't be far away.'

'We've tried calling, Fruit,' said Indeedy. 'Chris and Zach left Boddy in the bakehouse porch and went off on deliveries. They locked the door. When I got back from dropping you two at the hatch, I saw the bakehouse door was open. The lock had been forced.'

Chris rose and placed one hand on Summer's shoulder, the other on mine. 'We've notified the police. I'm sure everything will be all right.'

'She's been dognapped for certain,' said Zach, 'but why?'

'That would be Meat Loaf and his villains. Have they not made clear their intentions?' Summer turned to me. 'Remember what he said? *Dogs don't have nine lives.* If they have taken her where I fear, we must be very quick.'

'But where do we start?'

'Follow me.'

We tore up the lane, calling, 'Come by, Boddy! Boddy! Come by, good girl!' and cut off to our left over a stile into Wellings' wheat field.

'Boddy! Come by!' Then, 'Listen!' Did I hear her? No. It was a cow or a lamb or something.

'This way,' Summer said.

'I have to slow down, Summer,' I panted, out of breath. 'Where are we going?'

'Wellings' slurry pit.'

There was no time to ask what a slurry pit was. We kept running. I could see Mr Wellings' barn and found a second wind. 'Boddy! Come by!'

Clear as anything, a wolf-like howl rang out. It was like nothing I'd ever before heard from my dog.

'Behind the barn!'

By the pit was a sign.

DANGER OF DEATH. KEEP OFF.

And there Boddy was, drowning. Her head and one forepaw were just above the crusted and fetid surface of the open slurry pit.

'Boddy! Stay. Wait.' Oh, why hadn't I taught Boddy a 'don't move' command? I rushed towards her.

'Robin, listen carefully. Do not stray too close to the pit,' Summer warned. 'Keep the *jukel* calm and I shall fetch a crook from the barn.'

Boddy began to struggle more. Her forepaw disappeared under her.

'Shh, shh, Boddy,' I forced my voice to a whisper as I crawled to the edge of the pit, trying to catch her collar and pull her out. She was just out of reach. Boddy began to struggle again.

'Good girl, Boddy, shh. Good girl.'

I wanted to shout Summer to hurry, please, but …
I couldn't.

I felt faint in a way I'd never felt before.

I reached out again for my dog and then …

From the darkness, I heard a voice, Summer's voice, far away.

'Robin, Robin. Your *jukel* is safe.'

The effort to open my eyes took all my concentration. Boddy is safe? Summer Locke held me, stroking my face. 'Your *jukel* is safe. Look.'

There she lay, my noble hound, hawk eyes unblinking and fierce, her coat covered in brown smelly slimy stuff. Summer had rolled me away from the edge of the pit. I stroked Boddy, not caring that I was getting covered in slurry too.

'How are you feeling now?'

'Dizzy but OK.' Summer helped me to my feet. 'I'm fine, I think.'

'Boddy is exhausted. I shall carry her. You walk ahead.'

When I tried to walk my legs felt wooden and rigid. Summer said something about putting the crook back in the barn. 'Do not wait. I will catch you up and bring your dog.'

13

Lurcher

Head like a snake, neck like a drake;
Side like a bream, back like a beam;
Tail like a rat, foot like a cat. Who am I?

Ding-dong on the doorbell. Zach loped to the front door. A stocky bespectacled man in Skullduggery leathers greeted him with a smile. 'Mr Swallow?'

'Yes. Are you plainclothes police?' Zach's tone and expression was inscrutable.

'You jokin'?' Removing his safety helmet, the young man extended his hand. 'Winitoo here, thought you'd like news of your dog.' His civility and soft Borderland accent contrasted with the Skullduggery leathers.

'Oh.' Zach seemed disconcerted but his expression softened. 'Well, we already have news. Good news. Boddy's been found. Please come in and take a pew. Cup of tea, coffee? Cold lemonade?'

'Lemonade would be lovely, ta. Whatever's easy.' Winitoo moved to an empty chair by the coffee table. Zach came into the kitchen where we were making a big fuss over Boddy, all washed clean of filth and covered with a fleece blanket. The pong of the slurry pit lingered.

'How can we get rid of that rotten smell?' gagged Zach, then, lowering his voice, 'Summer, this chap's a Skullduggery. Is that OK? I'm not really sure what he wants.'

'Yes, I see it is Winitoo. He is sound.'

Winitoo's winning smile was as unlike the Skullduggery image as a puppy's from a rattlesnake. Indeedy introduced herself and Chris. 'Pleased to make your acquaintance,' said Winitoo. He pulled a tobacco tin from his pocket. 'Mind if I skin up?' Without waiting for a reply, he placed the necessaries tidily on the coffee table, rolled and lit up, inhaling deep. 'Toke, anyone?'

'No, thanks. We're non-smokers here. I used to smoke twenty a day,' said a conciliatory Indeedy, adding, 'but I'm still a keen passive smoker.'

I could see Chris's face speaking louder than words: *Indeedy, I realize you are a laid-back American but have you gone bonkers? Do you realize this twit is lighting up illegal substances? In front of your children?*

Indeedy tugged at the end of her ponytail.

Winitoo seemed to notice the silent exchange and smiled. 'No worries.' He took one more long pull on the joint, then put it out but held onto it as he spoke. 'Now. Your dog.'

'Wait. Robin, is it OK for Winitoo to come into the kitchen?'

Summer nodded at me. Yes.

'Do come in, Mr Winitoo. Here she is.'

Winitoo crouched by Boddy, who whimpered and licked his hand. 'Here is one sound hound,' he said. 'How did you find her?'

'Summer Locke here knew where she was likely to be. Wellings' slurry pit.'

I told Winitoo how I had fainted but that Summer had saved the day by moving me away and fetching Boddy out with a shepherd's crook.

'Wellings' grandfather died in that very slurry pit trying to save his collie about three years back,' Winitoo said. 'You and your dog have made a lucky escape.'

Summer Locke nodded.

'You don't look like the other bikers,' I blurted. Here was a man with kind eyes, dimples, shiny long hair and clean fingernails.

'Maybe that's why they give me such a tough time,' shrugged Winitoo.

'Why'd you want to join in the first place?' asked Zach, offering a frosty mug of lemonade.

'The bikes. They don't tell you it's about more than bikes until it's too late. I've been trying to break away for a long time now, and they know not to include me with the bad stuff, but it's not easy.' There was a loaded silence. 'Do you mind my asking if my so-called biker mates hold a grudge against anyone here?'

Summer said quietly, 'Yes, I fear they do. It is I.'

'And now us, too,' said Indeedy. 'We fired them on my daughter's birthday, actually.'

The sound of another engine intercepted Winitoo's response.

'I'll see to it,' said Zach, checking at the window. 'Deffo the police this time.'

Chris flailed the pungent herb-laden air with a tea towel, motioning wildly at Winitoo. 'Put that thing away!' Winitoo moved with dreamy deliberation, forgetting the tin and dumping the contents into the pocket of his leather jacket. Summer and I heaped into a giggly scrum.

Winitoo looked at Summer vaguely. 'What they got against you, then?'

Summer, still giggling, looked at the floor.

Indeedy called to us, 'Robin, Summer, join us in the lounge, OK?'

'No problem, Mum.'

At Zach's side stood a dimpled, sandy-haired police officer. 'This is Police Constable Corteena.'

Constable Corteena removed his hat and nodded. I'm thinking, he is gorgeous.

'Hello, Winitoo. Winitoo and I are well acquainted,' the police officer said. He twitched his nose just noticeably enough to let the assembled know that a) he could smell the weed and b) he would be ignoring it. 'And Summer Locke. And Ms Lamb, the Lois Lane of Borderland.' He smiled warmly at Chris then turned back to Indeedy. 'Now, about your dog. We are making every effort—'

'Constable, we —'

'— and we need a few details, normal procedure if you don't mind,' continued Constable Corteena imperviously, taking a notepad and pen from his pocket. What time did we discover Boddy was missing? About 10.30 a.m. Were there any signs of breaking and entering? Yes, the lock had been forced. Any damage to the premises? Only the forced lock. Anything else missing? Nothing noticed so far.

Eventually Indeedy said, 'Constable, I've been trying to tell you – we have found our dog! Well, to be accurate, Robin and Summer found her. Boddy is safe here in the kitchen. Robin, pour some lemonade for the constable, please.'

Summer and I followed Constable Corteena back into the kitchen. He crouched down and made a big fuss over Boddy. 'To be perfectly honest with you, I am glad you didn't wait for the police to search and find your hound.'

'Well,' I said, 'we had to do something.'

'How was it that you chose Wellings' slurry pit?'

'Summer just said to me let's go and so we went. How *did* you know where to go, Summer?'

Summer's eyes twinkled. 'It is my Romany instinct.'

'I'll drink to that,' said Constable Corteena, taking a healthy swig of lemonade. 'You were lucky. Open slurry pits like the one on the Wellings' farm should be illegal. They are a major cause of death or serious injury on farms.'

I'm thinking, worse than quicksand, my scariest nightmare. 'But why did I pass out?' I asked aloud, my mind racing.

'How long were you unconscious?'

I looked at Summer, who said, 'Not more than a minute or so. I carried Robin away from the edge and then fetched the *jukel* free.'

'To be blunt, young lady, a slurry pit's a nasty deep pool of faeces, a runoff from the buildings that house the animals. Eventually it goes back on the land as fertilizer.'

'Sort of a "swim-in-poo"?' quipped Zach.

'Very good. What isn't funny is that slurry pits have claimed human lives. The farmer may be overcome by noxious gases, like you were, Robin, and hundreds of animals have been killed in similar circumstances. Wellings' pit is deep enough to drown an animal twice the size of your dog here. Dry weather was on her side – the crust on top of the slurry presumably kept her head above the muck.'

'Do you have any leads as to who did it? I mean the dog-nap?' Chris asked.

'We do have our reliable sources. The problem will be credible evidence beyond a reasonable doubt.' Constable Corteena grinned and nodded towards Winitoo. Sniffing Boddy, he crinkled his nose. 'She may pong for a while, but she's back in good hands now.'

Constable Corteena emptied his glass and rose. He handed me a Neighbourhood Watch pamphlet then looked around the room.

'Just one more thing. It might be quite a good idea if you all put your minds to enhancing your security requirements. Better safe than sorry and all that.' He smiled beamishly and headed towards the front door.

Indeedy grimaced and pulled on her ponytail again. 'Yes, the country idyll and its evil underbelly. Seems we're getting more than our fair share of underbellies at the moment.'

Constable Corteena opened the door and saluted us. Boddy jogged from the kitchen and presented her elegant self as if to say goodbye, accepting adoration with a graceful, snake-like circle dance. She twirled her long tail, stretched a graceful demi-plié and deposited herself at Zach's feet, nose propped on front paws, amber eyes glowing.

When the constable was out of earshot, Winitoo convulsed with helpless laughter. 'Enhance your *security* requirements! The nearest cop shop is forty miles away, and most of the time that one's closed. You speak into this phone in the wall to someone. Get caught behind a tractor or two and it's an hour minimum. *And* it's getting worse not better.'

Indeedy went to the kitchen, dumped a large portion of raw steak into Boddy's dish with some dog biscuits and set it down. 'Boddy, Boddy, just a little something special for our rescued she-ro dog, eh?'

Boddy twirly-tailed her way to the kitchen door, stretched her approval of the menu and wolfed her food.

'Robin, have you ever spitted that *jukel*?' asked Summer Locke, watching Boddy finish her food and lick her lips.

'Ever *what*?'

'Spitted her. Once you spit her you will never lose her to anybody. Just open her mouth and spit down her throat.'

'That is gross!' But I knew I would do anything not to lose my dog again. I saw her in the slurry pit again, my hands reaching out to her. 'But if you say so.' I gentled Boddy's jaws ajar and spat. She offered no resistance, but Boddy is very good at disgusted dog looks.

Zach stared, incredulous. 'Summer Locke asks you to jump off a cliff and you jump?'

'That Constable Corteena is brilliant,' said Chris, with a deft change of subject.

Zach looked at Chris. 'Meaning what?'

'Let's just say he has helped me with my work in the past.'

'Your journalistic investigations?'

'Yes. The dog will be fine now. Let's leave it at that.'

'True,' said Winitoo. 'But look, there's just one sound way to say what I must say and that's by saying it. Thing is, is that if Meat Loaf has tried to harm your hound, this won't be the end of it. His vendettas always start with man's best friend. Sad to say they don't end there.'

'This has occurred to us,' said Zach. 'As the alpha male in the house, I'm not particularly happy myself. I'm off to university in a fortnight.'

'Yes,' I said. 'And we begin school then too, don't we, Summer?'

'I shall be the first Gypsy at Oxford University,' Summer said.

'I'm sure there are dozens already,' Zach said. 'You won't be the first.'

Summer shrugged.

Indeedy fixed Winitoo with a direct gaze. 'So basically it'll be me, Chris and Mrs Spicer during the days. What do these thugs want from us anyway?'

Winitoo studied his hands. 'That is the evil thing. For you, there is no reason beyond bearing a grudge. What they really want, though, is young Summer.'

'I am feared of the men,' said Summer, 'and I now

live here. This is my family.'

Winitoo took in the wild and tousled Summer Locke. 'May I suggest you consider cutting your hair and changing your clothes?'

'Adopt a disguise?' Was he joking?

'Might be a good idea.'

Chris moved over to sit by Summer. 'Listen, chook, I think it's time you told us what's going on.' Summer stared at the floor, then, to my surprise, nodded.

'Indeed? Young Summer has something to tell us.'

Summer and I exchanged looks: *Don't tell them too much.*

Summer 'summer-ized' the story I'd already heard. How the danger came from Summer's time at Pucklethorpe with Brockton Wheatley. How Summer's kinship and deep affection with Papa Brockton grew over time. Lady Charlotte's animosity, her attempts to hurt the people who helped Brockton. Her accusations that the Gypsies were stealing valuables from the house. The years building up to such bitterness.

'She knew Papa Brockton would not move out of her precious house. He believed he was entitled to stay, and one day, it was I do believe not long before your arrival, she went truly *didlo*, insulting Papa Brockton's friend, ranting at me.'

'You need to go to the police with this information, my friend.'

'I have spoken with the *gavs*. But my people have our own ways of seeking justice.'

Chris shook her head. 'So do the Mafia. What about Constable Corteena? He's a good guy.'

'He is a fine man and tries to help as best he can, but in the end,' said Summer, 'he must uphold *gorgio* law. The *gavs* do not protect Gypsies.'

Chris kept shaking her head. Indeedy didn't speak.

Summer pleaded, 'Please try to understand, Miss Chris. The *gavmush* are bad *baxt* to my people. I have told my elders. They have called a *kriss*, and came to agree to deal justice our way. I believe that is what they are doing at this very moment.'

Zach was intrigued. 'What do you mean, Summer?'

Summer ignored the question. Silence.

Indeedy spoke up. 'I understand. Our laws are harsh to Gypsies. We remember our Jewish friends who died in Hitler's Holocaust but forget the nigh-on 300,000 Gypsies who died in that diabolical time. Gypsies aren't protected by our laws. But what do your people have against the bikers?'

'Aye, that I may say. There was one, from the European Skullduggeries, who even his biker friends would not allow to tarry with them for long. So he came to us. But we found soon enough that he was a housedweller, and housedwellers do not bide for long with us. We do not trust them.'

I was offended. 'Thanks a heap!'

'You are different and you know it,' Summer told me.

Winitoo nodded agreement. 'Yes. I remember. Name of Stinger. He stayed at mine for a while. That bloke could eat more than anyone I've ever met, some kind of disease. Thin as a rake he was ... speaking of food, I feel the munchies coming on myself.'

Indeedy grinned. 'Well now, I find that food brings calm to a crisis and it just happens I've whipped up something that'll fit the bill.'

Winitoo grinned back. 'Thank you.' Mum headed to the kitchen. 'Now, where were we?'

'About this Stinger chap,' Chris prompted. 'And why the bikers hate Gypsies.'

'Yes. As I was saying, Stinger, that's his Skullduggery name, after he crashed his bike playing chicken on the Green Man runway, he had to walk or hitchhike,' Winitoo said. 'He'd go into houses as if he owned them – some people in these parts still leave doors unlocked – and ask if he could "take a sandwich". Eventually we'd all had enough of his gluttony. His birthday was coming up so my girlfriend baked him a cake full of Senokot.'

'Ha! Laxatives to give him the trots! Perfect revenge,' said Zach.

'Aye. He ate the whole cake without sharing a single piece. Sick as a parrot for days, he was.'

Indeedy returned with a plateful of brownies.

'Laxative-free. Promise. Did Stinger discover who organized the prank?'

Winitoo demolished a brownie. 'MMM-mm, dee-LISH. He did, and it was hit and miss for a while as to whether he would get his own back on us – he was mad keen on Taekwon do, which was a worry.'

'What-kon-what?' I said.

'Taekwon do. Martial arts, the combat side,' Zach enlightened me.

Winitoo looked at Summer, who was staring at the floor. 'Anyway, that's Stinger. He went to the Gypsies for a while, and they got fed up of him too. Sorry, Summer, I got carried away. You were telling it.'

But Summer said no more on the subject of Stinger or the Skulduggeries, remaining silent.

'So, what should we do next?' Indeedy asked. 'I don't like this business with the bikers at all.'

'Precisely nothing,' said Chris. 'I'll keep covering the Brockton Wheatley case. It's too hot to drop. And we'll just carry on and ignore the Skulduggeries for now. We can't do any more.'

I breathed a quiet sigh of relief that, for the present at least, the pressure was off Summer Locke.

'Chris is right, Mum,' said Zach. 'Lady Charlotte is out of circulation for the time being, unlike your homicidal bikers. She can't harm Summer. Let's allow justice to take its course.'

Indeedy joined Summer on the floor then, sitting face to face, and tousled Summer's hair affectionately. She looked Summer square in the eye. 'Are you absolutely and positively sure we mustn't go to the police with your information about Lady Charlotte? I would go with you.'

'On my mother's life, I ask you not to do so,' said Summer.

Indeedy looked worried. 'OK. I recall an ethics question from one of my college teachers: it was a quote from a famous writer, E.M. Forster, I think. It went something like, if he had to choose between betraying his country and betraying his friend, he hoped he would have the guts to betray his country.'

'That's a good one,' said Zach.

'You are our friend, Summer, and we won't betray you,' Indeedy promised. 'But we must keep you safe from harm.'

'I'll do my best to help,' said Winitoo.

'Why do you want to help us?' I asked.

'You lot are sound, you are. It's the good you've shown young Summer Locke here. Sound.' Summer's smile lit the room.

'Remember Martin Luther King? Your mum will.' Chris burst in with a throaty contralto and Indeedy joined in:

We shall overcome,
We shall overcome,
We shall overcome some day,
Oh, deep in my heart, I do believe,
That we shall overcome some day.
We are not afraid, we are not afraid ...

'I am,' said Summer Locke.

'You're what?' Indeedy asked.

'Afraid.'

'Well, don't be,' said Indeedy. 'We're the good guys here and we will carry on. Besides which, we haven't a choice, really. That reminds me, Chris, we've left poor Mrs Spicer in the bakehouse, slaving away, and we've got orders to fill. Bradenfield Show is coming up and they're about to announce that we're doing the catering!' Indeedy squeezed Summer's hand, then rose to go to the bakehouse.

As Chris and Zach went through the door, Indeedy paused, and fixed Summer with a gaze again. 'Anything else we need to know?'

Summer's silence gave her the answer.

Summer and I sat still with Boddy, who had dozed off, silently looking each other in the eye.

Have you ever had a day that felt like it lasted a year? This was one of them.

14
Jam & Jerusalem

We are off to Bradenfield Fair
To breathe the perfect country air,
To fiddle and diddle and look at fine horses
And watch lads and lasses on dangerous
courses.

– anon

If anything truly marks the difference between town and country, folks around and about here agree it's probably county fairs. Back in London we had a city farm and I loved it, but here in Borderland everything about being rural makes sense when you go to the agricultural shows. Chris Lamb calls it 'Jam and Jerusalem time'.

Indeedy had never catered for hundreds of people before, but she was up for it. 'How cool is this?' She cleared her throat and began to read the organizers' letter in a painfully awful fake English accent: 'Ahem!

"Thanks to the continued generosity of the Dowager Viscountess Purrloyne, the Bicentennial Year of Bradenfield County Show will again take place on the grounds of the Purrloyne Estate."'

'Where's that?' I asked.

'Hold your horses. Let me finish, because here's the good bit! "In keeping with tradition and the continuing challenges of growth, we are pleased to announce the procurement of an outstanding firm of caterers for the main marquee, YES INDEEDY CAKES & BAKES." Then there's this PS: "To ensure speedy and efficient service, will members kindly make an effort to avoid the 1 p.m. lunchtime rush?"'

We all danced around like fools, laughing and miming the *My Fair Lady* song about the rain in Spain staying mainly on the plain.

'Mum, your English accent sucks.'

Chris chuckled, 'Oi! Give her a break, Robin! I do know what you mean about asking members not to go to lunch at lunchtime, Indeedy – only in England! But wouldn't you rather we were "polite" and "courteous" rather than loud and "bra-a-a-sh" like you Americans?' she said, switching from received pronunciation to an equally painful American twang.

For the next few weeks, mealtimes were even better than usual while Indeedy tried out her menu ideas. Other than the occasional 'Keep the capers out of the potato salad' and 'Use real apricots in the Coronation chicken' and 'Never, ever skimp on the pizza toppings; always go right to the edge', we pounced on the goodies like bears after hibernation. Chris Lamb produced and printed the menus: 'Created from delicate and delicious products, 90% locally sourced and reflecting the very best of Anglo-American culinary tradition.' Mrs Spicer would make three hundred Scotch eggs. Three hundred!

It turned out that the Spicers were long-time stars of Bradenfield Show. They had entries across the board: Mrs Margaret Spicer, in Open Cookery, always entered her raspberry jam and a steak and kidney pie 'Fit for royalty, if I do say so myself'. Mr Toby Spicer's premier offerings were in the Corn, Hay, Sileage and Barley sections, while their two grown sons, Andy and Ben, entered the Shireton Sheep classes and the 'One Man and his Dog' herding competition. All in all, they were always trophy winners, the Spicers, and with very few yellow ribbons to blemish the reds and blues over the years. Jealous competitors called them 'The Spicer Syndicate' behind their backs.

Towards the end of summer, Zach seemed more and more remote and I didn't like it one little bit. A rare concession was the occasional evening with Summer and me, poring over Brockton Wheatley's journal. We took notes on the aerial view of Pucklethorpe. Something was emerging from the puzzle, but there remained a missing piece or, probably I should say, pieces.

Then one night, just a few days before Bradenfield Show, a crucial piece plunked into place. Summer and I were sat as usual on the floor of my room with the journal between us, open to Summer's sketch of the Pucklethorpe grounds beside it. Summer made me jump straight out of my skin.

'ABRACADABRA! Why did I not think of this before!' Summer Locke's eyes appeared fit to pop.

Summer started tracing around the perimeter of the aerial sketch with a forefinger. 'How might we define the borders of Pucklethorpe Manor?'

'Easy.' I followed the border of topiary. I noticed that Summer's dotted lines included our place as well as Chris Lamb's.

'Robin, I must say sorry for both of us. In all the excitement of your birthday party day, when we were up in the sky ...' Taking the pencil, Summer made a new sketch of our pond, and further topiary shapes. 'See, Robin. The grounds as they were before they divided the land and sold it off. And look. When we include your pond, the one here at the cottage, the Jesse Tree in the cellar is duplicated. Do you see? The pond – your pond, Robin, would be right there, at the top of the tree.' Summer looked at me. 'We could only see that shape from the air.'

That was it. The patterned landscape of the manor's garden joined up with our pond at the cottage, to form the outline of the Jesse Tree in the cellar of Pucklethorpe Manor. A nice neat garden design that extended to include the old borders of the original estate, now complete.

I did not understand, though, what we had learned. It was still a mystery to me.

'But what about the Latin poem?'

'I do not know.'

Next day, after breakfast, our minds turned to more immediate matters. Summer thought we should check things out at the hatch.

'Bibi Esmeralda makes fair takings at Bradenfield Show from her *dukkering*, but every year she moans she is too old to go again. Shall we persuade her? If we are successful, we might be allowed to travel in the waggon with her.'

I needed no persuasion myself, not one little bit. 'You bet! C'mon, Boddy!'

The hatch was heaving with hens running loose and dogs waving their tails and barking a welcome in the morning sunshine. Tethered ponies and goats cropped the shiny grass. Wee Ghostie and Goblin neighed a greeting as Esmeralda groomed them in the shade of an oak, plaiting their silken manes in red and gold ribbons, her long skirt hiked between her legs and tucked into her apron's belt. So, she was going anyway and we would not need to persuade her. The hatch seemed otherwise absent of humans but washed bright following a night of winds and light showers. Summer seemed wary.

'Where is everyone, Bibi?'

'No worries, my chavvies, they have *jollered* off for a Romany fair in Wales. It'll be just our cousin Comfort Boswell here once't we've set off. Comfort will see to the creatures when I'm off for Bradenfield. Yes, I *am* going – before you chide me, my chavvie – and yes, I know the fair is tomorrow. We shall travel today and be rested and well ready for all the excitement.'

She said 'we'. I poked Summer.

'May we travel with you, Bibi? We wish to help.'

Esmeralda plucked her clay pipe from the bend of the adjacent oak tree, sucked thoughtfully and continued plaiting Goblin. Moments ticked by in slow motion before she said, 'You'll be attending school with your young *gorgio* friend then, my chavvie? Tidy up your mind and then teach your Bibi to read and write properly?'

Summer frowned at the change in topic. 'I do not know, Bibi.'

'Well, now then. I'll strike ye with a bargain. You attend the housedweller's school, Summer Locke, and I'll allow you to ride with me – the both of ye.'

Summer looked long and hard at Esmeralda, and then at me, green eyes like saucers. *Please, please, say yes*, spoke my silence.

'Yes, then. I will attend the *gorgio* school, Bibi.'

I tried to sound nonchalant. 'This is so cool! I'll go back home right this minute and tell, I mean ask, Indeedy if it's OK. Back in a tick.' I dashed off, ran a few metres, then stopped in my tracks. 'May we take Boddy to the fair with us, please?'

At the sound of her name, Boddy twirled round Esmeralda, showing off.

'Sorry, my dog loves attention.'

Esmeralda smiled and stroked Boddy. 'A champion *jukel* you have here. You may. Now be off. Young Summer will stay with me and we shall be set fair to be off by midday.'

I was away by the shortcut. Indeedy said yes, and I was packed and back in a flash, rucksack ready, Boddy dancing with excitement. Wee Ghostie was already hitched in the waggon shafts. His elaborate harness carried white metal buckles, clips and collars. The buckles were horseshoe-shaped and the reins were plaited with an abundance of red Morocco detail. Goblin stood alongside as the 'sider'. Summer was effortlessly hitching the traces.

'Wow, that looks complicated!'

Summer smiled. 'It is quite simple really. These reins run back to the swingle tree from the chest straps, see? If you didn't have the swingle tree to adjust, the horses would get rubbed and sore – it buffers the chafing when we are away and moving. Then, double-check all the tack. We shall be wanting Goblin's extra strength on the journey.' The clinking of the clips and creaking of the leather, and the sweet breath of the horses was altogether lovely.

'How far is it?'

'Just short of ten miles, but more like twenty due to the hills. And once we start up a long incline, we must not stop in the middle,' Summer said, seriously. 'If we stop with this waggon mid-hill there is no brake and we would end up sliding backwards. And we have to cross Beggar's Bridge, where once a terrible catastrophe beset us.'

'What happened?'

Summer ignored Esmeralda's *button your lip* glare.

'Well, a very long time past it was, but I always recall my prayers when we pass over Beggar's Bridge. It was a two-horse bow-top waggon. Something frighted the lead *grai*, who proceeded to jump over the parapet and be broken on the shallows below. The second was dragged over the edge and suspended in its harness until someone cut the poor thing loose. Both horses died.'

'How terrible.'

'You've nought to fear from my Ghost and Goblin,' sniffed Esmeralda.

Summer, chastised, explained that Ghost and Goblin, being light of bone and high-stepping like

Hackneys, were not typical Romany waggon horses or the mules of yesteryear. The favoured sort would be 'bomb-proof' coarse-coated cobs of about fourteen hands and accustomed to working in noisy traffic. Ghost and Goblin had been driven with waggons from the time they first set hoof on the road. The horses whinnied their excitement, stylishly pawing the earth.

Esmeralda beckoned us to mount into the waggon and climbed up nimbly, taking the reins. 'Now hearken, my *grais*, chuck-chuck, easy now. A bit eager for my liking.' She spoke over her shoulder. 'We like to say, "Keep the *grais* dozy for the journey and fizzy for the sales."'

Esmeralda clucked and we were off, stepping out smartly in the cool bright breeze. The waggon swayed side to side like a schooner in full sail. As we eased off the grass verge the iron-boned wheels grated on the tarmac. Ten miles to go, with luck at a pace of four miles per hour. Boddy trotted alongside the waggon.

Summer smiled. 'If your dog were Romany trained she would be walking beneath the waggon safe from traffic.'

Four miles an hour. Sow's Leap, Darky Dale, Beggar's Bridge – where I admit my heart skipped a beat – Muckminster, Cock's Bottom, Stagwardine. Esmeralda knew her route like the palm of her hand. *Clippety-cloppety-clop;* the sweetest sound ever.

We arrived at a ford bordering the upper corner of the show field. Esmeralda smiled as we approached the Women's Institute marquee. 'There's your jam and Jerusalem ladies, ready for us. These fine *gorgio* women always keeps me happy on fair days. Best cup of tea in all the shires. And scones. And cucumber sandwiches! Well, first things first. Let us set up our site and settle the ponies.'

We stripped the harnesses. Then on went halters and lead ropes while Esmeralda built the outdoor fire.

'Summer. Do you know, I've not ridden since we moved here from London. Indeedy sort of promised a pony, must've forgotten.'

'Long past time, then.' Summer Locke sprang catlike onto Ghostie's bare back. 'Let us be off!'

I led Goblin to a tree stump and clambered aboard, shouting, 'Wait for me! I can't vault bigger than thirteen hands,' as Summer went trotting away.

'You will learn with practice,' Summer shouted back at me.

I followed Summer, who was heading into the ford, riding Wee Ghostie upstream. 'Come along, Robin, there is some depth upstream where we can cool them down.'

Goblin walked willingly enough into the shallows of the ford, but stopped and began pawing the water, lowering his head and blowing ripples on the surface.

'Pull him up sharp, *rakli*,' Esmeralda called out from beside the waggon, 'or he'll be going down with ye!'

I tried to pull his head up but, as if on command, Goblin knelt down to roll, and me? I balanced for a second, desperately grasping a tuft of plaited mane, then managed to jump clear just in time, straight into the water. Summer, laughing, was upstream and still astride Ghost, who was shoulder-deep in the cool river. Esmeralda came close and threw a chamois in my direction. 'Never mind mounting the little devil again; he's got your measure, see? And he'll do it again. Wash him off with the cloth, chavvie. Then come dry yourself by the fire.'

'Thank you, Esmeralda. I'm fine,' I lied.

I felt hot tears well up as I led Goblin from the ford and cooled him with the chamois, hiding my face. Summer brought Ghost up to the bank. 'Are you sound?'

I nodded. I didn't look at Summer. 'I'm fine.'

'Well then, shall we bridle them up and take a walk round the grounds to dry us all?'

'Yes, thank you.'

'Then we shall return and brighten Esmeralda's *dukkering* sign.' Summer fetched two snaffles from the storage bin at the waggon's rear. 'There you are. Some necessary steerage.'

'Take that *kair jukel* with ye and see if she's any use catching us some *shushi* for supper, then,' Esmeralda called out.

'Rabbit,' whispered Summer Locke, whistling Boddy over, and giving me a leg up. We set off in the direction of bustling marquees. Here was a world in its own right – local crafts, a 'Taste of Borderland' stand, the heavy horse enclosure and goat ring. On to the fairground, teeming with construction – the Octopus, the Dodgems – my favourite – a Ferris wheel, Lover's Leap, candy-floss and burger stands. Then back round through the engine and tractor exhibits to the cattle and sheep lines, where Boddy suddenly streaked off like a flash into the adjacent field, caught a rabbit and broke its neck with nary a squeak from the poor thing.

Summer smiled. 'Well now, we have our meal.'

I felt a bit sick. 'That's her first kill.'

As if she sensed my revulsion, Boddy trotted straight as an arrow to Summer, who extended a hand as my dog surrendered her lifeless prey. I felt a shock of jealousy. So much for the 'spitting', she should've come to me regardless, I thought. I choked back my feelings.

We made our way back, past where Indeedy would be selling her meals tomorrow. We saw her bright new van, parked by the kitchen unit. The main ring was quiet now but by the next day at noon it would be a heaving metropolis.

'Well, *jukel*, we've a fine meal and thanks to you. You shall have your portion.' Esmeralda beamed and set to skinning, gutting and chunking the rabbit into the waiting pot. A few potatoes, carrots, onions and herbs followed. Boddy eased herself nearby, drooling. We went off to tether the horses in the lush grass behind the marquee.

Esmeralda's palmistry posters awaited our brightening with new paint. The sandwich board also needed the letters touching up:

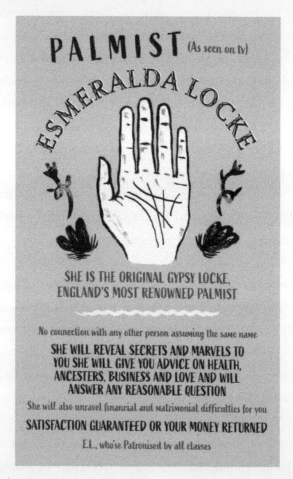

PALMIST (As seen on tv)

ESMERALDA LOCKE

SHE IS THE ORIGINAL GYPSY LOCKE,
ENGLAND'S MOST RENOWNED PALMIST

No connection with any other person assuming the same name

SHE WILL REVEAL SECRETS AND MARVELS TO
YOU SHE WILL GIVE YOU ADVICE ON HEALTH,
ANCESTERS, BUSINESS AND LOVE AND WILL
ANSWER ANY REASONABLE QUESTION

She will also unravel financial and matrimonial difficulties for you

SATISFACTION GUARANTEED OR YOUR MONEY RETURNED

E.L., who'se Patronised by all classes

On the second board was a brightly painted hand, the palm divided into Life line, Head line, Heart line, lines of Affection, Fate line, Health line and the line of Fortune. It would stand upright in the waggon in Esmeralda's driving seat.

'Not meaning to be rude, but do people really believe this stuff?' I asked, touching up the last lettering with permanent marker.

'I do not know,' said Summer. '*Gorgios* want to believe her.'

Then my troubled thoughts tumbled inside my head, recalling the way Mum waited so long to tell me the whole story of Daddy – and was it the whole truth? What is the whole truth of anything? I remembered overhearing a relative say that my parents' marriage had been going wrong 'ever since Robin was born', and I thought that it was true, and meant that it was all was my fault, that I was responsible.

What I said to Summer was, 'I think truth makes a difference. And houses make a difference and houses that stay in the same place make a difference. And things belonging to someone. Like, for instance, whose rabbit did Boddy kill?'

Summer, silent, concentrating on the lettering.

'Well?' I insisted. 'Whose rabbit?'

Still no reply.

In frustration I jibed, 'Plus there are two mistakes where you're fixing the sign. It should be "*who is*" or "*who's*", not "*who'se*".'

'Who says?'

'My English teacher in London, Mrs Avey.'

'And the other, then?'

'Spelling. *"Ancesters"* should be *-ors* at the end, not *-ers*.'

'I thank you.' Summer made the necessary corrections.

'Whose rabbit, I asked you?'

Summer sighed like an old person. 'Your Boddy is a fine Romany *jukel*. You've never taught her to make a clean kill without a sound and deliver the meal to the cook. That's her Gypsy breeding through and through. She knew. As to whose rabbit it is, it is God's bounty and our rightful borrowing of the good earth. Does the wild rabbit belong to Her Majesty the Queen Lady Day? No. Our people have been killed for nothing more than claiming God's gifts. Were it true that your fine *jukel* here were born yesteryear she would have a forefoot chopped off by their majesties to keep her from hunting the king's royal deer! You know how I believe. You may keep your law of property and possession. It is not mine.'

Summer Locke, full marks. Robin Swallow, nil.

Summer gathered the brushes and pens, turned away and walked towards the waggon. Esmeralda called out, 'Come along now, chavvies, for some good stew and a story and a sound night's sleep.'

The cool August air, misted and made pungent with the open-air fire and the smell of freshly cooked food, calmed me down. Esmeralda spread a tablecloth on the ground and dished out the stew, a bowl for each. Boddy would share in the bounty, but would have to wait. Summer and Esmeralda crouched round the *yog* on their haunches. Suddenly chilly, I retrieved a jumper, spread it on the ground and settled down cross-legged. We ate the delicious stew in silence. Boddy lay beside me, staring intently at my steaming bowl.

Esmeralda cleaned the last of her stew with a piece of bread. 'Now then, chavvies, would you like a story before we take ourselves to sleep?'

Summer brightened. 'The story of the Gypsy and the crucifixion, Bibi, please?'

'Well then now, ask your Bibi the question.'

Summer read my mind and explained. 'Every story begins with a "why" or a "what happened when". Like this: Well now, Bibi, why are the Romany forever wandering?'

Esmeralda's features glowed in the firelight. 'Now then. It was when the Lord Jesus was here on earth. There were in Jerusalem these evil priests, and they gave money to two Roman soldiers for to buy four strong nails to crucify the Lord. Well, these Romans they spent half the money getting drunk as skunks and they forgot the nails. By time they remembered, the darkness was heavy.'

The darkness was falling now around us, slowly. Esmeralda talked on.

'They hurried on along to an old Jewish blacksmith. "We want four strong nails for to crucify Jesus." The old blacksmith said, "Why do you want these nails? For to crucify the King of the Jews? No, I will not do it." So! The drunken soldiers they stabbed the old blacksmith and they killed him.

'Now then, then they found another Jewish blacksmith who told them the money was sufficient only for very small nails. Well! They frighted him into forging the nails by setting his beard alight. So he set to working, and the soldiers said, "Make them good and strong, Jew, for at dawn we crucify Yeshua ben Miriam." Hearing the name of Jesus, the Jew ceased his work. And Lo! the voice of the first blacksmith that the soldiers killed came faintly to his ears: "Do not make the nails. They are for one of our own people and he is innocent." So! The second smith refused to continue with his work and the soldiers they killed him.'

Warmed by fire and a full stomach I felt the torpor of exhaustion wash over me. My eyes felt heavy and I wanted the story to finish. 'Are there are no Gypsies in the story?'

'Harken!' Esmeralda silenced me kindly. 'The wicked soldiers finally came upon a Gypsy with an anvil by his tent. At point of sword they ordered him to forge the four nails. Now. The Gypsy pocketed the money they offered him and made three nails without delay. While he was working on the fourth nail, they told him that the nails were made to crucify Jesus. Then a miracle! The Gypsy heard the trembling voices of the dead blacksmiths begging him not to make the last nail. The soldiers also heard the voices, took the three nails and ran away.'

Esmeralda paused. Summer was looking at her expectantly, knowing how the story went on.

'Now then! Terrible to tell, the Gypsy he finished the fourth nail and waited for it to grow cold. But harken! The nail remained red-hot as if straight from the fire. The Gypsy poured cold water on it, but it continued to glow, a terrible bright glow like lightning. Well now. The Gypsy was terrified. He packed his tent on his donkey and fled from the nail. After some distance he pitched the tent between two high sand dunes, but there at his feet he saw the very same glowing nail! Throughout the night he poured water and sand upon it but in vain.'

I was hooked now, Esmeralda's storytelling reeling me in.

'By now the Gypsy was gone wild in the head. He again packed his belongings and fled further into the desert, arriving presently at an Arab village. But Alas! The nail had followed him. An Arab approached the Gypsy and asked him to repair the iron hoop of a wheel. Quickly the Gypsy used the glowing nail to do this, and then watched the Arab driving away with it. Well now, he believed he was rid of the nail. But Alas!'

– Esmeralda paused dramatically – 'sometime later, a man brought him the hilt of a sword for repair. Harken! Within the hilt, was the glowing nail!

'The Gypsy packed and fled again, but even after his death the nail always reappeared within the tents of his descendants. Thus the Gypsy must forever wander.'

The firelight illuminated Esmeralda's face, the scar on her nose picked out in the contrast of shadows.

'Now, hearken, chavvies. You'll know this story to be true, for the Lord Jesus was crucified with three nails, and the one was used to pierce the both of his feet drawn together. And the fourth nail wanders from one end of the earth to the other, in pursuit of the Gypsies whose forefather forged the other three.' Esmeralda stopped, then said, 'There now. I've done!'

'That is a very sad story, isn't it,' I said, 'because the wandering is like a curse?' I struggled to repress a yawn and cast a pleading look in Summer's direction.

Summer ignored me. 'Tell about the shadow of the cross, Bibi.'

''Tis simple. If ever we see the shadow of the cross at a stopping place we move on.'

'Thank you, Esmeralda,' I said. 'I need to sleep now.' I could hear the sounds of motors and muffled shouts coming from the fairground, readying for tomorrow.

Summer smiled. 'Shall we sleep under the stars, near Ghost and Goblin? I have a groundsheet and blanket.'

'I've brought my sleeping bag. But won't the noise keep us awake?'

Esmeralda smiled. 'I should think not, and I will sleep the better for solitary slumber.'

Boddy curled underneath Esmeralda's caravan, one ear perched on the listen. Wee Ghostie and Goblin were snuffling and grazing the sweet summer grass. Summer and I, snug in our sleeping bags, lay beneath a star-spangled sky.

15
Arson

Gypsy woman, with eyes emerald green
Dark hair tossed across her face in
your dreams
Beautiful temptress, bringing kings to
their knees

     – 'Gypsy Woman' by Colachloe

Summer Locke, startled from deep sleep by … what? What sifted through *my* dreams first? Ghostie and Goblin whinnying in terror? A smell? An alien sound? An instinct?

Summer's eyes open. An orange light. Fire. FIRE!

'Robin! Robin, wake up!'

'I am awake!'

'Bibi's waggon is alight!'

We fumbled from our covers.

'Dial 999! Where is the phone?'

Everything is a blur. Run to members' marquee? No time to lose. Scream for Esmeralda. ESMERALDA! Can't find a way into the waggon, the heat is too great. Round to the back. Esmeralda is slumped halfway out of the back window, trying to escape the inferno surrounding her. Summer seems immune to the heat and pulls with superhuman strength. Esmeralda rolls on the grass, her clothes alight. Don't stop rolling Esmeralda, good good good! Summer falls and rolls her over and over and over. Security guard with two-way radio: 999! Fire! Fire! North-west entrance of showground well alight. Persons reported on fire. Figures running towards us from every corner of the show field, fire extinguishers.

The scream of a fire engine sounded its way to the burning waggon as a cockerel crowed from the fur and feather display at the other end of the fairground. I squatted alongside Summer Locke, huddled in the dawn inferno, cradling Esmeralda's head. Her charred clothing raggedly burned from her slight body. We covered her with a blanket.

'My chavvie, you will attend the *gorgio* school.' The words were whispered, weak but lucid.

Summer nodded yes. 'Please dear God,' prayed Summer aloud, 'and Jesus and Mother Mary and Joseph and all the angels please let my Bibi live. Please, please in all the heavens and moon and stars, save her life. Please and thank you, dear God. Amen.'

Two paramedics from the air ambulance knelt with a stretcher and a silvery blanket. Tenderly they lifted Esmeralda – 'You're light as thistledown, Miss Locke' – and carried her to the ingenious patient's hatch at the rear of the helicopter, constantly speaking softly to her: *Can you remember your name? Are you able to move your legs? Arms? You are strong. We'll look after you, no worries.* Then they were away as suddenly as they arrived.

We stared the helicopter out of sight and sound.

'Summer, have you seen Boddy? She was under the waggon when we …' I could not bear it.

'There she is.'

Boddy was lying some distance from us. She was in a strange position.

'Boddy! Come by.' No movement. 'Oh no!'

Adrenaline kicked in and I tore away to my dog. Breathing? Her ribs are moving up and down. Come by, my lovely Boddy, what have they done to you? Will you be like a cat with nine lives? How many more will you need? Oh, come by, my lovely bravest and best dog in the world. I will hold you, I will stay by your side until you wake.

I barely registered Mum as she and Chris arrived, breathless, frantic. I cradled my dog, and Summer stared at the smouldering waggon.

By the time the sun was up the firefighters had gone. Hazy sunlight outlined the smouldering carcass of

Esmeralda's caravan. Only her Queenie hostess stove stood sentinel in the ruins. Ghostie and Goblin had found temporary refuge with the Shire horses near the horsebox lot. Speculation over the cause of the fire, at first of the 'Old crone probably dropped off while her pipe was alight' variety, very soon moved away from the accidental. *Arson.*

Despite it all, the show must needs go on. Indeedy and Chris catered to record crowds, but the fire, combined with too many gawpers and bad news about the extent of Esmerald's burns, cast a pervasive pall over the one-day show. I watched helplessly as Summer Locke joined me while I sat vigil beside Boddy, who for ages either slept or stumbled about, still shaking off the effects of whatever abuse she had received. As evening drew near we carried her to the main marquee, made her comfortable, intending to help Chris and Indeedy pack for our return home.

'Poor, poor bonny *jukel*,' Summer said, cradling Boddy as we set her down, still groggy. 'Who has done such a thing to you?'

Boddy raised her head, staring intently at Summer's face, ears pricked.

'It's like she's trying to tell us something, Summer.'

'Yes, she is telling us. Listen.' Summer began to speak quietly, staring steadily into Boddy's amber gaze:

It is not my lurcher way to bark a warning. My hackles lift. I rise silently, and I wolf-trot towards the sound and

*its smell, a human whose scent I recognize and hate. I wait.
My keen eyes see the human carrying a container. I wait,
crouching to the damp ground as if to meld with the grass.
When the human approaches I spring. The human drops
something but knees me in the chest as I go for his throat.
The human grasps me round the neck, pulling a bag from
his pocket with a free hand and slipping it over my head. I
struggle but I cannot stop breathing in a sick-sweet tingly
smell. This is all I remember. When I wake, my humans hold
me. I cannot walk at first but you, my humans, look after me.*

I stared at Summer in amazement. I cannot explain my
feelings properly, but in this moment I believed Summer
genuinely and completely understood dog language.

Summer stroked Boddy. 'Poor, brave *jukel*. Just one
more thing. The slurry pit. Was it the same human then?'

*I cannot speak of this. It is a dog's worst nightmare and
I will never roll in sheep's poo again.*

'Wise *jukel*,' said Summer, smiling ruefully.

Oblivious to my amazed silence, Indeedy called to
us from the entrance. 'Nearly finished, and then we can
get you home. I expect you're both in shock.'

'Well,' I said, 'I am not shocked.'

'I said "in shock", Fruit.' Indeedy came over to us and,
squatting beside me, took my face in her hands. 'The
most important thing is to stay safe and try to be back
to normal as soon as possible.' She called to Chris, 'We
have clear suspicions about the culprit, don't we, Chris?'

'We do, but it is a mistake to jump to conclusions,' said Chris. 'What do you think, Summer Locke?'

'I cannot think at this very moment, Miss Chris,' said Summer, ending the conversation.

I wished someone would ask me what I thought, even though I was not sure what it was, as Indeedy took my hand and nodded to Summer to come along with Boddy to the van.

'Normal' is what happened next. Day followed day in a humdrum, slow, silent sadness. Summer Locke made daily trips to the hatch to follow Esmeralda's progress. We managed to keep up our nocturnal pow-wows. This is Summer's information, direct from Mr John Pockett and through Summer to me.

Esmeralda lay in intensive care for days. Mr Pockett and Norah Boswell returned from their Welsh fair, sharing shifts by her bedside round the clock. Esmeralda seemed to turn a corner towards healing. Then, late one night and without warning, pneumonia. Her breathing became laboured and ceased during the midnight shift. John Pockett looked about him, made certain he was not observed, and unhooked Esmeralda from her electronic monitors. He would take her body home with honour and dignity. He murmured a Romany prayer as he wrapped her tenderly in a blanket.

'It goes like this,' Summer told me. Summer Locke's voice was sweet and chorister-clear:

> *'Under the leaves, the leaves of life*
> *There I saw maidens seven,*
> *And one of them was Mary mild*
> *As was God's Mother from Heaven.*
> *They asked me what I was looking for*
> *All under the leaves of life;*
> *'I am looking for sweet Jesus Christ,*
> *To be our heavenly guide.'*

John Pockett slipped through the maze-like corridors of Borderland Royal Infirmary, carrying Esmeralda in her blanket, and hailed a taxi to take them to the Romany Road hatch. Norah Boswell greeted John, took one look and, without a word, retrieved an ornate death rug, spread it on the curtained bed and helped Mr Pockett lay out Esmeralda.

'I could not help but reflect,' said Summer, 'the times past I had lain in that very bed. And then Norah said, "Blessing be on her, Bibi is smiling. And she is smaller."

'Then Norah Boswell, she laid Esmeralda out in a fine frock and fit dancing slippers on her feet. She placed an ounce of tobacco in one hand, a box of matches and clay pipe in the other, her snuff in an apron pocket and a squeezebox on her belly. And then Norah she sat at the bedside, humming more tunes she'd learned from Esmeralda. I asked Norah, what will happen now? "Well now, my chavvie," says Norah, "back in the day we would burn our Bibi's *varda* to show our respect, but … what has burnt cannot burn again."'

Summer stopped. I knew not to press her but to wait for the end of her telling.

'So I said, "What about the lot of her possessions, Miss Norah?" and Norah told me, "Aye, 'tis hard but we, her friends and kin, we would destroy all that did not burn, and whatever will not burn, we would smash." Whatever will not smash would meet with the sledgehammer. Jewellery will be buried. Nothing whatsoever can be sold. Only one single ring left to a daughter or female next of kin, and this ring may stay in the family line forever.'

'Even money? Is money burned too?' I asked.

'Ah now, money is the exception. Money would be kept,' Summer said. 'Then I asked Norah what I most feared to ask. "Her animals? Her ponies, Miss Norah? Goblin? Wee Ghostie? What of them?"'

Summer stopped again, then said, 'It sorrows me this very moment to tell, Robin, but the horses would be shot, and any other animals.'

'Oh, Summer! This is horrible!'

Summer would not meet my gaze. 'I shall try to explain. Our Roma forebears would have meant this as a sign of respect. Thankfully the other customs have passed away and we will keep the horses after all.'

'Well, to me that isn't respectful. But they can't burn her caravan because it's already done. Am I allowed to attend?'

'Aye, that you may.'

By mid-afternoon of the following day it was clear that Esmeralda's passing would be a gala occasion. She had long asked to be buried beneath her oak tree at the Pucklethorpe hatch. That day you couldn't squeeze a thin chicken in at the hatch or fit another animal, waggon or chrome caravan. Families parked under every available tree, settling into a routine. The open area filled with groups sitting on the ground, chasing down slabs of unbuttered bread with steaming mugs of tea. A number of the men tugged at bottles of Guinness. Standing regally beside Esmeralda's oak tree was, in Summer Locke's words, 'The one, the only, the great Prince Petal Petulengro.' He was in full regalia, holding a newspaper and pointing something out to a circle of admirers. Hearing word of Esmeralda's death, Petal had rushed across from the continent by ferry, bringing with him a smart pick-up and leaving the other elders to the task for which they had gone in the first place. Seeing us, he hailed, voice booming, 'Well now, my chavvies, you have arrived at the best moment. Come, read this for me.'

'When the papers want to write about our people,' Summer told me as we walked over, smiling at Petal, 'to be sure it is Petal they wish to photograph.'

I could see why – his shiny crimson shirt was unbuttoned to belly point, spotted scarf knotted round his neck, a great mass of grizzly silver-black hair, full beard down to his chest. Round his middle Petal sported a leather belt several inches wide and studded with magical signs made of brass. Petal bear-hugged Summer Locke, and gestured, who was I? Summer said, 'This is my friend Robin.' Petal nodded OK and pointed to the pick-up. He had purchased a coffin for Esmeralda on his journey home. It was in the back there, see. He paid cash in hand for the coffin, see. This newspaper Summer's holding will explain, see.

'Now then. Read this out for us, chavvie. You know I've not got the book learning.'

Summer took the newspaper and read solemnly.

"GYPSIES SEAL OFF PART OF A11 FOR DAWN HORSE RACE. Police in Kent are looking into complaints that Gypsies closed off seven miles of the Great Channel Road with their vehicles and turned it into a racecourse. Villagers nearby said yesterday the 250 Gypsies, some from the Continent, closed the road for thirty minutes while two families decided which of them owned the better horse. Each staked £2,000 on the race, and side bets totalled several thousand pounds. The trotting race, run at 6 a.m., was won by a striking dark bay stallion called Bruno, from the Welsh borders ...'"

A cheer erupted. Summer read on.

"'The winning horse completed the course in nineteen minutes. After the race, the winning owner rejected an offer of £3,500 for Bruno. Police said, 'We did not know it was happening and we are looking into it. No one has the right to close a trunk road, certainly not for horse racing.'"

'We done it for Esmeralda,' said Petal. 'She loved them road races.'

Summer Locke returned Petal's newspaper. Friends thumped Petal on the back, roaring approval. Two men lifted the coffin from the back of Petal's van. It was a handsome box, bright mahogany with fine brass fixtures catching the rays of the afternoon sun. I could not but be struck by the general merriment.

'Why are they laughing?'

Summer drew a deep breath. 'I have not the sense of it, but Gypsies do not like anything dull and drab, even in death. King teaches us that death should be the same as a wedding and a part of life. It is a great thing to be old and dying, says he. You go into a new experience, a new life says he, invisible to those left behind.'

'You've not followed your elder's advice the last few days!' I think I sounded more harsh than I felt. 'I mean, you *have* been pretty miserable, Summer.'

'I could not help myself.' Summer's eyes brimmed tears. I love the way Summer is not ashamed to cry.

'Well,' I said, taking Summer's hand, 'a lot of people love your Bibi, that's for sure.'

And I love you, too, I almost said.

We followed the coffin bearers into the house and moved to a corner of the room where children clustered. White dimity curtains festooned the windows, set off by shutters of green picked out with panels of bright red. The room was carpeted and partitioned at the far end to house the bunkbed, built like a ship's berth. The bed was curtained like the windows with white dimity. In another corner stood the 'gavver in the corner', a stove with a narrow chimney passing through the outer wall of the house, surrounded by a small larder, several storage cupboards, a milk churn and articles of gleaming crockery. In the room's centre stood a huge oval dining table of dark oak.

The men placed the coffin on the dining table. They moved towards the deathbed, picked up the tall candles and placed them at the two ends of the table. There was no sign of strain as the bearers lifted Esmeralda's frail body. Picking up the corners of the patterned throw that would be her shroud, the men took care not to come into contact with her body. Gently they moved Esmeralda to the waiting coffin. From a corner of the room, a young woman sounded a clear alto:

'Cold blows the wind for my true love,
Cold blows the drops of rain,
I never had but one true love,
And in green wood he was slain.
I'll do as much for my true love,
As any young girl may,
For I will sit and weep down by the grave,
For twelve months and a day.'

As the song wafted around the room and other voices joined in, Summer Locke moved towards the coffin.

'When twelve months and a day were gone,
This young man he arose;
'Why do you weep down by my grave,
That I can take no repose?
O fetch me a nut from a dungeon deep,
Or water out of a stone,
Or white, white milk from a fair maid's breast,
Or from me begone.'

Summer Locke was sitting sentinel at the coffin, gazing into it.

'How can I fetch a nut from a dungeon deep,
Or water out of a stone.
Or white, white milk from a fair maid's breast,

When fair maid she is none?'
'If you have one kiss from my lily-white lips
Your days will not be long,
My lips are as cold as any clay,
My breath it is earthy and strong.'
'One kiss, one kiss from your lily-white lips
One kiss from you I crave.'
'The cock does crow and we must part,
And I must return to my grave.'

As the song ended, Summer turned round slowly, quiet, calm, pale, to face the assembled. 'Fetch me a mirror, please.'

Summer placed the mirror close to Esmeralda's face. 'Our Bibi, she is alive.'

No response. Heads down. I waited in the corner, gesturing to Summer, who smiled like an angel but didn't move. What I thought was, my beautiful magic Summer Locke has now gone truly bonkers.

Again, calmly, 'Our Bibi is alive. Moving her mouth to the words of the song she was.'

Summer turned back to the coffin, tucked an arm under Esmeralda's head and gently lifted her to a sitting position for all to see. Esmeralda opened her eyes, blinking like a creature emerging from hibernation. She spoke in a harsh whisper. 'Fetch me a drink and loose me from this bonebox!'

By dusk Esmeralda was well enough to sit round the *yog* near her beloved oak tree, nursing her healing burns with ancient remedies and telling the story of her journey to death and back. The scene in the caravan after Summer had lifted Esmeralda had been astonishing to me. To be fetched back from the darkness, from the coffin itself, as was Bibi Esmeralda, seemed truly miraculous. Summer's extended family accepted it as such, and entirely without question.

'Praise to *Mooshabove*,' Petal Petrulengo had intoned.

'PRAISE TO *MOOSHABOVE!*' chorused the assembled. And that was that.

Stunned, I had thought about Daddy, that we had never held a proper funeral for him because we had never found him. Not that I know what a 'proper' funeral is, but the outward trappings of this Romany ceremony seemed quite similar to ours. And yet still this was not a proper funeral – Bibi Esmeralda was not dead, after all.

'Now, this is what is on my mind and what I have learned,' Esmeralda was saying to the assembled crowd, 'I wasn't fearing to die, because I believe that this life I've been living is a dream and that the real life starts when we're dead, when the spirit leaves the body.'

Esmeralda nodded, summoned more tobacco for her clay pipe, and, with great deliberation, filled and lit it, sucking long and deep and staring into the embers of the fire.

'Well, now. I've been dead before so I know what I'm talking about. You've first got to experience a thing before you can discuss it. Here is what happened this time.'

You could have heard a leaf drop.

'I had gone to my rest, having readied for the show,' Esmeralda began. 'So fatigued was I that I did not say my prayers or consult my cards. Now you *dukkerers* hearken. I should've said my prayers no matter how tired. But I did not. When the chavvies took themselves off to sleep under the stars by Ghost and Goblin, I was too tired to do anything but lay me down and close my eyes, with the *jukel* resting beneath me. I drew my curtains and off to sleep was I like a wee babby.'

Esmeralda paused to tug on her clay pipe. Summer Locke leaned forward.

'Bibi, the villain must have known our movements. We found Robin's *jukel* lying prone. Next morning she was staggering around like a drunken *didekoi*. Then we discovered a sack with a sicky sweet smell. He doped Boddy.'

'Well now, there you are. That would be chloroform. As I was telling, it must've been in the wee hours of the morning, the dark night of the soul time, when troubles wake us, when I heard a rustling. I waited for the *gorgio* girl's *jukel* to sound warning. Nothing, and now we know why. So I drew my curtain back a pinch and what did I see, did I see a dark shadow running off or was it nothing? So I lay me down again and out like a soggy match I was in no time. Next I know I'm in the devil's own kitchen and choking on the smoke. The door of my *varda* was solid flame so I took to the window by my bed. And do I misremember you pulling me out of the fire and rolling me like a sausage, Summer, my chavvie?'

'You remember rightly, Bibi.'

'Well now, there you are, and I am grateful for you putting my light out.'

Esmeralda smiled broadly, her maimed nose shining like a puppy's. Faces around the fire glowed, eager for the rest of the story. Dusk closed in quickly, and I was conscious we would be walking home in the dark. I nudged Summer. Summer shhh-ed me. Esmeralda spoke again.

'I was on a table in the hospital and the doctor was giving me the kiss of life, and he told me later that I had the heart of a lion, otherwise I would not have survived, for I'd been dead for five minutes. Smoke inhalation. I said, "Look, doctor, I've been over the border. All my ancestors were waiting, pulling my spirit towards them, and I came back."'

A child's voice whispered in the dusk. 'What was death like, Bibi?'

'Well, now. I can tell you about death and it'll cost you nothing. Death was just like a dream. I thought it *was* a dream. You get people dreaming in black and white and some dream in Technicolor. The one who dreams in Technicolor is psychic, and also dies in Technicolor. When I died both times it was as if I dreamed beautiful flowers, beautiful trees, beautiful girls in different coloured dresses. Why the only bad part was this very time, waking up and finding myself in a bonebox! Well now, you remember this when my turn comes, as it will for us all. Death is a new experience and now I know it. None of your *gorgio* "Rover dead all over".'

I returned Summer's glance with a glare. 'I'll ask Zach what he thinks,' I said through gritted teeth. 'Summer, we must go home. Indeedy will be worried.'

'All right.' Summer turned to Esmeralda. 'Bibi, I thank God, and you, for your coming back to life. Now we must be returning to Robin's house.'

'Don't you be thanking me, it's not my doing. Well now, you take care, the both of ye. And that *jukel* of yours, Robin Swallow.'

Petal stood. 'I will give you a lift. It's dark.'

We hopped into the back of Petal's pick-up. For the first time since Esmeralda's death and sudden resurrection, Summer thought about asking news of the elders and their mission to Belgium.

'Petal, sir, have you any more news of the elders?'

Petal shot a sideways glance Summer's way. 'Well. Yes I do, now you mention.' Then silence.

'Do not tease, Petal, sir. I would have news of Stinger if news there is.'

'Yes, and so you shall have.'

Silence.

Me, Miss Mouth Almighty. 'Well? Cut to the chase! Please?'

Silence.

I think Petal likes to build up suspense because he pondered and pondered. Then, 'Well. We were not far off when I was called back.'

'Far off from where?'

'Far off from working our trap. By now they may well have snared your killer.'

Summer asked no more questions. I gave Summer a look.

'That is very good news,' said Summer, avoiding my gaze.

When we crunched up the gravel at Limberlost Mill, Winitoo's motorbike was parked in the drive. He greeted us at the door.

'Hey up, the pair of you! Good news. Meat Loaf's going down to prison for a long while. Arrested for arson and attempted murder, remanded in custody until the trial comes up.'

So. It *was* Meat Loaf. 'How'd they catch him?' I asked.

'They took him in that very same night of the fire,' Winitoo said. 'He near enough collided with a fire engine on the lane near Beggar's Bridge, and he had the goods on him. Petrol canister, chloroform, the lot. Confessed right off.'

'Am I safe now?' Summer asked.

'Don't you mean "we", Summer?' I reminded.

'Yes. We,' Summer agreed.

'Well, I should think so, but who knows?' Winitoo said. 'Rock On and Twitch don't work without a leader, they're, like, total copy-cats for certain. And it looks like the police don't intend to continue further questioning.'

'I hope he never sees the light of day again,' I said hotly. 'Winitoo, have you seen my mum and Zach?'

'I have. Indeedy's gone off with the tall lady friend looking for you two at the Gypsy site. When they arrive they'll find out you've got here, won't they? Well then, I'll be getting on. *Hasta la vista*, mateys.'

Winitoo sashayed off to his bike, hips swaying.

Summer beamed. 'Perhaps good news is like bad news, coming in threes?'

'Miracles, more like. What a relief!'

Summer smiled a radiant smile, turned to the stairs and went to bed.

16
Catalepsy

Q: What does a dyslexic, agnostic insomniac do at night?
A: Stays awake wondering if 'dog' exists.

Zach's birthday and departure for university was approaching fast. Almost overnight he got more moody and not a very nice sort of person. It's true that he was often a bit pompous, but witty with it. Now he just seemed plain arrogant. His appetite grew enormous, to such an extent that Summer Locke, not usually one to speak out in criticism, could scarcely repress telling Zach stories about Buddhist hungry ghosts. 'Your brother has an appetite like the nasty Mr Stinger,' Summer whispered to me.

'Have you got tapeworm?' I asked as a tease, but Zach just scowled. He ignored us mostly but when he did notice us, it would either be to be bossy or to avoid us.

Indeedy teased him too. 'Irritable Soul Syndrome – is there a cure? Short of amputating a vital organ, perhaps a spate on a desert island?'

Zach's nose was in a book as usual and he ignored her.

'Seriously, son, do you think university will do you any good?'

Zach lowered the book. 'Indubitably. We are at the dawn of the Third Industrial Revolution. Robotics.'

I couldn't resist showing off that I too knew what Zach was talking about. 'Yes. Mrs Avey says we will be having a revolution, but Mrs Spicer says they're a flash in the pan and no better than the people who make them.'

'Such views are only too predictable, I fear. Would you like me to draw you a diagram? Sum up the distinction between mechanical, electronic, analogue and digital?'

Zach can be such a smuggy!

Indeedy assumed her long-suffering parent look. 'Another time, honey.'

Zach was on a roll. 'I was trying to say, Mum, that I don't really give a monkey's what Mrs Spicer thinks about this stuff. This is bigger than rockets to Mars. Soon our entire lives – communication, transport, information of all kinds – will be, well, automatic. And oh, one more thing about your geriatric Gypsy lady. I've been reading up on her apparent death.' He picked up another fat book from the floor, the *Concise Medical*

Dictionary. 'Her condition has a name, "catalepsy..."'
Zach ran his finger along the text. 'Says here, blah blah,
ah, here: "The subjects of catalepsy are in most instances
females of highly nervous or hysterical temperament."'

Summer Locke frowned. 'Bibi Esmeralda is
not hysterical.'

'Let me finish. "The word *hysteria* derives from the
Greek and means 'wandering womb'. Sometimes the
typical features of the disease are exhibited in a state of
complete insensibility. In this condition vital functions
appear to be reduced to the lowest possible limit
consistent with life and to such a degree as to simulate
actual death. The attack may last for many hours and in
rare instances persist for several days." So the old trout's
body just played possum. Simple as that. To say that she
died is a pseudo-scientific and gross misrepresentation.'

Summer's loyalty was unswerving. 'She died twice.
She said so, and Bibi Esmeralda does not lie.'

'Twice? That smacks of carelessness,' sneered Zach.

There was no sense arguing. I grabbed my togs,
whistled for Boddy and stomped off on my own to
the jumping-off place. A good plunge in the heart-
stopping cold water might clear my head. These days I
felt I couldn't even venture near Zach's bedroom. Soon
he would be gone entirely, like Daddy. I could not at
times remember what he looked like. 'Daddy's name
was Rory,' I recited to myself. 'He had dark brown eyes.

He used to take me horse riding and tell me his plans. He made toffee popcorn balls at Christmas. He was English and brave. He was …' Then memory fugged.

I jumped deep and opened my eyes to the brown-green water world.

Scrambling up the bank, I thought of Summer noticing that I had taken to stomping on insects.

'Please leave spiders alone, is all I ask,' Summer had said, finding me in a spree of red ant-stomping.

'Why should I?'

'Because they have done you no harm and it is bad fortune to kill a spider,' said Summer Locke. 'They weave the webs of our dreams.'

'These are ants! Oh, why don't you just go off with your … just … just go off!'

But Summer stayed put, regarding me in a solemn silent reproach that spoke volumes.

The weekend arrived which was to be, in Zach's words: 'The last three days of carefree youth'. He announced magnanimously that he could now spare time with the 'groundlings'.

'That's Shakespeare for riff-raff,' I explained to Summer. 'Us.'

Chris had booked tickets for herself and Indeedy to the Borderland Opera's production of *Tosca*. 'You don't mind if we just take off for the evening?' Without waiting for an answer Indeedy said, 'Just pop the pizzas in for ten minutes and they'll be perfect. There's green salad and cheesecake in the fridge.'

As Indeedy ran upstairs to ready herself for the evening's outing, Chris produced a bottle of champagne and removed the cork with a deft twist so that none of the lively liquid escaped onto her cream linen suit. 'It's high time we raise a toast to you, Zach. Robin, will you fetch some champagne flutes please?'

'Did you know,' said Chris, pouring the cheery champagne, 'that the opera *Tosca* is the unluckiest opera in the world?'

Me, I'm not keen on opera. It's too much like real life, all that shouting and saying things like 'Fare thee well, for I love another' and 'I'm leaving I'm leaving!' and then they don't leave and just keep saying the same things. But I wanted to be polite. So I said, 'Do you mean, kind of like *Macbeth* is the unlucky Shakespeare? Mrs Avey told us about how actors never say the word "Macbeth" because it's unlucky, so they always call it "the Scottish Play".'

'Sort of. Something bad always happens. Last time they produced *Tosca* in Borderland, Tosca was bashed by a bunch of black fake beachballs that were supposed to be cannon balls just as she tried to throw herself to her death from the parapet.'

Indeedy floated down the stairs.

Zach wolf-whistled. 'Mum in a frock! What a shock! You do scrub up well, Mum.'

Indeedy twirled. Swishy sea-green, low-necked, off the shoulder. She had rubbed her patent leather heels with Vaseline to retrieve the shine, and she smelled of her signature perfume, her hair swept up in a honey-brown swirl. She wore her garnet earrings from Ethiopia – Daddy's last gift.

Chris passed out the champagne glasses. 'Cheers to you, Zach, and to us all.' We toasted solemnly.

'You look lovely, Mum.' I said. 'Have a good time.'

Indeedy beamed *I love you*, and they were off.

After devouring an entire pizza on his own, plus half the cheesecake and a pint of milk, and ordering me and Summer to do the washing-up, Zach announced, 'Well, I suppose I'd better take a final look at Wheatley's journal then. When you've finished clearing up. And make us some popcorn while you're at it. Loads of butter and salt, no sugar thanks.'

We washed up, me muttering away *grunt-grunt* about Napoleon the hog – 'all animals are equal but some are more equal than others' – from that book I'd read in year seven. When we moved from the kitchen we found that Zach had set up materials on the dining table. He slouched in the middle with two chairs on either side.

'Take a pew.'

Summer placed the big brown mixing bowl on the table, heaped with hot popcorn.

'Where's the soy sauce?'

'You didn't *ask* for soy sauce.'

'You know I like it with soy sauce, Robin.'

'Just don't get any grease on Mr Wheatley's journal!'

'And bring a smaller bowl too!' Zach shouted back.

Summer and I had divided Brockton Wheatley's journal according to its separate topics: One: Domestic & Personal; Two: Historical; Three: Science and Blindness. We began at the beginning.

Part One: Domestic and Personal.

We had left out Brockton's long lists of spending and details of shopping and who would be visiting.

Summer said, 'Papa was certain that someone was visiting the house by an entrance he couldn't seal off. He knew Charlotte's threats were real, he knew that furniture was disappearing, but Papa felt helpless to stop it. When he confronted Lady Charlotte she told him to follow the "Gypsy brat" to catch any thieves.'

'Oh well,' said Zach. 'To proceed: "Part Two: Historical." Let's see … the bulk of writing concerns the history of the house, which he duplicates in the notes for his book,' Zach said. 'Quite plausible sounding, not really my area.'

'You have an "area" now, do you, Zach?'

'Of course. You must have an area at university these days. Competition and all that. Moving on …'

Part Three: Science and Blindness.

'This category I skimmed,' Zach said. 'Mostly entries about the cures of blindness, which were quite tedious.'

'As in *boring*?'

'As you know full well, Fruit, I don't accept boredom as a valid experience.'

'Papa was hoping to bypass the eyes and "see" directly from the brain,' said Summer.

Zach appeared unimpressed.

Part Four: Notes towards a novel.

'He got only as far as a plot summary and a first chapter. It's a romance, set in Arthurian Britain, Camelot transposed to Borderland. No surprises here,' Zach told us.

Summer frowned. 'There is no need to mock.'

'But what's he really writing about?' Zach pondered.

I shrugged. 'I haven't got a clue.'

'You?' Zach targeted Summer with his academic look.

'I do believe it is about romantic love.'

'Huh. Look, do you want to know my take on the journal or not?' Zach asked.

'Yes.' I meant to say 'No'. Instead I said, '*I'd* like to say that the most interesting part, for me, is where Mr Wheatley wrote to a chap campaigning in America to save a sparrow from extinction. The last one died in a cage in the middle of Disney World, surrounded by Mickey Mouse and funfair rides. Mr Wheatley was gutted. Here. He quotes from the Bible: "Are not two sparrows sold for a penny? Yet not one will fall without the knowledge of your Father."'

'Yes,' said Summer. 'I too am moved by this little bird.'

'How'd it happen?' asked Zach. 'The sparrow becoming extinct, I mean.'

'It was called the dusky seaside sparrow. NASA flooded the marshes to get rid of the mosquitoes and the floods destroyed the sparrows' habitat,' I said. 'Then they built a motorway. You know, like that Joni Mitchell song where she says we're paving paradise to put up a parking lot?'

'I just might take up environmental studies.' Zach rose and stretched. Or robotics. Anyone for hot chocolate?'

'Yes, please.'

'You'll make it, then, won't you, Fruit.' Not a question.

I stomped off, muttering. What did your last slave die of?

Zach looked at Summer.

'I remember now. Mr Wheatley compared Gypsies to those sparrows. He doesn't exactly say "extinct is forever" but that's what worried him. Here.' Zach read directly from the journal. '"The Romany community are a case in point. The Criminal Justice Act. An outrageous misnomer ..." Then, this bit about property ... "My young Gypsy friend leads me to ponder about houses. Why do we live in houses, asks my young friend. Why does Pucklethorpe Manor with its rooms and history mean so much? My young Gypsy friend loves the 'room of the sky'. To my young Gypsy friend there are two kinds of people in the world, Romany and housedweller.'"

Summer nodded. 'Is this not true?'

I brought the hot chocolate.

Zach paused, blowing on the steaming drink.

'Your turn to read,' he said, offering Summer the journal.

'Where were you?'

'There. Still about houses.'

'"First one builds a shelter, one stashes it with necessaries. Like a squirrel one then begins to collect things, some unnecessary. Those outside the house may desire to possess the items and so one erects walls, then borders. Others of like mind gather round. Yet even travellers have a place from which they leave, a stopping place to travel from.'"

Zach peered at Summer. 'Is that true?'

'Yes. It is true.' Summer flushed. Was it sadness? Agitation? Summer changed the subject. 'Papa Brockton possessed an instinct to connect the ceiling and the poem although he did not know the shape of the Jesse Tree from the air. He kept digging holes, but had no proper plan.'

Zach produced his irritating know-it-all tone. 'Whatever. He was searching for Camelot. There was no question in his mind. The problem is yours, not mine. What I say is that what you need to ask yourself now is, what is the *point* of the poem? Being where it is and what it says about the Jesse Tree. There will be a clue. Finito, over and out.'

Summer reached across and took the journal. 'I thank you. We will be asking the point of the poem. And now, I would also like to take my rest if you do not mind.'

We made our way upstairs. Zach must have changed his mind because he flung together a Cheddar and Branston sandwich and switched on the television to a late night Open University programme.

It must have been an hour or more before the opera fans breezed in. My brain was keeping me awake anyway, and I could hear everything.

'How was it? Any disasters tonight?' asked Zach.

'Oh, we weren't disappointed, were we?' Chris said. 'You tell him, love.'

Indeedy giggled. 'It's almost the end and Tosca is in despair, waving a candle about. There's this villain called Scarpio. He's the sheriff and Tosca's promised to make love to him if he frees her True Love from prison, but Scarpio kills her True Love instead. Tonight her waving candle caught Scarpio's beard on fire. Scarpio carries on acting while madly trying to put out the fire, when a stagehand runs on and douses him with a bucket of water.' Indeedy laughed again. 'Bit of a damper, for sure. Anyone for a late snack?'

I stay in bed but I still can't sleep. What *is* the point of the Jesse Tree poem? One in three, three in one. That's the Holy Trinity. But the poem says 'golden trinity'. Why did Lord Pucklethorpe write that beastly verse? Why? Does it matter? Why are there no more dusky seaside sparrows ever again? Why are the Gypsies disappearing? I don't know I don't know I don't know.

17
Education Education Education

Q: What we love e'en more than life,
Fear more than death or mortal strife
The poor possess, the rich have need of
A contented person desires
The miser spends and the spendthrift saves
And all folk carry to their graves.
A: Nothing

Zach went off to university on a Saturday. Three duffle bags, his sound system, two tea chests of the most important books, bedclothes. A secret teddy bear. Piled in the back of the Yes Indeedy Cakes & Bakes van, they were off to digs in a city of seven hills and a big bridge. Indeedy said she'd be back before midnight. I pretended to be glad for Zach.

When Zach had gone, for me and Summer Locke, the riddle of the Jesse Tree, even Brockton Wheatley's murder, faded in the face of everyday-ness: school uniforms, hair cuts, pencil boxes, spiral notebooks, pencils, staplers and rubbers, highlighters and Biros.

'We'll have to get used to a routine, Summer.' I counted the cornflakes in my breakfast bowl that would float. Twenty-four.

'This is true.'

'Right. When we go to school Monday, we'll stick together.' I presented a brave front, but in truth I was anxious about sharing my friend, summer drawing to an end, and endings in general.

Summer Locke slurped the milk from the cereal bowl. 'Let us go now to the hatch. I would like to see Bibi.'

The Borderland sky clouded and billowed and breezed. Esmeralda was tying flowers to dry, hanging them on strings suspended from the branch of an oak tree. Parked in the place of her burned out bow-top was an almost identical shiny red, green and gold replacement.

'John Pockett found 'er. Grand, eh?' Esmeralda said. 'Now, my chavvies, what can Esmeralda do for you?' The scarring on her arms had faded to a shiny pink.

'I have a question, Bibi.'

'Have you now? And what would that be?'

Summer leapt into the caravan and fetched Esmeralda's pipe. She took it, blew it, packed and lit it.

'Ask away, Summer Locke.'

'Why is it do you want me to go to the *gorgio* school?'

Esmeralda tugged on her clay pipe. 'And why, my chavvie, do you want to know?'

Summer frowned. 'I fear I shall be hemmed in, Bibi.'

Esmeralda nodded sagely.

'Come inside and I shall tell you the answer to that. Robin, my *rakli*, fetch us cups of tea to hasten the telling.'

I swelled with pride to be asked.

'Well now. Travelling children in my time could not read or write because the *gavs* would evict us night and day so we could not go to school. My real-as Mammy – I call her "real-as", as she adopted me – well, my little real-as sister had died, God rest her little soul. This was a terrible shock to us all. It very nearly killed my real-as Mammy. She cried for a whole week till no tears were left. Then she called to me and she said, "Will you go down to the convent, Esmeralda, and ask the nuns for a borrowing of a crucifix to put in the waggon?" I said yes. And she gave me tuppence for the bus fare. I was in my bare feet. I had some big rips in my clothes. I felt like a clown I did.'

I brought the tea. Esmeralda sipped from the steaming cup.

'I came to the convent. I knocked on the door and I could hear footsteps and a little nun appeared. She was dressed in black robes with a white front. I told the nun the whole story of how my little sister had died of pneumonia. The little nun said she was sorry to hear that and her lovely eyes, wide like saucers, they brimmed with tears. She was truly sorrowed. Then the little nun asked me to come in.'

'Were you frightened, Bibi?'

'Well now, as I walked down the big, long hallway the noise of my two bare feet was echoing all over the place, like the noise of a big heavy duck walking: *clap, slap, clap, slap*. Finally we came to a big room and straight in front of us in the room was a lot of nuns sitting around a table big as this very waggon. They all stared at me. So I took courage. "How the Devil are you?" says I.'

I grinned at the thought.

'Well. They all crossed themselves. I tried to change the words to, "God bless you sisters," but I was so embarrassed you could roast a *hotchiwitch* on my face, it was that hot. So, "It's a grand morning," says I. In fact it was evening. They asked me all about where I lived and how old was I. One asked me, "How many horses have you got, Esmeralda?"

'"Not many horses, sister, but we have the world of donkeys, all in red harness, and two caravans." Then, says the little sister with the big eyes who greeted me at the door, "Have you ever been to school, Esmeralda?"

'"No, Sister, I never went to school but I would like to go to school only the police and corporation won't let us stay for long."

"'Well, I will teach you, Esmeralda," says the little sister with the big eyes, and she presses a crucifix of wood with a gold chain in my hand. "You come here next Monday week at seven o'clock in the evening and I will see to it that you will know all your letters.'"

Esmeralda's face lit up at the thought.

"'Yes, sister, I will come" says I. As I was leaving I said, "Tell me, sister, when will I know it's seven o'clock?" and "Ask someone the time and they will tell you," said the nun. So. Home I went with the crucifix. I handed the crucifix to my mother and she said, "God bless you, Esmeralda."

'They buried my real-as sister next day. Hundreds of Romany were at the graveside. They came in lorries and motor vans, the flashy ones with shiny chrome metal and all.'

Esmeralda paused to refill her pipe and sip the cooling tea.

'On the Monday I was in an awful hurry to get on my clothes. Clean shoes I wore and I put on my good skirt and blouse, all embroidery it was. All day I was asking the time. An old lady was passing and I asked, "What is the time, missus, please?" The old lady said it was twenty to six, so I washed myself and I waited for the bus.

'When it came I got on and the conductor said, "Fares, please." I gave him my penny. "What time is it, conductor, please?" "Twenty to seven," said the conductor. "When will it be seven o'clock?" says I. "In twenty minutes," says he.

'I arrived at the convent and I got off the bus. I knocked at the door and the little nun with the big eyes opened the door.

'"Come in, Esmeralda." And that was the first time I ever was at school.'

Esmeralda closed her eyes and rocked gently.

'Did you go to a class with other children, Bibi?' Summer asked.

'Not in the beginning, my *raklo*. I were on my own. 'Twas but a day or so and I could write my name. At home during the day I would sing all the day to the tune of "Twinkle Twinkle Little Star": *ABCDEFG-HIJK-LMNOP-QRS-TUV-WX-Y and Zed, If you sing along with me, you will learn your A-B-C.* Two days and I could tell the time of the clock myself. Then the little nun asked me, would I like to go to a real classroom with other little girls? I said yes, so the next day for the first time in my life I was in a classroom. When the girls of the class saw me I could hear them whispering to one another, "She is a gyppo."

'I was nearly mad, I was. I shouted, "Ah, shut up your big mouths." It was wrong to treat young ladies that way, but I was glad of standing up for myself, and after a while that day I got settled down to the class.

'Well now, sad to say I was ashamed of my life. But the girls became to like me and we became great pals.

'I really enjoyed being at school. But the *gavmush* and corporation gave my real-as Daddy three days' notice and I had to leave school. One night, when I came back to the waggon, my real-as Daddy said, "Esmeralda, tomorrow is your last day at school." Just like that.'

I tried to imagine what it must have felt like. Esmeralda carried on.

'I was angry, then. "What?" I said. "I am not going to stop going to school." But my real-as Daddy told me, "Well, if you do not stop going you will have to follow the waggons a very long road."

'"Why?" says I, and he says, "Because we are being shifted on Saturday."

'I could not sleep that night. The next morning at school, I told the teacher that this was my last day. She was very upset. At playtime the girls gathered round me, "Please don't leave, Esmeralda." Some of them was crying. I said my goodbyes.

'Well, now I would not be able to go to school. So I said to myself, "I will learn myself how to read proper." Every sweet paper or box with writing on it I would collect them all day. I would stay at the shop windows reading everything. Big words like SURGERY, and BIRMINGHAM and PERSIL AUTOMATIC. What made me angry was words like KNIFE or KNOWLEDGE or PNEUMONIA or CZECHOSLOVAKIA that had silent letters; I would say to myself, the person who made these up was a fool.

From then on, everything I bought, I bought for the words on the wrappings. The rubbish dumps was my teachers. I would collect old newspapers, comics and books. I would rather collect than go to the cinema.'

Esmeralda could make a short story long and a long story longer still. Not boring, just long.

I looked at Summer and Summer looked at me. I had never thought about reading as something you didn't just, well, *know*.

'Well now,' she smiled. 'I can thank only one person for the knowledge I possess, and that person is the little nun. She taught me how to defend the rights of the Romany people. Her work was not in vain. Strange to relate, I never knew the little nun's name. I say God bless her. Now you know why I wish for you to go to the *gorgio* school, Summer Locke, and now my story is ended.' She paused. 'Just one more thing. Never be ashamed of who you are. I was, and now I am ashamed of being ashamed.'

Esmeralda gazed into her teacup, swilling it gently.

'I will go to school, Bibi, and I will never be ashamed.'

I wondered to myself why Summer did not tell Esmeralda that Papa Brockton had taught a lot about words already. Summer had the rudiments of knowledge but without the bad side of schools, without the bullying, the gangs, the exams.

'Well, my chavvies, another thing you will not learn in school. The tea leaves have a picture for you too. See here.'

I looked into her cup. 'A picture?'

Esmeralda pointed with the thin end of her spoon. 'A box shining with treasure. It is deep and it is not deep.'

Well, perhaps I was not looking properly. I didn't say, but all I could see was a little pile of tea leaves in the bottom of Esmeralda's cup.

18
Revelation

You can trust a Romany for your best friend
You can trust a Romany to the end.
He won't rob you, he won't lie,
You can trust him 'til you die. But hate,
betray him and you'll come off worse,
For he may haunt you with a curse.

— anon

Rain poured down on the first day of school as if it too had been on holiday. We galloped down the long drive, and, seeing Summer getting drenched and wearing no waterproof, I was secretly glad of my ugly orange cagoule. A small group of children, all strangers to me, huddled at the bottom of the drive. Indeedy had insisted on coming with us, even though I had begged her not to. She grumbled as the school coach squeaked to a stop, the windows opaque with mud. 'You'd think they'd at least clean the windows for the first week of term. Like going to school in a brown stain,' Indeedy said, wrinkling her nose. Inside, the driver stared at us, his last pick-up group, as we found our seats. I waved at Indeedy and Boddy through the mud-spattered windows. Twenty minutes of bendy blind corners taken at breakneck speed, and out we tumbled.

Summer and I registered in the same form. A kindly prefect directed us to our classroom. Summer Locke said, 'Let us sit here in the front.' A thin ray of sunlight shone through the windows, picking out dust and tiny specks swirling in the air. Students began straggling in, exploding with gossip and giggles. It was impossible not to notice how pointedly we were ignored.

A mad dash for desks at the back began as the Deputy Head entered. 'Good morning, class, and welcome back!' Mr Precious wore brown tweeds and gold-rimmed spectacles. You could imagine him living at the school, sleeping in the library, dusted down and smelling of paper like a beloved book. 'Remember the old saying, lads and lassies, if you want to sit up front be early, but if you want to sit at the back be even earlier!'

The class groaned. Summer Locke gazed downwards. I examined the contents of my pencil box and loosened my school tie, noting that the buttoned-up look was not 'in'. Mr Precious had no problem harnessing us into a semblance of order, being a bit like Mrs Avey – nice but also strict. He opened the green registration book and called out the names, proceeding with stern patience, stopping sometimes to make comment – 'My, my, four Davies in the form, a record, I believe' – and discovering who was missing already on the first day of term. Eventually he reached 'L'.

'Locke, Summer. New to us here, are you not?'

Summer Locke stood. 'Yes, sir, that I am, sir.'

'Tell us something about yourself, Summer Locke.'

Summer's promise to Esmeralda rang in my head.

'I am a Romany Gypsy, sir,' Summer said, 'and I am come to school to learn.'

A charged silence.

'And what would you like to learn?' Mr Precious enquired.

'Everything, sir.'

'And what would you like to do with this learning?'

'I would like to become a veterinarian, sir.'

'Welcome, then, and good luck to you, Summer Locke. You may take your seat.'

Mr Precious returned to the register.

'Scholefield, John. Smith, Emma. Swallow, Robin.' He paused. 'Ah, another new name.' Mr Precious peered over the top of the spectacles perched on his nose.

'Yes, sir.' I stood.

'And where do you hale from, Robin Swallow?'

'London, sir.'

'And you, young lady, are you happy with this move to the country?'

I looked directly at Mr Precious. 'Yes, sir, very happy. My mother has just started a food catering company.'

'How splendid. And your father?'

'My father is gone away, sir.' I just couldn't say *dead*.

'I'm sorry to hear that. And will you be a caterer too when you've finished your schooling?'

'No, sir. I would like to be a space journalist, or private investigator. Or an environmental pathologist.' I pulled the last one from thin air.

'Most intriguing.' Mr Precious smiled, closed the register and clasped it to his waistcoated middle. Without raising his voice, he recited to the class the monotonous necessities of school life: cafeteria rules, lunch passes, bus passes, playground restrictions, attendance regulations. 'Any questions?' Silence. 'No? Well then, wait here please for your new form teacher. Her name is Miss Withers, and she is also your R.E. teacher once a week.' At that he strode from the room.

He was scarcely through the door when, without warning, *thwack!* on the back of Summer's head from a heavy satchel.

'Gyppo,' snarled the source of the blow.

Without thinking, I sprang with a reflex leap and set about him with my fists. I was about to sink my teeth in his arm when Miss Withers entered.

'What on earth is – Enough!' she cried.

Summer Locke prised me from the new enemy. 'Sorry, miss. It was a misunderstanding, miss.'

'No it ain't,' growled the mousy-haired assailant. 'This one's a gyppo and my dah says they are all thieving no-goods. They stole our chickens last year.'

'Please, miss, but I would like to say that some of my own people are suspicious of housedwellers.'

'Well, you are both wrong,' Miss Withers said. 'What is your name, young man?' she demanded.

'Alan Jones, miss.'

'And your names, please?'

I told her through gritted teeth.

'Sit you down, all of you, this minute,' said Miss Withers. She was a kindly looking dark-haired woman just a bit short of pretty. Frowning, she said, 'I will see the three of you at the end of class and we shall sort things out.'

Miss Withers then asked us each what we would like to learn from her – how to be a pop star, miss, how to be a millionaire, miss, how to be a superstar footballer,miss. She distributed neat green exercise books and instructed us to write our names and our form in the upper right hand corner of the book, black ink please.

'Your first written assignment will be: "What I would like Miss Withers to know about me?". Due next Monday.'

Sighs of 'Homework, already!'

When the others had left, Alan Jones joined Summer and me at Miss Withers' desk.

She asked us what we thought a bully was.

Alan Jones answered first, looking down at his feet. 'My dah is a bully, miss.'

'And you, Summer?' she asked.

'A bully is ignorant and cruel for fear of someone different.'

'And you, Robin?'

'I think a bully thinks that they are stronger and so they torment someone they think is weaker.'

'All these things may be true, but I forbid bullies in this class. I would like you all to shake hands.'

Summer was first to extend a hand. I reluctantly did the same, and Alan Jones followed.

'Thank you,' said Miss Withers. 'I look forward to seeing you all tomorrow.'

I was glad that she didn't say she'd have to phone my mum.

Indeedy had cooked Maryland chicken with mashed potatoes, mushroom gravy and salad. Summer and I were quiet, and Chris Lamb shifted the conversation from 'First day at school' to local news.

'So, team, let me fetch the paper – there's something you'll find interesting. Pucklethorpe Manor may go up for auction as early as Christmas time. And, on page three ... Hey, my article's in. Shall I?'

Chris read aloud:

"'A Case to Answer: Aristocrat to Stand Trial for Murder. The peace of rural Borderland was recently shattered when the brutally battered body of Brockton Wheatley was discovered at Pucklethorpe Manor. Members of the public and interested parties waited in the pouring rain on the final day of committal proceedings being held to establish whether Lady Charlotte Wheatley *née* Bullwar-Lytton should stand trial for the murder of her ex-husband, the historian and local eccentric Brockton Wheatley. After hearing the evidence, prosecuting counsel concluded that "The place of the killing was the kitchen of Pucklethorpe Manor, the house over which the defendant and her ex-husband fought for many years and where the victim lived alone. The defendant was despairing of ever getting her hands on the property. The prosecution aver that the evidence discloses a case for this defendant to answer."'

'So she'll definitely stand trial?' I asked.

Chris closed the newspaper. 'Yes, Robin. I think it most likely that she killed him. But we must accept that she's innocent until proven guilty, as well as taking into account other possibilities, that is, a killer who is *not* Charlotte Bullwar-Lytton, unless she disguised herself in male apparel. There's Winitoo's story of … what's his name – Pricker?'

'Stinger!' I laughed.

'I'm intrigued. What makes you so certain it was Lady Charlotte?' said Indeedy.

'On the balance of probabilities,' Chris said. 'Three reasons. One, she hated her ex. Two, it's on anecdotal but reliable record that she wanted rid of him. Three, there's a direct link between her and the probable murder weapon. And lastly, it may be hearsay, but someone said she hid in the grounds until Dr Whelan left.'

Summer smiled. 'You said three reasons and that's four.'

Chris ignored Summer. 'Her legal team plan to dismiss all the circumstantial evidence as "colourful tales". This is all *sub judice*, as they say, and it could be just bravado and a good legal act. She also asked the court to consider whether there might have been another person in the house after the invited visitor left – perhaps a "border itinerant"?'

Chris paused, eyes directly on Summer Locke.

Summer, eyes averted. 'Is that the end?'

'There's more, quote: "As the magistrates gave their verdict at the pre-trial hearing, Charlotte Bullwar-Lytton showed dignity, her face pale and expressionless. The trial is set for late October in the Crown Courts."'

'Summer,' said Chris, 'why won't you just go to the police and tell them what you know?'

Summer didn't look up.

Chris's agitation flushed her face. 'Summer Locke, you may be the only person on this planet who knows what happened. If you do know something it is your duty to tell the truth. I'm a journalist. The truth matters. People should know.'

No response.

'Tell you what, I'm going to pull all the stops out, speak to Lady Charlotte again.'

That made Summer look up. 'Miss Chris, at this very time, my elders are seeking the guilty person and I am bound to respect the ways of my people.'

Indeedy reached for Summer's hand. 'Would it help if I went to the police on your behalf? You can tell me what you know, and I will tell them.'

'Won't work – hearsay,' said Chris.

Summer shrank away.

'If you do that, Mrs Swallow, I will disappear and you will never see me again.'

What exactly *did* Summer know? I was not sure but I felt fiercely protective of my friend.

'Please, Mum. Please. We must wait.'

And so we did. Like priests keeping silence over a confession. Indeedy and Chris trusted us. Is this rare? I don't know, but they did. We waited.

Later, together and out of earshot of the grown-ups, Summer opened up.

'She did not put her own hands upon Papa Brockton. She did much worse.'

'What? Trust me, Summer. You can tell me.'

"T'was blood money.'

I sensed Summer wanted to tell me, I just needed to push at the door a little. So I did.

'Do you want to tell me, Summer? Finish from where you left off, a million years ago?'

Summer looked at me. Then nodded.

'So, after Dr Whelan was with Papa Brockton on that day, I went to the hatch, as you recall. I was no more than an hour and then back to Papa. When I returned, the kitchen light was lit and the outer door open. Papa *never* left this door open. He had changed the locks and gave me the extra set and all.'

Summer tugged on the leather thong necklace and pulled out the keys, as if to demonstrate.

'So I knew something was not right. I ran swift-like but quiet as a stone, to the door. Robin, you remember I told you about the crowbar? Well, the crowbar was *gone*.'

'Was it definitely there when you went off to the hatch?' My mind raced. It was weird the way they said Lady Charlotte carried it around with her like some people carry a walking stick. 'You said you saw Lady Charlotte leave when you went to the hatch?'

'Aye it was there when I had seen her go, and then it was not. I heard a rustling noise, like rats scuttling across a ceiling. I slipped in the entrance. The inside door stood ajar, open this wide.' Summer made a two-handed wedge. 'I drew courage and peered round the edge of the door.' Summer paused. Then, 'Blood there was, Robin, blood in pools on the floor, spattered on the legs of the table, on the top amongst the vegetables.'

I wanted to say 'Stop, enough', as if by stopping Summer from telling me I could prevent what had happened.

Summer captured my eyes and did not flinch.

'I saw the sole of Papa's shoe; jamming the door, it was. I could not stay my eyes and where they took me.'

Then Summer began to tremble all over.

'Here,' I said. 'Sit right here.' I put my hand in Summer's cool hand, held it. 'You don't have to tell.' A big part of me didn't want to know. But the small part won. 'And you were in danger for your life,' I encouraged.

Summer nodded yes. 'There he was. A man with scragetty hair and a headband, bending over Papa. He was doing something to his face.'

The colour drained from Summer's face.

'Robin, I believe that he *sensed* me watching. He jumped up, fit as a cat he was, and moved to the kitchen window. I hid in the shadows. Then, sudden like, as if he stopped worrying, he moves back over to Papa dead on the floor and mocks, "Now, sir. *Now* may I take a sandwich?"'

'A *sandwich*?'

'Papa Wheatley had a custom of inviting ramblers and the like to take tea and a sandwich,' Summer said.

'The man was covered in blood, all calm. No more did he wash his bloody hands than did he look at Papa's body. He gobbled the sandwich like a wild starved thing. Then he picked up …'

'The crowbar?'

Summer nodded, yes. 'He began to come towards my hiding spot, but something stopped him. Did he entertain second thoughts? Was he thinking to make his exit through the same door he entered? I shall never know in this life. Anyway he slipped his boots off, picked them up and turned round and tiptoed through the kitchen door into the hall and to the front door.'

'Do you think he saw you?'

'If he had, I would not be here now. But sure I am that he sensed another pair of eyes was watching.'

I thought, no, Summer is wrong, it isn't possible that if he sensed it the killer would not come back to look for the 'pair of eyes'.

'Robin, have you ever seen a dead person?'

'No. Just birds and such like. And Bibi Esmeralda – but she turned out not to be dead after all.' It wasn't a good time to mention my many failures at saving baby birds.

'I had to see if Papa still breathed. So, I waited until I heard the front door close, and in I went. The blood was everywhere. At first I was sure he was breathing and so I spoke to him, "Papa, Papa, you will be mended. I will phone the ambulance for you." But he could not move and he was not breathing. And the man who killed him had ... had ...'

'Had what?'

'He had taken the photograph from Papa's eyes,' Summer said.

'What do you mean, Summer? No riddles, please,' I begged.

Summer sighed. 'He had poked Papa's eyes out.'

I felt a wave of nausea sweep through me. 'But Mr Wheatley was blind! I don't understand.'

'Some believe that a Romany who has sunk so low as to kill another human being would poke the eyes out,' Summer said. 'Then the dead one would not have a picture of the murderer to carry across to heaven and damn the killer forever. But this man was not a Roma. I recognized him, Robin. I know who he was. It was Stinger.'

'And you didn't phone the police!' I was struggling to understand. Summer Locke knew who the murderer was?

'What I did was this: I raced across the back fields to the hatch. King brewed me some cowslip tea, held me in a hug and tucked me away on the bunk. Then he called out to the waggons of the three elders for an emergency *kriss*. They thought I was asleep but I was not. I turned my face to the wall and stared at it.'

'You should have phoned the police! We can do it now! Or at least tell my mum. Let's go!' I repeated.

'No and no and no! How many times must I say to you that my people have our own laws, supreme and above yours?' Summer Locke seemed to visibly sag, and moved to get up.

I plumped the pillow and slid into my bed. 'Here, take this. Don't go to your room.' I suddenly did not want to be alone. I knew I would not sleep, or I would dream of the horrors Summer had described. 'We can top and tail it here. That way we have a bit more room.'

Summer accepted. In no time, we were prone. I tweaked Summer's toe.

'What did they decide? The elders?'

'To make a plan.'

'Plan?'

No answer. Summer Locke lay still, toes stuck close to the head of the bed and next to my pillow. And before I could even make a feeble joke about smelly feet, we were both sound asleep.

19
Veracity

You have to make up your own rules and follow them; that's not as easy as it sounds.

– attributed to Mark Twain

Summer Locke lapped up school like a thirsty puppy. We did not speak again of what Summer had told me, and by unspoken agreement we did not visit the manor again. Instead, we spent our time devising our own subjects: geography (the hills all alive); biology (bodies, natural and otherwise); maths (looking out of the window, a lot); history (Gypsies haven't got it in this school); English (ripping yarns).

Summer's favourite was Miss Withers' RE class.

'Cain must have been a Romany, miss.' … 'Abraham must have been a Romany, miss.' … 'Moses must have been a Romany, miss.' … 'Jesus, he must have been a Romany too, miss. Look, miss, it says here, "The foxes have holes and the birds have nests but the Son of God hath no place to lay his head.'"

'No wonder they crucified the geezer,' muttered Alan Jones to a chorus of chuckles. Miss Withers' gentle protestations about historical inevitability and the rise of cities and houses being really quite useful impressed Summer Locke not one little bit. Miss Withers took to calling us 'teacher's pests', a term of endearment, she assured us.

Discussion time took an interesting turn with the Ten Commandments. Miss Withers distributed her version of the "Moses Code": 'I have paraphrased the commandments, class – meaning that I'm putting something into my own words.'

1. Choose one God and stick by your choice.
2. Don't be tricked into worshipping things like cars, or money or buildings or people (idols).
3. Don't swear.
4. Put your feet up at least once a week. God did.
5. Respect your parents; parents respect your children.
6. Do not kill.
7. Only have sex with your beloved (no adultery).
8. Do not steal.
9. Telling lies is wrong.
10. Don't waste time wishing you had something that belongs to someone else.

She asked us to take the Moses Code home and think of something Moses had left out, preferably a rule in our own homes. 'Ask your families what they think.'

I liked this idea, and Indeedy was full of ideas, of course, but for our class it didn't work very well. Country children apparently did not talk around the dinner table like city children. I was the only city girl. Even so, a few of them brought in a commandment Moses didn't think of.

Ellen Davies, daughter of a Baptist minister, raised her hand.

'Yes, Ellen.'

'I have not made a rule, as my dah says this is the Word of God and we've not to add or subtract from God's word.'

Miss Withers smiled. 'You're quite right to point this out, Ellen. This exercise was not intended as a challenge to your faith but a way of understanding things a bit better.'

Alan Jones was certain he knew. 'I know a command old man Moses forgot.'

'Is it a bit disrespectful to say old man Moses, Alan?' Miss Withers never called God *Him*.

'Mr Moses then. I know what he forgot.'

'And what would that be, Alan?'

'Spare the rod and spoil the child.'

'Raise hands all who agree with Alan's rule.'

I didn't raise my hand but Summer did.

'Robin, you disagree. Would you like to say why?'

'My mum never hit me or my brother Zach, miss, and I don't think we're spoiled.'

'That's what you get for doing your own thinking,' mocked a voice at the back.

'My people love spoiling us. We run wild as the foxes,' said Summer. 'But if we fall foul, our elders will give us a thump, no doubt.'

'Any other rules?'

Summer's hand shot up, keen to participate as always. 'Summer Locke?'

'I have thought of three,' said Summer, opening a notebook. 'One: never be cruel. Two: if you do not want to be hurt, you must not hurt anybody. Three: do not dwell in a house unless you must.'

Miss Withers sighed. 'Thank you, Summer Locke.'

I put my hand up. 'I have one, Miss Withers.'

'Please tell us, Robin.'

'Don't look down on other people.'

Miss Withers nodded and gazed out of the window. 'The best and most difficult of all rules.'

Half-term coincided with the trial of Charlotte Bullwar-Lytton and everywhere buzzed with gossip. Chris was going to cover the story. She said we should come along too, that we'd learn something. My first court trial, ever. Indeedy packed us a lunch.

'Are you sure you're up for this, Fruit?'

'Yes.'

'Well, take your school satchels and exercise books. That way, if anyone objects about your ages you just say it's an assignment from your teacher.'

Chris grabbed her cheese sandwiches. 'See you there, then. I've got to get there early.'

'Where do we go?'

'Bus stops in the square, you can't miss it. You should be there in good time but don't mess about. I've heard seating is dire, only about twenty for the public gallery.'

I ran upstairs to get dressed.

The Borderland Rover bounced roughly along the lanes. Summer had brought a copy of *Animal Farm*, one of the books we had been set as homework.

'I've already read everything on the list,' I bragged.

'Well, then you will be minded to help us all, to be sure,' said Summer.

A huge statue dominated the city square. 'That statue,' said Summer, 'is William Wilberforce, who ended slavery in England.' The statue's left hand extended directly towards the Crown Court. The entrance hall hummed with black-robed barristers swooping like crows. Men in grey suits with tense faces and books under their arms darted between groups. In one corner was a trestle table where handsome women in winter coats and woolly hats served steamy drinks. A cardboard sign read 'Tiptovia Womens' Institute'. They get everywhere, I thought. We marched into the fray just as a long black limousine pulled up beside the grand entrance.

'That's the Red Judge come,' said someone.

'What is his name?' whispered Summer to a kindly looking person.

'Why, child, that's Lord Justice Fieldsend.'

Indeedy need not have feared. A steward directed us to the public gallery, no questions asked. Narrow stairs led to a cramped balcony with five rows of wooden benches. The gallery door squeaked noisily.

'Look, Summer, you can see your breath it's that cold.'

'Leave your coats on, chooks,' whispered someone behind us. Mrs Spicer! 'Couldn't miss it either, now could I?' She winked, and nudged Summer, removing a tea towel from her wicker basket: Scotch eggs, chicken drumsticks and fruit. 'A little something to keep us going,' she beamed.

'Thank you, Mrs Spicer.' It would be rude to say we had sandwiches already.

'My Toby's collecting me at four. Would you like a lift?'

'Yes please.' This way I'm thinking, it won't matter if we miss the one single afternoon bus going our way.

The vastness of the court contrasted sharply with our cramped space in the gallery. Opposite where we sat, on a rostrum in the curve of the court, was the High

Judge's chair like a throne, above it a tall canopy topped by a dusty gold crown on a purple velvet curtain with the initials 'ER II'. There was a second chair too, less grand but in a design matching the Judge's seat. Along the right-hand gallery were the journalists, mostly men – recorders and notebooks poised. Chris Lamb arrived, joined them, saw us and winked discreetly.

Mrs Spicer groaned and shifted on the bench. 'Just be happy you're young, the both of you. It's only the first day and already me bum is numb – bring a cushion next time, I will.'

In the centre of the court was a sort of fancy open trap-door contraption. 'That's the dock. They don't make 'em like that any more,' whispered Mrs Spicer. 'All the cells are down there, under the floor.'

Just then the trap door opened. The top of a head, then a whole person in uniform emerged. Then Lady Charlotte herself, followed by another uniformed officer. She looked just like her pictures in the news, sort of pale and fragile but quite pretty for an old person if I'm honest.

Lady Charlotte took her place as defendant and set her spectacle case, pen and notebook in a tidy row on the table. She did not remove her coat. Then the jurors filed in. Until then, Lady Charlotte had seemed unaware of her surroundings, but as they took their seats she lifted her spectacles and stared at each juror as if she were examining creepy-crawlies. We all stood as Lord Justice Fieldsend entered, bewigged and in a red gown crossed with a broad black sash and white kerchief at the throat. We were invited to take our seats.

We sat, but nothing seemed to happen. I fidgeted. 'When's it starting properly?' I asked a trifle too loudly.

'Shhh-hhh!' from all around me.

They read the murder charge against Lady Charlotte Bullwar-Lytton. Mr Roger Scrivener, QC, for the prosecution, boomed *basso profundo* like a Shakespearean actor.

'The deceased, Brockton Wheatley, was a man whom the defendant had grown to hate, because he would not leave the house owned by the defendant and shared throughout their marriage. The defendant came to despair of his ever voluntarily vacating the premises.'

The next bit was very hard to listen to. Summer held my hand while Mr Scrivener went into detail about the way that Mr Brockton Wheatley died. It was a blunt instrument to his head and neck. The fatal blow was to the side of Brockton's head and also possibly the throat. He told how for mysterious reasons the victim's eyes were gouged out, possibly after his death – an act made more grisly because Mr Wheatley was virtually blind. There was no apparent forced entry to the house on the night in question. Nothing was stolen. Brockton Wheatley had been found dead on the floor with a modest amount of cash left untouched in his pocket. There was, however, the QC argued, clearly a motive to see Mr Wheatley dead: profit.

There would be two primary witnesses: Dr Rupert Whelan, who would appear in due course and confirm that on the night of the murder the defendant had behaved in an unreasonable and threatening manner; and Mr Wheatley's secretary, who had found the victim's body.

I nudged Summer sharply with my elbow and whispered, 'Only two main witnesses!' For once my mouth engaged my brain and I didn't add the obvious. Summer winced at my unspoken reproach.

Mr Scrivener was very persuasive, and at this early stage it seemed clear to us that Lady Charlotte would be found guilty. But she didn't seem bothered one little bit. She just sat there, cool and still, sketching on her notebook pad and occasionally smoothing her shiny hair.

In fact, it transpired that there were more than the two main witnesses to listen to. There were members of Borderland Constabulary in charge of the police end of things, including Constable Corteena, who glanced our way, rewarding us with a small nod. Constable Corteena brought up suspicious behaviour; Lady Bullwar-Lytton had swept her chimney on the weekend in question. Was this necessary in order to burn evidence? She had painted her crowbar with

Hammerite that weekend. Was this to disguise any forensic evidence? Brockton's cleaning lady was called up, and reinforced the impression of Lady Charlotte's continuing unkindnesses, as had his secretary, who went into detail about discovering Mr Wheatley's body and the horrifying fact of defiling the eyes of a blind man. Was this to deflect suspicion in the direction of the Romany Gypsies?

Dr Rupert Whelan testified next. The archaeologist was tall and dapper with his white handlebar moustache. Exactly what time did he arrive and leave? He recalled that as he approached the house Lady Charlotte 'emerged as if from nowhere' with a crowbar over her arm. When Dr Whelan enquired as to the purpose of the crowbar, she claimed it was 'for clearing brambles'.

What impression did Lady Charlotte leave with him?

'She was quite aggressive,' he testified, 'particularly when we were in the cellar – threatening, shouting and raving.'

Did Brockton Wheatley seem disturbed by his ex-wife's behaviour? Dr Whelan thought not – Mr Wheatley had said that his ex-wife's erratic behaviour was unfortunately the rule rather than the exception.

Did Mr Wheatley expect any other visitors that evening? Yes, perhaps. There was a young Romany who had been present when he arrived but left before him. Brockton Wheatley was expecting someone, possibly the young Gypsy, to return, or perhaps someone else.

Dr Whelan was not certain whether Mr Wheatley had meant the same evening or another time. He observed that he may have been the last person to see Brockton Wheatley alive. However, when Dr Whelan left, he was certain that Lady Charlotte was still on the property.

No more questions. Dr Rupert Whelan clicked his heels, military fashion, bowed his head to Judge Fieldsend, and made his exit.

We had all been listening avidly in the gallery as Dr Whelan spoke, particularly when Summer was mentioned.

'He is a very kind man,' whispered Summer.

Last, on what was beginning to seem the longest day ever, came the forensic report. Enter the expert witness, a Dr Norman Wigglesworth. He hoisted a massive folder of notes onto the witness box. His forensics team had taken two hundred samples of fibre and hair from the kitchen and surroundings at Pucklethorpe Manor. Some of these samples remained unaccounted for. They had examined the body of the deceased on the scene. In a monotone voice, Dr Wigglesworth described the position of each of the injuries to the body. You'd think he was reading a laundry list or something, he was that deadpan.

In Dr Wigglesworth's opinion, a crowbar, or similar implement, was most likely to have caused the victim's head wounds. 'If wielded by a man,' he said, 'I would have expected a skull fracture.' The grisly mutilation of the victim's eyes was most likely executed by 'human digits'. The crowbar that Lady Charlotte possessed had been analysed for forensic evidence. Dr Wigglesworth concluded that he could find no positive forensic or DNA connection with the accused. At that point, Charlotte looked up, with just the hint of a smile, first at Dr Wigglesworth, then at the jury.

Mrs Spicer whispered, 'One big point to the defence.'

As Dr Wigglesworth left the court, I was dead certain I saw him wink in Lady Charlotte's direction.

'Now, Robin Swallow, might you begin to understand why my people have no truck with *gorgio* laws?'

That night I dreamed of ghoulish creatures all in black, flitting like bats. I woke, troubled, wondering what it was all for. Summer had retreated to bed early and silently. The world of trials and lawyers seemed far too complicated. I could not comprehend what seemed to be the facts of the matter: that if Lady Charlotte Bullwar-Lytton were not proven to be a liar in court, and found guilty of murder, it would not be because she was *not* guilty. Plus, the actual killer would still be on the loose. Surely she *was* guilty? But would a court of law *find* her guilty of murder if they concluded that she did not commit the murder *with her own hands*? If Summer saw clearly, and spoke truthfully, it was someone else with blood on their hands. But wasn't she still guilty? I began to comprehend that the law, with all its majestic courts and grand judges, might be unable to deal with right and wrong, because what would be right and proper would be a second person, the hitman, right there in court, standing beside Lady Charlotte Bullwar-Lytton.

But Summer Locke alone knew the whole truth. And Summer Locke had no trust in *gorgio* law.

I knew there was nothing I could do. Summer Locke would never tell. So neither could I.

Right or wrong, I would be keeping my promise to Summer Locke.

Shhh-hhh.

20
Litigation

The first thing we do, let's kill all the lawyers.

– Henry VI Part Two, William Shakespeare

Do you ever wake to a day already worn out? The next morning Summer seemed OK, but I felt fuzzy, vague, listless. Like Aunt Martha used to say on those tired, tepid Tennessee summer days, my get up and go had got up and gone. Indeedy noted my demeanour at breakfast, my favourite pancakes and maple syrup, and tried to persuade us to stay home, which made me feel guilty. No! I protested. I must be there, with Summer.

In the courtroom, the second day began with us in the gallery counting dust motes on the ceiling while in some back room they showed a police film of the murder scene. It was to be viewed only by the jurors, a selection of journalists and the rest of the main players in the case, including Lady Charlotte herself. Finally they all filed in. Day two. The turn of the defence.

Charlotte's barrister opened the proceedings. Katherine Burt, QC, had a barrister's wig perched atop a flame of red hair.

'Lady Bullwar-Lytton has asked the court to accept that she does not wish any of her children to be called as witnesses. This is because she does not want them to suffer the trauma of giving evidence on her behalf. Her son, who was with her on the day of and following the incident, will not testify for this reason.' Then she referred to Lady Charlotte's alibi – she had gone home to watch a detective film, '*Inspector Morse*, was it not?' With a wry smile and a nod to the jurors, the barrister remarked, 'Perhaps we could benefit from the good Inspector's investigative skills now?' Quiet murmurs and smiles from the jury greeted this observation.

Lady Charlotte was called to the stand. She moved to the witness box confidently like a ballet dancer walks when not performing, toes turned slightly outward, balanced, very erect. When she spoke, her voice was quiet and precise. Justice Fieldsend asked her to speak up. She claimed she could not speak more loudly, so the judge suggested she be moved closer to him to the seat on his left. This seat, whispered Mrs Spicer, was where visiting dignitaries would ordinarily sit. Summer and I exchanged glances. It didn't seem right that someone accused of murder should sit next to a Red Judge.

'Suit her fine,' humphed Mrs Spicer. 'Thinks she's the almighty still small voice, she does.'

'She possesses a big voice when she wishes, like a honking goose,' said Summer Locke. It was nice to be the one saying Shhh-hh! to Summer.

Lady Charlotte continued to speak so quietly that I was trying to lip-read. Even the court clerk requested a microphone. The judge gestured that Lady Charlotte take a seat, but she refused.

'Your Honour, I prefer to stand. My ex-husband once beat me so hard that I suffer severely and the pain is much worse when I sit.'

Could this be true? The accusations got worse. She painted a very crude picture of Brockton Wheatley, claiming he was increasingly aggressive, an unloving husband and father. That he liked wearing lipstick and make-up 'when we were alone in the house'.

Scrivener: 'Objection, your Honour.'

Judge Fieldsend: 'Overruled.'

I was confused. Summer was frantic. 'What is this to do with anything?'

'Shush,' calmed Mrs Spicer. 'She is trying to make out he was … well, er … that he was a man of unusual tastes.' She paused. 'Come to think, though, Father Michael wears a long frock every Sunday and nobody minds.'

Lady Charlotte continued her testimony. 'My ex-husband was frequently unreasonable and sullen. He neglected our children over the years, unless he wished to attend to thrashings, calling it corporal punishment. He was a sullen and mean person and we had no social life whatever.' All was spoken in a tiny monotone.

'Thank you, Lady Bullwar-Lytton,' Katherine Burt said. 'That is all.'

Judge Fieldsend called a recess. As the jurors filed out, I looked at Summer. 'You should be speaking on his behalf.'

'They would not believe me.'

I thought, Lady Charlotte has drawn a picture of Mr Wheatley as a monster and torn his character to shreds, which was not fair, not one little bit. That was not the man Summer Locke described as the kindly Papa Brockton. Why were no friends given a chance in court to contradict Lady Charlotte and stop her turning him into a monster?

'Who else knows what you know, Summer?'

'No one but the elders,' said Summer. 'But it makes no difference. The *gorgio* lawyer asks all the wrong questions.'

'*You* could've helped him ask the right ones.'

After recess came what's known as cross-examination. Mrs Spicer poured out tea from a steaming flask and passed us the mug.

'The real test comes now,' she whispered.

'Lady Charlotte, is it not true that you hated your ex-husband?'

Lady Charlotte was calm and confident. 'No, I did not hate him. I felt shocked and thwarted that he would not leave my home because I needed to sell it.'

Scrivener peered at her over the top of his spectacles. 'There was, was there not, a persistent war of wills between you?'

'Yes. I think you are correct in that view.' Her eye contact was calm, impressive and unblinking.

'You were obsessed by the notion that he was going to stay there as long as he could.'

'"Obsessed"? No. I was just entirely fed up.'

'You are a woman of persevering character?'

'Yes. In my life, perseverance has been necessary.'

'You say your ex-husband had mistreated you and the children?'

'He had, yes.'

I looked at Summer, who shrugged, *I don't know.*

'Any love that existed before had gone out of the marriage long ago, had it not?'

'Yes.'

'Did you think him insane?'

'Yes.'

'Since when?'

Lady Charlotte spoke to Roger Scrivener as if addressing a tiresome family servant. At one stage I thought she might yawn. 'Since approximately a year before I began divorce proceedings, Mr Scrivener.'

The barrister ignored her disdain. 'You were both furious and out of control with your ex-husband on the night of his death, were you not?'

Under her breath: 'Dog's bollocks, Mr Scrivener.'

There was another shiver of gasps and titters throughout the courtroom. Lady Charlotte's stage whisper carried more clearly than her other responses. I thought it was the 'out of control' bit that pushed her buttons.

'Order in the court!' Judge Fieldsend reprimanded.

'I beg your pardon?' shouted Scrivener, voice several notes higher than his customary baritone. Then, with rapier timing, Lady Charlotte replied. 'With due respect, I say you are incorrect, Mr Scrivener.'

Judge Fieldsend wrote something down, face averted. Roger Scrivener rubbed his chin and repeated his accusations of anger on Charlotte's part.

'This is just a case of a roomful of men ganging up against a woman,' accused Lady Charlotte.

'With all due respect, my honourable colleague and your lawyer,' responded Scrivener, gesturing towards Katherine Burt, 'is clearly not a man.'

'She might as well be,' said Charlotte, seemingly unaware that she was insulting her own team.

'Clearly she is not a man, but I have had more than my share of men turning against women. As the firstborn child I should be entitled to the family legacy. But it was passed on to a feckless younger sibling who is male. And to think, my forebears were the pioneers bringing the vote to women in this country.'

Mr Scrivener ignored her outburst. 'Please simply answer my questions, madam.'

Muffled whispers stirred the courtroom again. Judge Fieldsend glowered. 'For the final time, silence in the court, please! Mr Scrivener, will you simply address the subject at hand?'

'Apologies, your Honour.' Scrivener strode over to Lady Charlotte. 'You despised your ex-husband, did you not?'

He's repeating himself, I thought.

'No. I did not. I was exasperated by him, but I did not hate or despise him. I felt nothing for him any more.'

'The evidence we have heard from witnesses is that on that Friday night you were angry.'

'I suggest the evidence is wrong. I am telling the truth. I do wish you would get it into your little head, Mr Scrivener, that I was *not* angry.'

Little head! This woman had nerves of steel.

Lady Charlotte turned to the jury. 'Why should I hold affection for those who wished me ill? There was one in particular, a young Gypsy who moved into the house and was the bane of my life, who brought ponies and goats to graze my land. This child insisted on taking visitors round my house when it was in a most appalling state. I am all for visitors going round my home when it is clean and tidy, but not when it is a complete slum. I think it sets a terrible example of how one should live.'

Summer sank low on the bench, but Roger Scrivener ignored Lady Charlotte's outburst and the Gypsy reference.

'I do not suggest you planned over any length of time to kill Mr Wheatley. I am however suggesting that things were building up in your mind so that you had a confrontation with him that Friday night and that is when you killed him, because you felt extremely stifled and frustrated.'

'No. I was *neither* stifled *nor* frustrated. At no time that day was I stifled.'

'You were still somehow sad over the end of your marriage, however?'

'Yes, perhaps one always regrets failures.'

'And you realized that when two people both regarded the other as mad, one was bound to be injured by the other? Which is why you carried the crowbar?'

I quite liked the way most of Mr Scrivener's questions sounded like statements of assumed fact.

'No, it was not. My ex-husband was determined never to move from my house. I regarded him as even madder than in the past. On the night of his death I did wait for his visitor to go, but not so I would know that he was alone. My son and I were in fact just going for a little walk to admire the work we had done on the house.'

I poked Summer. 'She didn't answer about the crowbar.'

Summer shrugged once more. *Shh-hh.* I *shh-hh*-ed Summer right back.

Roger Scrivener appeared tired and a little distracted, but also he seemed to be trying to put words into Lady Charlotte's mouth. 'I put it to you that there was no reason for you to be there other than watching your former spouse to ascertain that he was alone in the house.'

'You are painting a false story.'

Things were getting nasty. Mr Scrivener rocked back and forth from toe to heel.

'You went there the next morning because you knew your ex-husband was dead.'

'No. I did not.'

'You went to Pucklethorpe Manor the next morning with your son when Brockton Wheatley lay dead. You returned to the scene of your crime.'

'That is not true. We returned, but for entirely innocent reasons.'

Very strangely, it seemed to me, Mr Scrivener didn't ask about Lady Charlotte's 'entirely innocent reasons'. He changed his approach, pointing out inconsistencies between her first and second interviews with the police.

Lady Charlotte replied sharply, still without raising her voice. 'There is no inconsistency no matter how much you twist it. Now. You must stop it, Mr Scrivener!'

Because she was standing in a high place, and beside the Red Judge, she seemed somehow taller than the Crown Prosecutor, and, to me at least, believable. Still, there was a collective gasp from the assembled, presumably at her impertinence. Her barrister, meanwhile, remained silent.

Mr Scrivener attempted to regain dominance, but Lady Charlotte seemed more and more confident. The following assertions and questions – that she returned to the scene of the crime in order to remove evidence; that she swept her chimney over the weekend at her cottage for the same reason – had lost their edge.

'Summer, he forgot the crowbar!' I said again, outraged.

Shhh–hhh.

'I suggest to you, Lady Charlotte, that you returned to Pucklethorpe Manor that morning to see that Brockton Wheatley was dead and to remove any remaining evidence.'

'You may suggest whatever you wish and until hell freezes over but your suggestions do not make it true. It makes no sense whatsoever, Mr Scrivener, for me to have killed him. The courts were going to see him evicted. I believed it was finally happening for the first time in many years. This was a crime I had nothing to do with. I didn't even have a motive.'

Mrs Spicer tutted. 'There's your jury going for not guilty, hook line and sinker. You just watch.'

I was horrified at the prospect. Surely not?

By now Lady Charlotte was on a roll. 'Listen. I agree I had the opportunity and a weapon, but there are millions of crowbars in the world. Why should I have killed him? Think of all the hassle I have had since. It would have been much easier to let the courts deal with him. I was stunned when they arrested me. I am innocent of this charge.'

These were Charlotte Bullwar-Lytton's closing words. Court adjourned until the next day.

Outside, I felt a second wind, eager now to get home and chew events over in private. I had so much I needed to say. We bumped into Chris Lamb.

'Chris, why has the gold bar thing not come up in court?' I asked the first thing off the top of my head.

Chris ran her fingers through her hair. 'Good question. I'm not sure. Perhaps they think it's not relevant? The prosecution seem to have leapt on all the wrong points, anyway. Remember Gordy Garden? She could've knocked him off too because he knew something. Look, not meaning to be rude but shall we talk about this later? I've got copy to finish for tomorrow.'

'OK. But just one thing, Chris. Summer says Mr Wheatley had lots of friends who would say how lovely he was, nothing like the monster painted by Lady Charlotte. Why didn't anyone have a chance to speak up for him?'

Summer had disappeared over to the bus stop.

'Another very good question. Don't know the answer, Robin, and from the sound of it neither does Summer. Who were these people who would speak for him? He kept himself to himself, as far as I know. What I do know, though, is that this is pretty typical; courts are often prone to summoning the wrong people and missing out those who can actually help. Anyway must rush, *ciao*!' Chris was off.

I joined Summer at the bus stop. We returned home, silent. Summer went upstairs as soon as we got back. I sat with Boddy for a while, stroking her in front of the Rayburn.

Later, when I checked upstairs, Summer Locke was fast asleep.

My sleep came slowly. Guilty? Not guilty?

Tomorrow seemed a million years away.

21
Verdict

Q: I am often broken without being held. What am I?
A: A promise.

The final day of the trial dawned. At breakfast I couldn't eat anything and none of us even attempted our usually chirpy small talk. I wouldn't say I felt ominous, but I definitely didn't feel like dancing a jig. Once outside the courthouse, Summer and I walked slowly, quietly. My empty stomach growled like an angry puppy.

We barely squeezed inside even though we were early. Mr Scrivener was up first for his final address.

'Ladies and gentlemen of the jury, five questions face you. First, when was Brockton Wheatley killed? Almost certainly on the Friday night. Secondly, who was at Pucklethorpe Manor at around the time he was killed? Lady Bullwar-Lytton and her son, who by the defendant's request has not been called to this trial as a witness. A young Romany who has been questioned and cleared by the police. And Dr Rupert Whelan. Why was the defendant watching Brockton Wheatley's visitor? Was she waiting until Dr Whelan left? If so, I put it to you that there was ample time for her to confront and attack her ex-husband.'

The barrister paused and moved to stand closer to the jurors, looking at them before he spoke again.

'Third, how was Brockton Wheatley killed? The size, shape and angles of the injuries inflicted by the murder weapon accord with a crowbar or similar implement, and we have heard that Lady Charlotte habitually carried a crowbar. In addition, the aforementioned mutilation of Wheatley's eyes would misdirect suspicion to the Romany community, who were eliminated early on in police enquiries.

'Fourth, who was most likely to erupt in fury? This was not a premeditated murder. There was a battleground – the property – and an unplanned explosion of temper.' Scrivener strode over confidently and looked directly at Lady Charlotte. She returned his gaze without a blink. 'The defendant knew that the proverbial leopard would never change his spots. There was no other visitor that night.'

'Wrong,' whispered Summer Locke, who had started fidgeting and looking towards the gallery door as if planning a quick exit. *Shhh-hhh!* I hissed.

Scrivener spun round on his heel and moved to the jury.

'Fifth, and final point. Who benefited from Brockton Wheatley's death? Who had motive? Once he was out of the way, the defendant would have her house back. The overwhelming weight of evidence points to the defendant and to her alone.' He paused, then, 'I rest my case.'

Katherine Burt adjusted her wig as if gazing into an invisible mirror, while smiling sweetly at the jurors. Her bouncy red hair pushed the wig up, creating the effect of a little white-tailed cloud following her about.

'Ladies and gentlemen of the jury, we have before us an ex-wife whose former husband has been killed and who has been advertising to all and sundry her animosity towards him. A wife who will gain by his death. However. Is it not far too easy *not* to look any further?'

She left her question to hang for a moment before continuing.

'Permit me, please, to explain something to you about murder. You all have been chosen because you are honourable, intelligent and normal members of society. But murder is no respecter of what is normal, intelligent and honourable. Most murders are pretty simple to solve once one knows what to look for. Any detective will tell you this. In the majority of cases the culprit is caught within hours, or days. Why? Because the murderer is usually known to the victim and there is a clear motive. And that motive? Almost always, the motive springs from a domestic source.'

She seemed to be saying that her client is a perfect guilty party. I was astonished.

'I put it to you, however, that this case cannot be judged like "most" murders,' Katherine Burt went on. 'My most respected tutor in law school made clear that property is a much more powerful motive for murder than passion. In fact, property, money and then passion, in that order, are the most powerful drivers behind domestic crime. Consequently, with all due respect, the lazy – and, to my mind, mistaken – notion is that the defendant is the culprit,' she said, looking directly at Roger Scrivener.

A murmur blew through the court.

'Yes, it is strange, most of us are of the impression that crimes of sexual jealousy are the chief cause of murder, but I put it to you, members of the jury, that this notion is not borne out by careful analysis.'

Katherine Burt smiled at the jurors, as if she were confiding with a close friend.

'Please return to your point,' urged Judge Fieldsend.

'My apologies, Your Honour. Curiously, many murder victims will have known their killers better than other people in their lives. That is one sort of murder. More difficult are the school shootings that plague our neighbours in North America, the serial killings – the Moors Murderers, the Yorkshire Rippers of this world, who strike without warning and seldom know their victims for long. A critical mistake by these types of killers most often leads to their capture.'

Katherine Burt held the courtroom mesmerized in the palm of her hand.

'However. Worst of all are the random killers, one-off attacks lacking method or motive. Attacks with a touch of the bizarre; the ones that slide away from easy categorisation. I say to you, for example, that investigators were unable to find a mysterious stranger seen in the vicinity at the time of the murder.'

Summer grabbed my arm. 'Stinger! Someone else saw Stinger!'

Shhh–hhh!

Katherine Burt glanced in our direction. 'This stranger was, to my knowledge, never located. There is no reason to suggest that Mr Wheatley knew the person if and when he opened the door to him. Most of the evidence, ladies and gentlemen of the jury, has been revealed to the police by Lady Charlotte herself, and her evidence has been largely consistent.'

Katherine Burt again eyed Roger Scrivener as if he were a naughty schoolboy in short trousers, and she a prefect.

'The Crown Prosecution has, with all due respect, emphasized the trivial and circumstantial. Just one trace of blood, members of the jury, *one single trace*, on the crowbar that has featured so prominently in this trial, and my client's story would be exposed as false. But there was none. My client has been grilled by the police and cross-examined at length by my honourable friend here –' Katherine cast yet another condescending, almost flirtatious glance in Scrivener's direction – 'and not once has she given way. There is not *one iota* of solid evidence to incriminate her.' She paused. 'I therefore assert that the prosecution's case rests entirely on circumstantial evidence.'

Lady Charlotte smiled. She looked almost ethereal in that moment.

'I am therefore confident that you, the jurors, will, in fairness and prudence, find my client not guilty of the murder of Brockton Wheatley.'

Katherine Burt's robes swirled as she turned around gracefully and took her seat.

I thought it was all over, and not a minute too soon, but Judge Fieldsend started up with a lecture on the difference between murder and manslaughter. When Summer poked me I sat up straight.

'What is it called when you pay another person to kill someone?'

'I don't know. *Shhh-hhh!*'

Eventually Judge Fieldsend broke for lunch. After lunch would come the summing up, and the verdict.

We made our way down to the foyer and outside the courthouse. Mrs Spicer spread a picnic lunch on a bench. I was hungry as a horse by now but Summer was restless.

'I thank you, Mrs Spicer, but I am not hungry just now. I would like to walk about.'

Summer dog-trotted away across the square and out of sight.

When the time came to return to the gallery, Summer hadn't come back. Did I have time to run and search? No. Then, at the very last minute, Summer appeared through the door, eyes shining with excitement, radiant.

'You OK, Summer?'

'Yes, I am well, very well.'

I squeezed Summer's hand. Something lovely must have happened and I was dying to ask but it would have to wait, because the Red Judge had returned.

Lunch break must have done Judge Fieldsend good. His cheeks and nose were bright pink; even his monotone became more expressive.

'This is called the "Summing Up",' whispered Mrs Spicer, as he began to outline the facts of the case for the jury once more.

Judge Fieldsend asked the court clerk to pass to him Exhibit A, the crowbar.

'The accused has spoken of a war of wills. Was she frightened when armed with this instrument?' The judge waggled Exhibit A above his head. 'Was this the weapon used by the murderer? Or was it simply a tool in common use around the gardens of Pucklethorpe Manor? Members of the jury, a guilty verdict requires that you must be certain *beyond reasonable doubt* that Lady Charlotte Bullwar-Lytton murdered her husband Brockton Wheatley deliberately. If, on the other hand, you find she was provoked in a way to cause a reasonable person to act in the same way, then she is guilty of manslaughter. Please take all the time you require, ladies and gentlemen of the jury.'

The jury retired, eight men and four women. The courtroom throbbed with the waiting. Would they take a long time? Opinion varied over whether taking a long time to reach a verdict was a good sign or not. We watched Chris Lamb file out along with the other journalists. Summer seemed fit to burst, so we tore downstairs, and then outside.

'Something good has happened. Robin, come aside.' Summer's green eyes shone. 'King and the elders have returned. They have found the killer of Papa Brockton!'

But before I even had time to respond, the bell rang, calling us back into session. The jury had reached a verdict.

Too quick? Or not quick enough?

The quiet in the room was like a held breath. The jury filed back in.

'Do you find the defendant guilty or not guilty of murder?' asked Judge Fieldsend.

'Not guilty.'

A noise erupted, something like a timid cheer, mixed in with gasps of surprise.

'And do you find the defendant guilty or not guilty of manslaughter?' asked Judge Fieldsend.

'Not guilty.'

This time the gasps ran loudly around the courtroom. Someone in the gallery pitched a bouquet of roses at Charlotte's feet.

'Who threw the flowers?' I asked Summer, incredulous, shocked.

'I believe that is her daughter.'

Lady Charlotte stooped to pick up the bouquet, smiled to the gallery for the first time and waved, just like you see Hollywood celebrities do at the Oscars.

Lady Charlotte Bullwar-Lytton was a free woman.

Summer Locke sighed and said, 'What has gone around will come around.'

'What is *that* supposed to mean?' But Summer would say no more.

Mrs Spicer shook her head as she gathered up her things. 'Well, I never. Now she can sell her unhappy house.'

The courtroom emptied quickly and we found ourselves waiting on the court steps to witness the acquitted

Lady Charlotte's appearance. Cameras clicked and flashed as she stepped outside into the chilly October air, attended by her beaming barrister. A black limo with a private hire sticker slid into position at the foot of the court steps.

Katherine Burt cleared her throat. 'My client has asked me to express her delight with the outcome of this case. She is most relieved that it is over. She is also aware that a criminal is still on the loose and she has expressed her hope that the murderer will be speedily apprehended.'

Summer Locke, eyes fixed on a distant point, seemed to ignore the drama taking place on the steps.

'Robin, please look after my satchel. I must attend to something.'

I watched Summer gallop down the steps two at a time and across the square, heading in the direction of a big white van. I strained my eyes to see the driver. It was King. To my shock, Summer jumped in the van and they drove off. I stared after the van as it went out of sight. Where was Summer going?

Just then, as Lady Charlotte got in the waiting limo, I heard the beep of a horn. It was Mr Spicer come to collect us. I grabbed Summer's bag along with mine and got in the back. In the front, Mrs Spicer regaled her husband with the details all the way home.

As we pulled up into our drive, I gazed up the rise to Pucklethorpe Manor.

'Look! All the lights are on. It looks like a fairy castle.'

'Party, I expect,' Mrs Spicer said disapprovingly. 'Celebrating Herself's freedom. Like I said, it's hers now to do what she likes. But innocent? My giddy aunt, if she's innocent, I'll be the next Pope!'

I thanked Mr Spicer for the lift and made my way to our house. Indeedy opened the door and gave me a big hug.

'Heard the verdict on the radio,' Indeedy said, tired and tender. 'Where's Summer?'

'Don't know.' My eyes filled. 'I love you, Mum.'

'Love you too, Fruit.'

My tummy churned. Where did Summer go? Would there be danger if King and the elders had really found the murderer? Would Summer be in danger too? Would I ever see my friend again? My strange, beautiful friend. Nothing in the world – not treasure or houses or anything – is more important than a friend.

My throat felt tight. 'When we got outside, Summer just shot off across the square and jumped in a van. I think it was King who Summer went with.' I paused. 'Mum, Summer told me the elders had caught the real murderer and brought him back.'

Indeedy didn't say anything to this revelation. She put her arms around me again and held me tight. Then, 'What do you want for supper, Fruit?'

'Not hungry, thanks, Mum. Will you take me to the hatch, please?' I wanted to go right now.

No, she would not take me to the hatch.

'You're exhausted, Fruit. You'll overtire yourself.'

I saw it was pointless arguing. And I was tired, truthfully.

'In the morning?'

'When you've rested up and finished your homework.'

'It's done,' I lied.

'OK. Want some hot chocolate?'

'Please, yes. I love you,' I said again.

'Love you too, my darling Fruit.' Twice in a single day.

22
Extinct is Forever

Who tonight can say where our Romany is?
Our Gypsy has left behind on the green
Two blackened stones and some blue-ish dust
And a smell of smoke where he's been.
Our Romany is not tied to a house in a street,
And life is sweet as may be.
Our Gypsy can roam through life's long path
And die where God may decree.

– anon

I ran a fever over the weekend, and spent it in bed. I mostly love remembering my dreams, but not this one.

Summer Locke reaches for me across a brook, holding a transparent globe. Inside the globe is a house full of coloured lights and miniature people moving around, like those snow globes – but not. I can see every single detail. The brook churns like white water, and I am frightened I will fall. A red raft bounces by. It is Rory. My father reaches for me, arms outstretched, balancing like an acrobat.

'Daddy! Daddy!' I call. Rory rafts out of reach.

'Jump!' says Summer Locke.

Monday morning is cold and my stomach aches. Plus, I almost never get headaches but now I do. Indeedy makes porridge and prunes for breakfast, which doesn't help.

'Please, Mum, take me to the hatch now. We can go there and still get to school on time.'

Indeedy says no. I don't argue, but she sees my tears.

'Listen, Fruit, meet me outside the school this afternoon. I'll be there at half three to pick you up.'

I think, Mum's turning English, Americans say three-thirty.

'OK.'

Even after a weekend in bed, the double whammy stomach-ache-headache doesn't stop. Miss Withers is kind and tries to make me laugh. 'You look like a wet Wednesday, Robin. Where is your friend Summer?'

'Not well,' I lie.

'I'm sorry to hear that, Robin. Tell Summer to get well soon.'

It is bad luck for me that on the first day back after half term I have to go first reading out my homework: a report on the court case. I am not prepared. I brace myself. Yet another day of difficult things and I must make an effort.

'My half term report is on English law. I attended a murder trial with my friend, which was held at the County Court in Tiptovia. It is a very big building, which makes you feel small. I went every single day. The jury decided the verdict was not guilty.'

'How fascinating, Robin. You are speaking of Lady Charlotte Wheatley's trial, are you not? All Borderland has been talking of little else.'

'Yes, Miss Withers. But she has a new surname, Bullwar-Lytton, which is her family name. She is very pretty for an older lady and a bit like a movie star, but sad and mean. She would be older than my mum, I think. We went to this trial because the old man Mr Brockton Wheatley was killed in the house next door to my house, where we moved to. He used to be her husband. My friend Summer Locke was Mr Wheatley's best helper. But you are innocent until they prove that you are not. The judge and the jury came in. There was a woman lawyer for the lady they suspected, who you call the defendant, and a man lawyer for the accusers, who was the persecutor.'

Miss Withers smiled. 'The word is "prosecutor", Robin.'

'I meant prosecutor. The lady lawyer had pretty bouncy red hair but her wig looked silly. The court was crowded every day. I learned a lot and I'm glad I went. That's all.'

Miss Withers rose from her desk, quite cuddly in her Argyle pink and grey angora jumper.

'Thank you, Robin. Any questions, class?'

Their questions I mostly can't answer. Why do they wear wigs? Do they say the ten commandments? What was the make of the limousine they drove off in?

Worst luck, I am chosen again in biology. The frog report. All I had written down in my notebook was that frogs breathe through their skin, that toads have bumps with poison in them that makes cats foam at the mouth if they lick a toad, and that there is a bug that can suck a frog empty like a deflated balloon. Mr Bowerman frowns as he ticks something in the class register.

At lunch there is red in my wee. My first period. I put a coin in the machine. Broken. So I fold up toilet paper and put it in my knickers and head for the school nurse's station. I am not ready.

I think about growing up, what adults say about it: the adventure, the changes, the uncomfortable bumps. Indeedy says it's a jolly trip, a journey, and I always believed her, but that's not what it feels like just now. Chris Lamb told about someone who held a party with presents and new clothes and what did I think? They're a bunch of old hippies, I think. I want the opposite, to fend off all signs. Summer Locke dresses like a boy but doesn't seem like other boys. I want to be like Summer Locke.

At the long last end of the day, Indeedy is there where she promised. I push through the other children and climb in the van. Boddy is on the back seat.

'What's up, Fruit?'

I cannot say anything. The words stick in my throat.

'Look at me.' Indeedy tilts my chin up, takes my face in her hands, which annoys me but which I love. 'The dreaded period, yes?'

I nod.

'Well, congratulations, darling. Do we need to stop by home before going to the hatch?'

'No, thanks, Mum. I saw the nurse.'

We speed down the lane towards the hatch. I sense the emptiness as we arrive. The silver-sky autumn wind whistles. It is very cold.

'Mum, what's the opposite of when you feel like someone's watching over you?'

'What do you mean, Fruit?'

'When there's no one there to help.'

'If you're talking about the hatch, it's not a feeling. Look.'

The picket gate is padlocked. Boulders block the drive. There is a bolt on the main door and the windows are boarded up. Boddy trots around the mess, tail up over her back, sniffing, growling, turning to us as if she wants an explanation. The five-bar gate to the field is clamped shut by a chain with a Yale padlock. Some mean person has knocked down the tidy woodpile.

There is a notice nailed onto a stake by the gate. It ends:

By order of Borderland District Council
MOVEABLE DWELLINGS ARE PROHIBITED.
Signed,
B. E. Heavy, Clerk of the Council.

'This stinks!' I said. 'They'd rather keep it empty than let it be used. And the house! Summer said it was derelict before the Gypsies made it tidy. What's wrong with them being here, anyway? Why do people hate them?'

We hear a motorbike and soon it pulls up behind us. Indeedy says, 'I do believe it's our friend the dimpled detective, Fruit.'

'He was in the court, Mum. I hate him if he has anything to do with this!'

Constable Trevor Corteena removes his crash helmet and tousles his flattened hair with a free hand.

'Did you do this?' I ask, looking daggers at him.

'Uh, no. Hello.'

'Robin is very upset, constable,' Indeedy began. 'Her —'

Constable Corteena gives his trademark grin as he interrupts. 'Understandable. It's the County Council, not the police. But you must realize that they are only doing their job. Legislation on travellers and such like. I am sorry.'

'You could stop them from making the Romany go,' I say hotly.

'I'm afraid not. My job is to uphold and defend the law of the land, whether bad or good.'

'Well, the law stinks on this one.'

'Personally I'm with you, Robin,' the constable says. 'I am against anti-nomadic measures. But this started a very long time ago. Open land began to be barred to travellers, even land used by the Gypsies for hundreds of years, and I must admit, sometimes they are their own worst enemies. These days they are fined when they stop, to pay for the cost of them using the land, I suppose, sort of like the rates your mother pays on your house.'

Constable Corteena reached to stroke Boddy. She leaned against him, slid down, rolled over on her back, a big grin stretching her grey whiskery face.

'Look, I'm off duty now, so please, the name's Trevor. Looks like Pucklethorpe Manor will be on the market in no time. The family organized a party for Lady Charlotte in the big house.'

'We saw.'

He smiled at me. 'And your young Gypsy friend?'

'We're looking for Summer now,' I said. 'I thought we would meet up at school, but no luck. And to be honest,' I say, realizing that I only ever say "to be honest" when I'm not going to be, 'I haven't got a clue. I'm freezing, Mum, can we go home now?'

'Yes, it is cold,' Mum agreed. 'Please feel free to join us, Trevor, if you want to talk some more.'

'Thank you, I'd like that. Actually, I chased you up here for a reason.'

Back at Limberlost Mill, Chris Lamb is cooking a vegetarian shepherd's pie. Lovely smells of garlic and onions and herbs waft our way. Seeing Constable Corteena, she grins broadly. 'I've a hunch why you're here, constable. Been listening to Radio Borderland.'

'Trevor, please.' He smiles, and pops a raw field mushroom into his mouth from a pile on the butcher's block. 'What did you hear on the radio?'

Chris gives Indeedy a peck on the cheek and points to the pile. 'Picked those from the back paddock this morning.'

Suddenly Trevor staggers, clutching at his throat, eyes rolling up in their sockets. 'ARRR-GGH!' he cries as he collapses in a writhing heap on the floor.

'Oh my God!' shouts Indeedy, jumping over to hold him upright. 'Robin, phone 999. NOW! Ambulance!'

Trevor goes still, opens his eyes, and then struggles to his knees and doubles over laughing. 'Joking!' he says.

'If you think that's funny you need a lobotomy!' Indeedy sounds annoyed, but she turns her back on him so he can't see her smile. She examines the mushrooms.

'People still die around here, mistaking field mushrooms for death caps.'

Trevor grins sheepishly. 'Sorry.'

I'm thinking that, for a cop, he is extremely cute.

'Chris, we've just been to the Romany site,' says Indeedy. 'County Council's wrecked and barricaded it.'

'Oh, I'm sorry to hear that, but not surprised. No sign of Summer?'

'No.'

Trevor Corteena straddles a dining chair back to front and leans forward, chin on forearms. 'Do you think the two events are related? Her Ladyship's acquittal, I mean, and the Gypsies going?'

Chris shrugged. 'Who knows?' She assembled all her ingredients and popped the shepherd's pie in the Rayburn. Yum.

'Call me a romantic,' said Chris. 'Do you think the words "romantic" and "Romany" are related? Anyway, nothing will ever make them conform, despite the Council's efforts.'

'Personally,' says Indeedy, 'I think they will be extinct within a generation.'

'Well, the official view is already that they don't exist,' Trevor says. 'The way the men in suits see it, they have no identity, no passport, no National Insurance number, don't pay taxes. And no fixed address.'

I'm thinking about the dusky seaside sparrow. Why be a space journalist when the Earth is in such a mess? Extinct is forever. Conversation returns to Lady Charlotte.

'I expect by now,' says Indeedy, 'she's hopped into a private plane and flown herself up and away to Santorini or somewhere.'

'Probably. That pie does smell proper good,' says Trevor. 'Nudge nudge.' He grinned.

'May we have the pleasure of your company for supper, Trevor?'

'Thought you'd never ask!'

Later, full up and satisfied, we gather in the sitting room. The woodburning stove glows with seasoned logs and pine cones. Trevor asks if there is a guitar about.

'I'd like to sing you something. Just got the words from a mate at the pub. It's a Gypsy song about the old ways changing.'

Like a lot of folk songs, it's long and sad and about injustice and stealing the king's royal deer and dying for the crime of it. Trevor has a good voice. I feel better now, and sleepy.

'Do you think we can help the Gypsies not being disappeared?' I ask.

Trevor returns the guitar to its case. 'I don't know. Sorry, Robin.'

23
The Key

He who binds to himself a joy
Doth the winged life destroy.
He who kisses the joy as it flies
Lives in eternity's sunrise.

— 'Eternity', William Blake

Indeedy knocks on my bedroom door. There is frost on the inside of the French windows.

'Goodies in the post this morning, Fruit.' She sets a mug of tea on the bedside table and brandishes a brochure in front of my sleep-filled eyes. 'Look. Pucklethorpe Manor is on the market.'

The photos of the manor are airbrushed to nobility, clean of its sinister history, blood and bones.

'If we had the money would you buy it?' I ask.

'Not for all the tea in England, Fruit. Even if we had the purchase price, the upkeep would be our downfall.'

'Why'd they send you this, then?'

'The estate agents? I saw them running around a few days ago with their clipboards and cameras. It was quite funny. They caught old Toby Spicer red-handed, treasure hunting with his metal detector and spade; he tore off like a blue-arsed fly. Anyway I asked for the brochure.'

Indeedy is beaming her *I've got a surprise* for you smile. She produces a large airmail envelope. 'If I am not mistaken, you have a big fat letter from Summer Locke. Here. I'll go rustle up some breakfast.'

A bright Irish stamp, County Mayo in the franking space. No return address. I open the envelope carefully, so as not to tear the flap.

Summer Locke's handwriting is crowded top to bottom and right to the edges.

Dear Robin, my friend,
It sorrows me I left so quicle and could not say 'devlesa' to you. Our van boarded the cargo ferry Innisfree, bound for Rosslare. The journey was rough. I sat myself in the front seat between King and Petal. In the back of the van Stinger the killer man was sat on a mattress, bound hands behind his back. King had removed the gag and the bolsters with which he was hidden to pass through Customs and he was not visible to anyone who might peer through the rear windows of our van. We are now nearby to Galway Bay. The

Irish Romany are very kind, but they are much poorer than we English Gypsies. The fields are small, with a cow, or some with sheep. They have stone fences. We are near the ocean. On the beaches are smooth stones and pebbles. I can hear the ocean singing now, the birds swooping and crying. I believe it is November, our Romany Return-of-the-Salmon month.

Please tell Miss Withers hello for me. I miss the gorgio school. Esmeralda will be very pleased I can spell words with silent letters, like Pneumonia and Czechoslovakia. Tell Miss Withers I plan to attend Oxford University someday. Tell her also this funny story. Yesterday Stinger asked for a newspaper. So I took myself to the paper shop in the village and I asked the lady for a newspaper. She asked would I like yesterday's paper or today's paper? So I said on balance I would prefer today's paper. So she said well then, you will be needing to come back tomorrow.

Stinger has confessed to his crime, in writing, and he has signed his confession. The elders have punished Stinger. The punishment is that he must work to eat even though he hates the work. He is not happy. He goes out only with guards and at night when no one will see him. I have asked the elders to bring Stinger back to England to be tried by gorjio courts. I pray this will be happy news, my friend. I try to make the elders laugh. I tell them that it would be an easing to us and a burden to the gorgios if we send this

doosh back to the housedwellers. Truly, he is great trouble
to us. We should bring him back to Borderland and drop him
in Darley Dale in the middle of the night and post the
confessions to the police station and tell the gavs where to
collect him. But I do not know what will happen.
Please tell Miss Withers this also. When I write something
now I've had schooling, I am very proud when I am writing
it, but when I see my own bad writing I get very fed up.
I have finished reading Animal Farm. I do not entirely
understand it. Some day you will teach me about it. I also
possess some thoughts about the Jesse Tree and the poem. You
will not be able to write me, Robin Swallow, but we will
always be friends. Please write me in your diary and when
we meet again I shall read it like a fine story. I will write
you whenever I am able. That is a promise.
Always your true friend, Summer Locke.
PS I cannot find Scotch eggs in Galway.
PPS I am learning the fiddle
PPPS This letter is too long and I would still like to write
more but I have run out of space.

    I tuck Summer's letter in my notebook. I vow to write
every day even though I can't send what I write. The letter
reminds me of my broken promise to write to Mrs Avey. I
will write to her too, and tell her Summer's story and how I
am keeping up my 'word of the day' book. I will send her a list

of Gypsy words. Then I take the key to Pucklethorpe from the drawer of my bedside table, put it round my neck and hurry into my clothes. I breathe a hole in the frosted window and rub a peephole. It is a perfect early winter day, bright and cold and clean. Into my backpack goes my word book and a torch, Brockton Wheatley's journal, and my pencil case.

Downstairs, at breakfast, Indeedy asks, 'How's Summer, then?'

'Fine. They're in Ireland.'

'Oh. OK.' She doesn't press me any further. 'So, what's on the agenda today, Fruit?'

'Stupid frog report.'

'They're still moving about on the pond, but probably not for long, not when the hard frost hits. Anyway, Chris and I have three deliveries, then we're free. By the way, your brother's coming home next week for a few days. With a friend.'

'Oh?' There's something in the way she said it.

'Girl called Jemima.'

'Nice name.'

I think, my brother will be a different person when he comes back and so will I. And it's OK.

I smile at Mum. 'Gotta go, frog watch! I'll take Boddy.'

I unlock the back door and prepare to enter the murder kitchen. There is a sour smell of fear, but I stand tall. No sneaking necessary now.

It was important to keep my last visit to Pucklethorpe Manor a secret, although I'm not sure why. Maybe because it will be the last chance before some rich squillionaire banker snaps it up and locks away its history beneath layers of modern paint and ignorance?

'Boddy, stay here.' She lowers her lank posterior reluctantly at the bottom steps, tail between legs, amber eyes glowing disapproval.

I pass through the kitchen and into the hall and pull on the brass ring, propping the cellar door against the wall. The cellar beckons, its familiar musty odour. I take my torch from the backpack and press the button. The beam captures dancing dust motes.

I go carefully down the slippery stone stairs and into the cellar. I shiver, and stretch myself flat on the dank flagstones, squinching my eyes shut, and aiming the torch ceilingward. I count to ten. Open eyes. The bright lineaments of the Jesse Tree gleam in the beam of my torch.

What is its secret? Is it all a fake? I think back to our plane ride; the grand design of topiary from the air. What does it mean? What are Summer's thoughts about the tree and the poem? Will I ever know? Will we ever work it out?

Lord Pucklethorpe surely would not have been pleased to discover that the part of his land with the pond now belongs to us peasants. His garden was so carefully planned, and then someone has chopped the top of the garden Jesse Tree off. This thought makes me smile. But they say he was a lovely man; perhaps he would have found it amusing? And I realize why I have come to the Jesse Tree. Not to forget, but to say goodbyes.

Goodbye, murder house. Goodbye, Skullduggeries. Goodbye to people who kill for money. And yes, goodbye to treasure. Goodbye to tall, blind, kindly Brockton Wheatley. Goodbye to sad memories of Daddy. Goodbye, too, to some good things. To Zach as my hero. To this first long summer with my friend Summer Locke. To first times of almost everything.

I rise. Up the steps I tiptoe as if someone is listening, watching, and close the trap door, the kitchen door, the outer door. I lock it. I call Boddy to heel, and head back towards our garden.

I settle myself on the pig bench beside the pond, frightening a frog who leaps and plops into the deep clear water of the pond, near the small island in the centre with the statue of the Virgin Mary.

I sigh. I don't want to write the frog report.

Do it, I tell myself. You can write here outside as long as the sunshine is warm.

My biology report is on *Rana temporaria*, the common frog.

'The first thing is that the common frog is not common any more. It is part of a growing list of endangered species. Frogs like to return to the same breeding place year after year. The frog family I see in my pond has been here for a very, very long time. Frogs make a lot of noise when they breed. They are mainly carnivores and eat slugs, snails and insects. They catch flying things by shooting out their sticky tongues, a clever evolutionary adaptation.'

I write on about frogspawn and tadpoles and predators. I want to digress and bring in the dusky seaside sparrow but can't think how. I want to write about things that disappear while you're watching, like shooting stars. I glance towards our house and catch Indeedy standing at the door, looking my way. I wave and return to my writing.

Chris Lamb beeps the horn.

'In a minute!' shouts Indeedy. Then, to me, 'Don't get a chill, Fruit. See you shortly!' Then she's gone.

Boddy and I are alone, together. Here we are, everything in this moment.

I remove the manor house key from round my neck and toss it into the pond. It plops with scarce a ripple, and disappears.

Rana temporaria *settles for hibernation in the muddy depths of the pond. The little frog, survivor of her first breeding season, digs herself in to the bottom. She buries herself at the edge of a large and wholly submerged metal box. The handle on the top of the box is coated with the slime and watery weeds of decades under water. Year upon year the ancestors of the frog have burrowed into the mud beside this very box. Ever since Lord Pucklethorpe hid it there, filled with forty-two bars of solid gold.*

Author's Note

The Jesse Tree is based on a real murder committed in the late twentieth century. The crime remains unsolved. Fascinated by the details of the case, a friend and I set about pitching a television documentary, but when we were unsuccessful I decided to invent a story using the true crime as inspiration. It has been more fun than I imagined, not least because fiction needs to be realistic, unlike reality, which is often so bizarre as to be inconceivable. There is something of me in every character in this story, villains included. Otherwise it's the irresistible and ageless alchemy of making stuff up.

Jesse Trees, however, are not made up. They exist in a variety of carved and stained glass depictions of Jesus's geneology scattered throughout Europe and the UK, and are probably the very first examples of family trees. The oldest is in Chartres Cathedral and dates from 1145 AD. A modern example is Helen Whittaker's wonderful stained glass masterpiece in St Mary's, Abergavenny in Monmouthshire. This book may well have remained a mere twig of a tale had not my friend Don Jesse taken me to visit a chemist's shop in Kingsbridge, Devon. There, in an upper room, was an exquisite plaster relief of 'The Tree of Jesse' on the ceiling. Lacking an idiot's guide to photography, I lay on the floor and photographed the very low ceiling with my Canon, taking at least ten shots and later pasting them together. Oh, for a zoom lens!

This book is my debut novel but although it is new it is also even older now than Robin Swallow herself. Its earliest incarnation was stopped in its tracks by a family tragedy, followed by the untimely death of my editor and mentor. Eventually, after publishing two more non-fiction books, and with the encouragement of beloved friends, the novel found legs again and Robin Swallow took flight in my imagination once more.

Thanks to agent Patricia White, to Caroline Press of Penguin Random House, New York for professional guidance, and to Suzanne Press for her generosity and networking skills. I also thank Andrew Buckley for his knowledge of Jesse Trees in Britain and Graham Dowell for translating the poem into Latin.

For publishing expertise: thanks to editors Emma Holtz, Emily Freer, and the magical Debbie Hatfield, whose detailed and nuanced suggestions remind me of the old days in publishing, when authors were mentored and gently reminded that we are not really omniscient guardians of a perfect and unchangeable text. I salute my publisher Helen Bowden, whose support of my work and investment in the project has been inspirational. I also thank Chris Knight for his wonderful illustrations and cover design. And to the entire team at Orphans Publishing, R-E-S-P-E-C-T.

For Gypsy, biker and architectural research: Veronica Bowater, Jo Corfield, Boo Dickinson, Andrew Dobbin, Ursula Freeman, Judy Harper, Laurie Kinsley, Patrick Jasper Lee, Harold Lock, Iris Lock, Bill Lock, Thirza and Marian Maynard, Stewart Myzinski, Caroline Price, Jeremy Sandford, Kitty Smallman, Sally Tudor née Dunn, Brigid Wright for knowledge of Gypsies in the Welsh Borders. James Smallman offered endless stories; very recently, Damian Le Bas, author of *The Stopping Places*, enriched the background research for the book and was kind enough to advise on dialect and custom, and Nicholas Pevsner's guide to the buildings of England aided me greatly. Pilots Graham George and my big brother Roy Gould flew me around the area to help me visualize the Jesse Tree code.

For legal and personal assistance: the BBC, Edmund Barber and Dr Ronnie Barber, PC Bill Bufton, PC Corteen, Gill Butler, Commander Carl Davis, Sue Dowell, WPC Anne Gutteridge, Don Jesse, Baroness Helena Kennedy QC, Terry Kirby, Thirza

Maynard, Julian Mitchell, Helen Osborne and Hillary Ratnasabapathy. I salute the young friends who read earlier versions and contributed ideas: Amelia, Dylan, Annice, Francis and Venice, who served as Robin's agnostic voice.

Dear Mrs Avey,

Here is the list of some Gypsy words I promised to send. I wrote them in my word book first, but not in alphabetical order, but I have fixed that here. The Gypsies don't usually write things down and when they do, spellings are often different. I remember that you said Shakespeare wrote his name a dozen different ways too. Also Gypsies believe words are magic and alive, and that to say them will make something happen, like abracadabra. Because they are secret, I don't know any of them, Summer Locke said that it was like when Devlah [God] made the world, saying, 'Let there be light and there was light.' Zach my brother says it's magical thinking and therefore a load of tosh, and that only children think like that. What do you think? I am not sure.

Love,
Robin

Robin's Romany Word List

atch: to stop, get down
barvalo: rich
baxt: luck, fortune, fate
bibi: auntie, but also baby
Bitee Fokee: fairies, or magical woodland people
bor: hedge
bosh: fiddle ('ker the bosh': to play the fiddle)
caer: house
carni: hen
chal: fellow, man
chavvie: child
cheriklo: bird
choom: moon
chored: stolen
cosh: stick, firewood
cushta: yes, good, nice
dadus: father
dei: mother
dell: give
Devlah: God
devlesa: farewell
didekoi: Gypsy
didlo: crazy, insane

dinlo: stupid
doosh: evil, bad, unlucky
drag: caravan, waggon
drom: road
dukkering: fortune-telling, palmistry
gavmush, gavs: police
gel: go
gorgio: housedweller, non-Gypsy
grai: horse
gudney: cow
hatchintan: stopping place, camp
hookapen: a lie
horri: penny
hotchiwitch: hedgehog
jogray: Gypsy stew
joller: go
jukel: dog
kair: house, or to make
kako: uncle
kanginga: hare
keelie: get-together
kom: to love, owe, or want
kriss: gathering of elders
Krissnatori: president of the Kriss
matchika: cat

Mooshabove: God is watching us

mora: bread

mullamoosh: a devil

nash: to run

nupe: a term of endearment

pand opre!: shut up!

parni: water

patrin: leaf; also clues for directions on the
        road

peg: to sell

Phui Dai: wise old woman of tribe

pikie: inferior form of Gypsy

pooka: ask

poove: graze

puro moosh: old man

rakli: girl, woman, friend

raklo: boy

rokker: speak

rukka: tree

sap: snake

sar shan: a greeting 'how are you?'

shushi: rabbit

skiving: dealing in

starry: prison

tatcho: good, true, holy

tinker: Scottish or Irish Gypsy
trash: to fear
trashed: frightened
vangra: money
varda: horse-drawn caravan
vass: hand
vudros: bed
yog: fire outdoors
yora: egg